TROLL LIFE

Alan Parkinson

ISBN: 978-1-9997402-3-8

To my writing friends, may you one day be my real friends.

troll
trɒl,trəʊl/

noun: **troll**; plural noun: **trolls**
1   (in folklore) an ugly creature depicted as either a giant or a dwarf.

2   a person who makes a deliberately offensive or provocative online post.

verb
1   make a deliberately offensive or provocative online post with the aim of upsetting someone or eliciting an angry response from them.

CHAPTER ONE

Darren edged up his sizeable right arse cheek, cursed the vindaloo that he had inadvertently sat in, and launched the carton across the room. He rested against the wall for a moment, surveying the scene of devastation around him. Clothes littered all over the place, empty cans and food wrappers scattered on the floor. Bedding that hadn't been changed for weeks, months even. A bedroom that wouldn't have looked out of place in Chernobyl. His pathetic existence was brought into sharp focus, but he'd lived like this forever. It hadn't bothered him before.

He never received visitors, didn't have any real friends and his only trips to the outside world were to the Job Centre, Aldi and Greggs. However, Greggs was now off limits after a slight misunderstanding with a hot pie innuendo. What a week this had been.

The can of Coca Cola, that he'd knocked over in the rush to switch off his computer, drenched the keyboard and cascaded to the floor. The PC monitor now blank after Darren had ripped the plug from the socket.

The World Wide Web was the world that Darren Updike inhabited and on there he was a success, even popular in some circles. Nobody online knew of the filth he inhabited; at least they hadn't until now.

He glared at the webcam sat atop his monitor; another gadget bought but never used. He'd purchased it during a brief spell where he thought he might try internet dating, but he'd never had the courage to switch it on and show his true self. Darren wasn't deluded enough to think anyone would find him attractive; sat there in his pants, scratching his arse and picking the remnants of takeaway curry from his chest hair. Outside of some special interest internet voyeurs in Germany, it was hard to see where his target audience would be. Now it was out of his hands. He didn't know if the webcam was active or if it had ever been switched on, but they had hacked everything else, there was no reason to think they hadn't hacked the camera.

"Oh Christ, how long has it been on?" he thought. *"What have they seen?"*

He scrambled about on the floor and found a stiffened white sports sock, hard enough to hammer nails into the wall; his face reddened. He prised the two sides apart and placed it over his webcam before slumping back against the wall. He wondered how much they knew but he already had the answer, they knew everything. Darren had no idea how long they had been watching him, but it was naive to think that they had just been deleting files from his PC, they will have taken copies. His spreadsheet, his database, the years of work he had put into ruling the message board, were now in the hands of somebody else. They had the power.

But it wasn't a fellow forum member who had hacked him. No, the message was very clear from those performing the cyber-attack.

From your friends at Phonetix Mobile.

Surely a pathetic call centre worker wouldn't have the skills to pull this off. This was big business taking its revenge; he had them rattled. It had all been a game to Darren, winding up the advisers, trolling the internet forums and social media. He loved getting a reaction and he was very good at it; the best. That had to be why they took him down.

He hadn't taken the internet crown without being prepared. He'd got to the top once, he could do it again. He had back-ups; this was nothing but a minor outage and he would soon be up and running again. Darren knew it was a risk switching the PC back on, but he had no choice. He crawled under the desk, heaving his belly through the debris like an icebreaker making its way through the Antarctic, sweat negotiating its way around his pockmarked face like a stream forging its path on a rock face. He replaced the plug before struggling to his feet and plonking himself on the chair. He used the sleeve of his sweatshirt to mop the Coke as best he could, then hovered his finger over the power button.

"Here goes."

The PC whirred into life and went through the normal start up process, maybe things weren't as bad as he'd feared.

But they were worse; worse than he could ever have imagined.

The folder where he stored the spreadsheet now contained several JPEGs. Snapshots taken from his webcam. They weren't flattering. He went to check his external hard drive but knew it was a lost cause. It had been plugged in when the attack happened, it was as vulnerable as the PC it was attached to. Sure enough it was blank. The internet connection still worked but he wasn't sure if that was a blessing or a curse. He had back-ups in his cloud server, but the password had been changed and he wasn't getting access.

He opened his email client but again, his password didn't work; they had been meticulous in their takedown. He could try recovery software but knew it was pointless. He wasn't getting his spreadsheet back, he wasn't getting his old life back. He'd been cast into the internet wilderness. Forever.

Darren should have switched everything off and walked away but he felt compelled to check the forum. The forum where he had been king until a couple of hours ago. He input his username and password but was denied access. He tried all the various aliases he had set up over the years but each one was the same. He entered the message board as a guest. Two threads dominated the top of the page. Each with over 10,000 views and 2,000 replies. The first, he had been posting on until very recently. **Armed siege at Phonetix Mobile**.

A gunman had taken over a call centre a few miles from where he lived. A call centre that he called daily, tormenting staff and demanding credits. One of the hostages was the very adviser that Darren had been battling with for weeks. His insider knowledge was internet gold, more than anybody could have dreamed for on the message boards. A once in a lifetime fast track to message board folklore.

But nobody had believed Darren, he was outed as a pathetic fantasist.

He had owned that thread until things began to unravel. That was the beginning of the end, and as tempting as it was, he couldn't bring himself to click on it again. Instead he clicked on the next one down.

See inside my new luxury flat.

Despite not being logged in, he could see who had started the thread.

DAZZLED, Darren's own username. He had started this thread himself. Except it wasn't him, it was whoever owned his account now. Picture after picture from his webcam showed the hovel that he lived in and the other forum users took great pleasure in his misfortune.

SIR STANLEY CUMMINS: Is this one of those films where the naughty maid comes in wearing stockings and suspenders?

ROKER REJECT: She'd need to be wearing a nuclear contamination suit to enter that place.

He could try and pass it off as a joke, but he knew he was beaten, his reign had come to an inglorious end; he was no longer king of the internet.

****

Humiliated, stressed and out of options, Darren closed the internet browser and stared at the blank monitor screen trying to work out his next step. But he had nothing. The message board had been his life and now he was a laughing stock. He'd had mishaps in the past, but he fronted them out, he wasn't sure that it would work this time. He had been in control before, in control enough to recover from whatever mistakes he made but not now; he didn't even have a log-in. His evening couldn't get any worse.

Then it hit him.

"No, no, no, not the photos."

He grabbed the mouse and clicked on Windows Explorer, he went to the pictures folder and one sub folder remained inside, the only pictures he owned. Maybe there still was a chance. He clicked on the folder named 'Nana' hoping, praying that they were still there. But they were gone.

There were only twenty of them, some of them black and white, scanned from the originals that he had borrowed without anyone knowing. Twenty photos of the one person who had ever loved him. Twenty photos of the one person who never judged him. Twenty photos that were now, like his Nana, gone forever. He put his head in his hands and sobbed.

Sweat patches formed in the armpits of Darren's grey sweatshirt and for the first time he noticed the smell. Not of the recent body odour but the stale sweat clinging to his clothes, the half empty food cartons, the unwashed bedsheets, the much-used sock covering the webcam. The stench of the disgusting mess he had become.

He tore off his sweatshirt and threw it to the ground, stamping on it. He swept the webcam from the top of the monitor, shattering it against the wall in its sock. The bed was next as he tipped it over, booted the bin and punched the walls in frustration.

All the rage he had kept bottled since his Nana's funeral five years ago, when the rest of the family ignored him as if he was a nobody. All the rage he had wanted to let out on that day but chose not to out of respect to his Nana. The rage that he was now taking out in a pathetic attempt to destroy his room. Because that's what he was; pathetic. They were right all along. He fell onto the upturned mattress and cried once again.

****

Darren rolled onto his back and stared at the mould on the ceiling. He felt like lying there forever but he needed a plan, he had to get the photos back. The spreadsheet and the database were no longer important, he just needed the photos. It wasn't like he looked at them every day, but it was comforting to know they were there. Now he had nothing. Nothing except his knowledge of the World Wide Web. If he was ever going to get the photos back, the answer lay on there.

He eased his hefty frame onto his knees and put his arm on the back of his swivel chair. He pushed up to stand but the chair spun away across the floor and he collapsed to the ground again like a fat Bambi. He let out a moan then grabbed the seat of the chair with both hands and stood up. Back in control of his furniture, he opened Google and began his search.

All the top hits were giving him advice he already knew, stuff he had already tried but he began with the most obvious. The back-ups. He knew they were gone from the external hard drive but there was a chance that he could find them on his cloud server, if he could get logged in. He went through the process for lost password but that sent an email to his locked email account. He attempted to unlock it but as he'd never got around to setting up the two-step authentication using his mobile number, that only sent an email to his back-up email account which was also locked. Round and round in a circle of despair.

"This is hopeless."

He knew there must be a way. He'd read about kiddy fiddlers being caught out when they thought they had deleted images; the police had been able to recover them by doing a deep search on the hard drive. Maybe he could get hold of the software the police used and find his Nana's photos. He had no idea what it was called, and he was very wary of a Google search asking how the police recover indecent photos of children. He didn't know who was still watching.

Had they deleted his files and gone away or were they sitting there recording what he was typing? Laughing at his misfortune? What if they were watching? What more could they do to him? He needed them to know that he wasn't afraid of them, that their bullying tactics would not work.

"Nobody trolls Darren Updike. I am the king of trolling."

He grabbed his mobile and clicked on the last call he made, the only call he ever made. The Phonetix Mobile helpline. They weren't getting away with hacking his life, he was fighting back. He had his fingers poised to navigate the menu but then he got a recorded message.

"The Phonetix Mobile call centre is closed right now. Please call back between the hours of 7am and 10pm or check on our website for further information."

It was then that he realised that it was the early hours of the morning. He had been so caught up with arguing on the internet that he had lost track of time, then the cyber-attack happened. It had been a stressful evening. Darren felt dizzy and grabbed the wastepaper basket just in time as he vomited vindaloo and Coke into it. The shock finally hit him and, exhausted, he stumbled back to his mattress and drifted off to sleep amongst the filth and chaos.

****

Darren awoke drenched in sweat. He'd been asleep, on and off, for about five hours with vivid dreams reminding him of the mess he was in. He wiped the sleep from his eyes and the crusted drool from his face and headed to the bathroom, grabbing his phone on the way. He'd usually have some breakfast and a mug of tea before making any calls, but this was an emergency. He sat on the pot and dialled Phonetix. He chose the lost and stolen phone option knowing that it bypassed the queue, he was put straight through to an adviser.

"Good morning and welcome to Phonetix Mobile, could I take your name and mobile number please?"

"You know who I am," said Darren, "get me your manager."

"I'm sorry, sir, I don't know who you are. If you could just give me a few details and we'll see how we can help you this morning."

"You can help me by giving back the photos of my Nana."

"I'm not sure I understand. Have you deleted some photos from your phone?"

"I haven't deleted them, you have. And they weren't on my phone, they were on my PC."

"I'm sorry, I'm not following you. We can't delete photos from your PC."

"Well you have, and you are all laughing at me. Put me through to Liam Grant, he is the one responsible."

It made sense to the adviser now, everyone knew who Liam Grant was; he'd been right in the centre of the armed siege the previous night. "I'm sorry but Liam Grant is not available, all requests about last night must go via the press office. I can give you their number if you like?"

"I don't want the number of your press office, I want my Nana back, her photos, give them back, NOW!"

"Could you please keep your voice down, sir? I am trying to help but you aren't giving me much to go on."

"Don't tell me to keep my voice down, you have stolen photos of my Nana. What sort of sick and twisted individuals are you?"

"What sort of photos were they?"

"What do you mean, what sort of photos?" said Darren.

"With you saying sick and twisted I thought they were, you know? Oh, never mind. I really am sorry sir but we don't have your photos, was there anything else we could help you with?"

"Anything else? Anything else? You've done nothing, nothing but ruin my life." With that, Darren let out a loud fart that reverberated around the bowl.

"Are you in the bathroom sir?"

"What's that got to do with you? You probably know anyway; can you see me? Are you watching me now, you sick pervert?"

"I'm sorry sir but I do not have to put up with this sort of abuse, especially from a Granny groper, I am terminating the call."

"You can't terminate the call, I know the rules and you can't end the call without getting yourself into a fuck load of bother."

"I am authorised to end the call under the three Fs rule."

"Three Fs?"

"Ferocity of tone, foul mouth and flatulence."

"That makes no sense."

The line went dead.

Darren stopped himself from throwing his mobile off the wall, he'd done enough damage, he let it slide into the sink. He needed a new plan and as much as he hated to admit it, he needed help. It was going to be painful and he had to be very careful, but it needed doing.

First things first. He needed to set up a new email account. After that was sorted he opened the message board. The same two threads were at the top of the board, now with over 25,000 views. He didn't click on them but instead clicked on the register button. He filled in the form, albeit not entirely honestly and he thought long and hard about his username. He didn't want everyone to realise who he was and he didn't want to use any antagonistic right wing names as nobody would help. He thought about giving himself a name the lefties would like but couldn't bring himself to do it. He realised that he didn't have time to care about such things, he was joining the board for one reason and one reason only. Once he had got the help he needed, he would be gone. Therefore, his username became the reason he was there in the first place. **'I LOVE MY NANA'**.

His account was set up and he received a confirmation email. He logged in and went to open a new thread, but he was blocked.

"Idiot," he thought.

You had to make at least twenty posts on other threads before you could post your own. He went about his task, trying not to draw attention to himself. He ignored the top two threads and started on number three, intending to write **I agree** against the last post on it.

The last post read:

TROTSKYREDANDWHITE: This country needs a return to traditional left-wing values, to start caring about each other again rather than the capitalist every man for himself society we live in today.

Darren's initial instinct was to ridicule the poster, but he couldn't get distracted, he had a job to do. He agreed and added similar dull responses to nineteen other threads. He now had the privileges he needed.

He posted his new thread entitled. **How to recover deleted photos.**

He needed to try and keep it low key. He knew the people who deleted them could be watching but it was a risk he had to take. He didn't want anybody else to know it was him asking.

I LOVE MY NANA: I've accidentally deleted some photos from my hard drive and external hard drive and really need to get them back. Is there any software I could use or anywhere I could take my PC to that could recover them?

It wasn't long before the first reply came through.

SIR STANLEY CUMMINS: I think that's how Gary Glitter got caught.

Then the next.

ROKER REJECT: I can see by your username that you are a connoisseur of the old Granny porn. Must be gutting to lose all your photos of cobwebbed fannies.

I LOVE MY NANA: It's not like that. These are photos that are very important to me, I need them back. Can anybody help?

Then one person offered to help, the one person he was least expecting; his old username again.

DAZZLED: Maybe I could help. In situations like this, I think it is always best to go back to the beginning and find out what I have done wrong. Only once I realise where I've made the mistakes can I begin to recover the situation. Hope this helps.

****

Darren's fingers hovered over the keyboard as he wondered how to reply. How do you reply to yourself? He didn't know who had control over his account, but he knew they had more than that, they had control over his life. He hesitated before replying, others weren't so reticent.

JULIOS SHIN PADS: What's going on here? DAZZLED giving out cryptic advice. Surprised to see him back after last night.

DON IN FARRA: He can't keep away, this place is his life. It's either that or he is having a meltdown.

"Both," thought Darren.

JULIOS SHIN PADS: Where's this Granny shagger fella come from as well? Surely an alias. Come on, own up, who is it?

There was no point in Darren replying. They were right, and they were wrong, he didn't understand what was going on himself. He returned to the post from his hacker and read it again.

DAZZLED: Maybe I could help. In situations like this, I think it is always best to go back to the beginning and find out what I have done wrong. Only once I realise where I've made the mistakes can I begin to recover the situation. Hope this helps.

Darren thought about it for another five minutes, tried to weigh up the pros and cons of replying but this was new territory for him. He was broken, he had nothing left to lose.

I LOVE MY NANA: What do I need to do to get those photos back? They are very special to me and I will do anything.

DAZZLED: As above, find out where you've gone wrong and change it. It's your only chance.

I LOVE MY NANA: So I have a chance of getting them back?

DAZZLED: Why don't you try it and find out?

JULIOS SHIN PADS: Think I drank too much Double Maxim last night, I can't follow this. I'm going back to bed.

Were the hackers playing a game with Darren? Was there a chance of getting his photos back or did he need to jump through hoop after hoop, so they could humiliate him further? What did they even mean by go back to the beginning? Where was the beginning? When he joined the message board? When he first started trolling the call centre? When his life first started to unravel?

He yanked at the drawer in the desk and began discarding all the old chargers, leads and batteries that filled it until he came across what he was looking for.

"How could I forget this?"

He went to grab it but then pulled his hand away. He scrubbed his hands clean in the bathroom. Days of muck, food and general filth swirled around the sink, adding to the grime that already coated it. He dried them on the towel hanging from the radiator. It was so hard that he could have sanded the floor with it and there were things growing on the towel that were nearly as old as him. It stunk but there was nothing else, it would have to do.

He reached into the drawer once more, taking the padded envelope and, using the tip of his thumb and forefinger, removed the plastic folder. He held it gently in both hands like he was handling a priceless antique in a museum. Amongst all the chaos in Darren's flat, in Darren's life, this was the one thing that was pristine.

He extracted the handwritten envelope from the folder; addressed to him, postmarked almost ten years ago. He removed the letter from inside it. He hadn't read it for nearly five years but remembered every word. He sniffed as he read it, he knew the tears were coming, there was no point fighting it. The end of the letter always got him.

I don't care what everybody else says about you, I know that you can be the best, you will be the best. Prove them wrong. Lots of Love, Nana xxxx

"I was the best, Nan," thought Darren, *"and I will be the best again, they won't defeat me."*

He replaced the letter with the same care and attention that he had removed it. They may have taken his photos, but he would always have the letter. The letter was his comfort blanket when the world conspired against him. Like the time he'd back heeled a dog when running for a bus. And the dog landed in front of said bus. It wasn't his fault, he didn't know it was there until he heard the yap of the dog, then its squeal matching the squeal of the brakes, then the thump as the bus hit it, then the scream from the owner. This was soon followed by the profanities of the bus driver, then another thump; this one on the end of his nose from the dog's now former owner.

Why did people always put the blame on him? The letter was a big help that day. It had helped him through some dark times and it would help him again. He'd ruled the message boards, he'd owned those call centre advisers. He had been the best.

Whoever had his account was right, they had set him a challenge. He needed to go back to the beginning, find out how they had managed to get the better of him and destroy them.

CHAPTER TWO

Spencer Proctor spotted his first target of the day. Everybody was a target, whether at work or out amongst the general public. He straightened his tie in the wing mirror of the Range Rover, considered whether the self-bronzing moisturiser he'd bought for thirty pounds really did make him look five years younger, and surveyed his prey.

The couple hovered outside on the forecourt amongst the second-hand cars; they hung about one particular Jaguar XF. It was clear that they had done their research online and had come for this particular motor. He liked people who had done their research, it always gave them a false sense of security. There was no need to go out and talk to them, they would come to him; they always did.

Sally, the young receptionist wandered past and his eyes focused on her breasts just long enough to make her uncomfortable.

"First victims of the day," he said.

He admired her legs as she walked away muttering "Dickhead," under her breath.

Sales had been slow recently and Spencer didn't normally deal with second hand cars. The junior salesman who did was at college for the day, so it was an opportunity for Spencer to kick start his sales.

As predicted, the couple came into the showroom, he pretended not to notice them. The timing here was crucial. Acknowledge them too soon and you were seen as desperate. Leave it too long and they could be gone, feeling humiliated. Spencer had to time it just right, so they would be grateful for anyone speaking to them and forget that he was the one who wanted to sell something. Just as they seemed to be considering leaving, he pounced.

"Good morning, my name's Spencer Proctor, was there anything in particular you were interested in?"

He followed up with a firm handshake for the husband then another for the wife where his hand lingered just that little bit longer.

"We were wondering if it was possible to take the black XF out for a test drive?"

"Of course, come and have a seat and we'll take a few details from you. Have you ever driven a Jaguar before?"

"No, he hasn't," said the wife, "it's always been his dream to own one."

"Too easy," thought Spencer, *"this isn't even a challenge."*

"Once you drive one, you will become part of the Jaguar family for life."

He'd get them signed up for extended warranties, service schemes, leather protector, the works, and stick it all on finance. That was the thing with virgins in the luxury car market. Whilst those at the top end argued over every penny, the first timers were desperately trying to prove that they belonged to the club and would stretch their budget as far as possible to keep up appearances.

He got them a coffee as he went through the motions, but he knew the deal was his. He knew people and he knew how to manipulate them. As he took the details needed by the garage, he engaged in idle chit chat about holidays, where they drank, where they ate, who their friends were. Whilst he knew this one was in the bag, he was in it for the long game. Make a connection and they will think they are mates and will come back time after time. Recommend him to their friends, even bring their kids here when they were old enough. Naturally, he expected to be running the place by then.

It was all in the detail. Everything they discussed now would be stored in his own little private spreadsheet. It was against the Data Protection Act, but nobody knew about it but him. The information might turn out to be worthless or it might turn out to be gold dust.

He looked at the wife again, she had clearly made an effort to come to the garage. Hair, nails and outfit all perfect if a little cheap. A touch older than Spencer, mid to late thirties he guessed. He didn't mind an older woman from time to time. He might well be looking up her information later.

After the husband's test drive, Spencer offered her a drive, knowing she would refuse but acknowledging her part in the decision-making process. After that the sale was a foregone conclusion.

The showroom was quiet once Spencer had got the paperwork out of the way, so he logged onto the message board for some fun. He'd been a bit busy last night and hadn't had a chance to go on so had missed the drama of **DAZZLED** being exposed as a fraud and the whole armed siege thing. Those two threads were dominating the board, so he wouldn't get much attention creating a new one.

Instead he did a search and dragged up an old thread where he and **DAZZLED** had clashed. About money, as always, and who had the most. It was clear to everyone now that Spencer was the victor in this particular spat. Admittedly most of his possessions, the multiple Rolexes, the Paul Smith suits, the Hermes ties, were bought with crippling debt but at least he could prove that he owned them; unlike **DAZZLED**.

He resurrected the thread with only one comment.

DB10: I'll just leave this here.

The message was clear. He was reminding everybody that he was top dog on the message board.

After a little bit fun on the forum, he moved onto more serious matters, his credit card bills. He tried to avoid looking at them, as if they would somehow disappear if he ignored them. But the debt wasn't going anywhere. He'd been shuffling money between them for months, but he was all but maxed out on every last one. There was no more room for manoeuvre. He closed the credit card websites and looked at his sales figures. It had been a slow month. Not because of his sales skills, he could sell a hog roast to a vegan, but the people weren't coming through the door anymore, today's couple were an exception. If something didn't change soon, they would start letting people go. Spencer would be safe, he knew that but Callum, the junior salesman, could be at risk. Maybe he could help make the decision a little bit easier.

He had a look at some of the deals that Callum had been doing, not bad considering he looked like a spotty teenage virgin. Must have been his mentoring that was turning him into a salesman at least that was the justification Spencer gave himself for what he was about to do next.

****

Charlie Blackmore could do without the interrogation this morning. She sipped her coffee as she tried to turn herself around, but the questions wouldn't let up. The grilling wasn't from the police, nothing as simple as that.

"They are making you go to work today," said her mother, "after all that has happened?"

"That's how employment works, Mam. I go in, they give me money."

"But what if there is another gunman?"

"There won't be another gunman."

"But how do you know? There was yesterday."

This was her mother's logic. Something happens once, therefore it must happen every day into eternity. She liked routine.

"The same way that I know there won't be someone taking pot-shots at JFK from a book repository. It was a one-off, big event. That's sort of why it was on the news."

"There's no need to be sarcastic."

"I'm not being sarcastic, just realistic. There won't be another siege, it's perfectly safe."

"But we worry."

"Mam, you worry if I go to the gym after work, you worry if I go for a drink with friends, you worry if I add a friend on Facebook who you haven't heard of. And don't think that I don't know that you snoop around on Facebook investigating my friends."

"I don't snoop, I'm showing an interest. There is a difference. Am I not entitled to show an interest in my only daughter's life?"

"I'm twenty-five years old, Mam. I'm entitled to a private life."

"And what is it that you need to keep private from me and your Dad?"

"I haven't got time for this, I've got to go to work."

"I can't believe that they are making you go in, today of all days."

Her mother did have a point. Phonetix could have given everybody involved the day off but today was likely to be busier than ever. There were all the calls that went unanswered yesterday plus all the additional people who phoned in to chat about what had happened.

Charlie had thought about calling in sick, but she preferred work to listening to her mother all day. She had never taken a day off sick. She tried once when a particularly heavy cold resulted in almost flu like symptoms. She planned a day in bed with a cup of Lemsip, but her mother had other ideas. She researched the symptoms on Google and had narrowed it down to either pleurisy or a rare tropical disease only found amongst the remotest tribes in the Amazon. Charlie had pretended to be better and struggled into work rather than wait for the ambulance and the stay in quarantine that her mother demanded. She wasn't making that mistake again. She grabbed her coat and bag and went to wait at the end of the garden path for her lift.

Charlie negotiated her way past the news crews in the car park and on arriving at her desk, she was relieved to see that her whole team had turned up. This made her life as Team Leader a lot easier. She'd expected at least a couple of them to phone in sick, but the lure of the gossip was strong, none of them wanting to miss out. There was a buzz around the call centre, this was their fifteen minutes of fame. She didn't need fame, she needed coffee.

"We'll have a quick team brief before we log in but if anybody needs a chat about yesterday, let me know. I'm getting a coffee, anybody want one?" said Charlie.

****

Charlie skim read her emails, they were as expected.

Refer all questions about the siege to the press office.

Encourage teams to work through breaks to make up for time lost yesterday.

We are expecting high call volumes today; Team Leaders be prepared to log-in to take calls.

She had been at Phonetix for three years now, the last two spent as a Team Leader. It said a lot about the place that even after an armed siege, she could predict what senior management would say. Nothing about staff welfare following a traumatic event, nothing about staff safety. Nothing about the shitty service that encouraged someone to walk into a call centre with a gun. Should life really be this predictable?

She heard the hurried, thumping footsteps, recognised them and knew what was coming.

"Morning, Michelle," said Charlie.

"Can you get your teams to log-in urgently, the queue is going through the roof?" Michelle, the Operations Manager and Charlie's boss, pointed at the electronic board on the wall with the call stats.

Michelle was barely five foot tall and nearly as wide. She had short spiky orange hair and an ill-fitting bra that made her breasts look like two carrier bags full of baked beans.

"They aren't due to start for another ten minutes and I want to have a catch up with them about yesterday, make sure everybody is okay," said Charlie.

"We haven't got time for that. If they don't log-in now we won't hit our targets."

"Is their welfare not more important than targets?"

But Michelle was already on the move, on to hassle the next Team Leader. She stopped for a moment. "And you, Charlie, all Team Leaders have to take calls. Management orders."

She grabbed her headset. "Sorry guys, they want us to log-in."

"But we don't start for another ten minutes."

"What about the team brief?"

Charlie shrugged and put on her headset. "Management orders."

She knew it was poor management on her behalf to blame those further up the food chain, but they were to blame, and her team knew it. The lack of compassion was as disappointing as it was expected, and Charlie wasn't going to defend it. The team recognised this and reluctantly donned their headsets as well. One by one they logged in. One by one they recited the script.

"Good morning, you are through to Phonetix Mobile. How may I help?"

Charlie knew she had a good team and they trusted her, but she hated the company. She needed to get out. Get out of the job, get out of Sunderland, get out of the country.

She glanced at the picture of Sydney Harbour taped to her desk, shook her head and logged in.

"Good morning, you are through to Phonetix Mobile. How may I help?"

****

Rebecca Proctor breathed a sigh of relief. Two children safely dropped off at school and nursery without major incident. There had been many minor incidents of course. The youngest having a tantrum because he wasn't allowed to dress as Spiderman. The eldest spilling cereal down her school dress, almost certainly on purpose. But these were everyday occurrences and as much as she loved her kids, she was relieved to see the back of them for a few hours. She had negotiated the traffic without any problems and was now safely in the office, ready to deal with the three hundred employees of cutting-edge software firm, Stratosphere.

As HR manager, she loved her job. It threw up different challenges every day and she was part of the DNA of the company. She'd joined seven years ago, straight out of university; and then she fell pregnant.

The company had been great with her and had gone over and above their legal obligations, letting her know that she was valued, and she would be when she returned from maternity leave. There was a mutual respect, and this was the relationship she tried to have with all the employees. Look after your staff and they will look after you. It seemed to work, the company had grown rapidly and had found its niche in a rapidly changing market.

A box of muffins lay open on the desk of the HR office. "Morning, they smell lovely, where did they come from?"

"Thomas dropped them in as a thank you for the help we gave him with recruitment. He's lovely."

Thomas was a favourite with the HR girls. He recognised the job they did and always remembered to thank them. A simple thank you was more than enough but cakes were always welcome.

"Sure he's trying to fatten us up," said Rebecca, "think I'll make a cuppa."

Rebecca headed into the kitchen where Thomas was filling the filter coffee machine.

"Thanks for the muffins, it was a lovely thought."

"Always keep on the right side of HR, you never know when you might need them. Coffee?"

"Yes, please."

They stood in silence as the coffee percolated. One of the young graduate trainees came in to raid the biscuit tin in lieu of a proper breakfast. His limbs appeared to be made out of Twiglets and could snap at any minute if the tin lid was too heavy. The pallid complexion and bags under his eyes suggested long nights of playing Magic The Gathering with his wizard pals rather than long hours spent in the office. There was an evident sense of relief when the tin wasn't full of Rich Teas.

Rebecca thought about how nice it would be to be that carefree, that your only concern was whether there were chocolate Hob Nobs in the biscuit tin. No kids, no husband, no debts to worry about. She'd never had that phase in her life. She went university, job, pregnant, marriage in that order. She wouldn't swap the kids for the world, but she did sometimes wonder what it would be like.

The beeping of the coffee machine brought her out of her daydream and Thomas poured her coffee. "See you at lunch?"

"Yeah, I've got meetings all morning but should be free about one. Got to dash."

She returned to the office with a smile on her face.

The day flew over and before she knew it, Rebecca was picking the kids up from the childminder, Daisy.

"I'm sorry to bring this up," said Daisy once they were out of earshot of the children, "but the cheque Spencer gave me bounced."

"Cheque," said Rebecca, "why's he giving you a cheque? We have a standing order set up."

"He cancelled it. Said that cheques were easier, tax purposes or something."

"How much do we owe you? I'll get it from the cash machine now."

"It's £200 but don't worry about it, give me it tomorrow."

"You sure? I'm really sorry, Daisy. Seems like we've had a bit of a communication breakdown. I'll speak to Spencer tonight and get it sorted. Sorry again."

"No problem, see you tomorrow."

Rebecca could feel the pressure growing at her temples when she got into the car, she'd never been so embarrassed. The kids fighting in the back seat weren't helping her mood.

"Will you two be quiet? NOW!"

They got the message and played in silence until she pulled up at the cashpoint at Sainsbury's.

"I'll just be a second."

The middle machine became free and she entered her card and PIN and tried to withdraw £200 so she would have it ready for Daisy first thing in the morning.

INSUFFICIENT FUNDS.

"You have got to be kidding me."

She tried again, same message.

Rebecca tried to process what was happening, it didn't make sense. Spencer and she spent a lot of money, Spencer mainly but they had good incomes, so it was never an issue. She couldn't understand how they were overdrawn. She'd check with the bank once she had got the kids home and made their tea.

Rebecca wasn't going to waste time trying to persuade the kids to eat healthily tonight so she put some chicken nuggets in the oven as they played in the sitting room. She fired up the iPad to log-in to the banking app, but her log-in details didn't work anymore. She tried again but was denied. She decided against attempting a third time in case she locked the account.

Her phone vibrated with a message.

Spencer: Playing squash tonight, will be late in.

She replied. **Have you changed the password on our bank account?**

Rebecca waited for a couple of minutes but there was no reply. She rang his number, but it went straight to voicemail. She hung up.

"Don't do this, Spencer."

Shouting from the sitting room alerted her to a more immediate problem and she went in to break up the fighting. The remote control was the source of the dispute, as it usually was, so she removed it from them and placed it out of reach. They were stuck with Peppa Pig whether they liked it or not. How a brother and sister could go from playing happily, to all-out war and then back to playing peacefully all within the space of a minute was beyond Rebecca.

None of this was in the marriage brochure.

****

Darren was in the zone. He may have lost his spreadsheet, but he had been battling with these people on the forum for years, he knew their lives inside out. It was the usual suspects calling him out on the thread about his flat and he was going to take them down one by one. He had to deal with the biggest and most urgent threat first though. Things had escalated since he last posted and the whole message board had worked out who he was. He posted a new thread.

My account had been hacked.

I LOVE MY NANA: My usual account DAZZLED has been hacked so I have had to start this one. The hackers are posting libellous stuff about me and my living conditions. I have instructed my solicitors to deal with it but in the meantime, I would like the moderators to lock the account and ban the IP address of the perpetrators.

Anybody posting on that thread will be hearing from my lawyers.

It was a little over the top and most would ignore it but the threat of solicitors should shake off a few of the stragglers. It wasn't long before the replies began flooding in.

LEFT WING LOTHARIO: The old "I've been hacked excuse." Never gets old.

SIR STANLEY CUMMINS: See you in court Dazza.

ROKER REJECT: Dust yourself down Dazza.

GINGER SNAPS: I think he will make a clean sweep of things.

CURLY WATTS GEGS: Will he be making a 'Pledge' on the bible when he's in court?

TROTSKYREDANDWHITE: Hope the evidence doesn't get brushed under the carpet.

This wasn't going as Darren had hoped, they had turned it into a pun thread. Every reply was a pun based on the state of his flat. Once a thread was a pun thread, they rarely recovered. It would take something drastic to get it back on track. Something drastic came in the form of the next post.

Moderator: We don't normally comment on such threads but as you are trying to clean up your act, we thought we would make an exception. We've checked the IP address of the person posting as DAZZLED and would you believe that it is exactly the same IP address they have always posted from? The exact same address that I LOVE MY NANA is posting from now. We've tracked it to a one bedroom flat in Southwick. Hope this 'clears things up'.

This couldn't be true. How could they be posting from the same address? Unless they had cloned his address, or worse, they were still using his computer, he just couldn't see it. He unplugged the PC from the wall. He needed a different strategy.

Darren needed to think, and he couldn't think on an empty stomach. He wandered to Southwick Green, the main shopping centre. It mainly consisted of bookies, bargain food stores and charity shops along with various food establishments. He avoided the cafes masquerading as coffee shops and found himself an old-fashioned greasy spoon. He ordered a large bacon and egg sandwich and a cup of milky tea and found himself a seat by the window. He watched the world going by, making judgements on everybody who walked by the window. Fat, slag, dole waller, thief, immigrant, senile, scruffy. It was easy to label people without knowing the first thing about them.

"Here you go, love." The waitress put down his tea and sandwich.

He didn't bother saying thank you before biting into the bun, spilling egg yolk down his front. He wiped it off with his sleeve and licked the yolk from his arm. The sweatshirt wasn't a clean one, so it didn't matter. His sweatshirts were rarely clean ones.

A group of young lads waited on the corner, sports bags slung over their shoulders. They laughed, joked, pushed each other and played around having fun until a mini bus pulled up. All the lads piled on, shaking hands with the occupants and each were handed a can of lager which they cracked open before sitting down. The bus pulled away and they were singing as they passed the cafe.

"Wankers," thought Darren. They were off on a stag do, footy trip or some other pathetic excuse for a lads' weekend away. Why did people need to go away to have fun? Why did they need to drink at 10:30 in the morning? Darren had never understood it. Darren never would. He'd not been out of the North East, never been on a stag do and had never had the friends who were likely to invite him on one. The closest people he had to friends were on the message board and the majority on there hated him without having even met him.

He looked out of the window again as a young couple went past, hand in hand. Yet another thing he hadn't experienced.

"Young love," said the waitress, "we were all like that once."

"Not me."

"You not married then, pet?"

Darren wasn't sure if she was goading him. "I don't have the time for girlfriends. It's all a con to get money out of you for flowers and shit."

The waitress raised her eyebrows. "Wow, someone must have really hurt you." She walked off.

He went to take another bite of his sandwich but somehow didn't feel hungry anymore. He gulped his tea, belched loudly and left the cafe, barging past an old man who was trying to push his way in through the door before he could get out.

He didn't want to go back to the flat yet and wasn't one for walking, so he plonked himself on the bench and tried to have some time to think to himself. It wasn't long before his peace was shattered as an elderly lady sat next to him.

"Eeee, it's nice to take the weight off. Lovely day, isn't it?"

"If you say so," said Darren.

"You're a talkative one."

"Aye, well, I was quite happy sitting here having a think until you came along." Darren watched the people on the bus stuck at the traffic lights and wondered where they were going, wishing he could join them.

"Who shat on your cornflakes? You're a young lad, you can't waste your life twisting your face around here."

"Aye, whatever."

"Cheer up Darren, you miserable bugger."

Darren looked the other way, trying not to engage. He sat for a couple of minutes attempting to clear his mind, but something came to him. "Darren? How come you know my name?"

But the old lady had gone.

****

Darren had gone against his normal principles and spent some money on getting his PC cleaned properly and anti-virus software installed. It wasn't fool-proof but it at least gave him a certain level of comfort that it was now secure and he wasn't being watched. There was nothing he could do about his message board account being hacked but it had been two weeks now and they hadn't posted anything from the **DAZZLED** username. Maybe the worst of it was over.

He'd slipped back into his routine, arguing online, ordering takeaways, not cleaning the flat. If he was to get back to being the best on the internet, he had to go back to basics. He created a new spreadsheet, filling it with whatever he could remember about users and adding to it as and when new stuff came up.

Despite the drama of two weeks ago, the forum had returned to normal with the usual insults and counter insults going backwards and forwards. He was no longer the centre of attention although, whenever he began to get the upper hand in a thread, the state of his flat would inevitably be brought up. Absolute denial that it was his seemed to be the best policy. As was always the case in these circumstances, the truth was never an option.

Apart from the day to day arguments he was having, one poster was pushing his buttons. **DB10** and Darren always rubbed up against each other. Arguing about who had the best car, house, suits etc. and more often than not, one of them getting a short-term ban from the board until they had cooled down. The past week had been a Godsend for **DB10** and he wasn't going to let it go.

DB10: You cleaned up those shitty undercrackers from the floor yet Dazza?

GINGER SNAPS: Hold on whilst I get some popcorn, this could get interesting.

I LOVE MY NANA: You couldn't even afford a pair of my pants. Get yourself down to George at Asda and get yourself three pairs for a fiver.

DB10: You still trying to convince yourself that it wasn't your flat?

I LOVE MY NANA: I don't need to convince anyone. Everyone knows I was hacked.

He fell short of blaming **DB10** for the hack. Whilst it would be good to throw some shade over the whole episode, he wouldn't like to give him the credit that he was capable of such a thing.

DB10: Yeah, hacked from your own computer. Who did it? Your butler?

This gained a few laughs from the onlookers via the use of emoticons. Darren hated it when they did that. If they didn't have anything to say why didn't they butt out of the conversation.

I LOVE MY NANA: We all know that you are jealous. Not noticed you put any pictures of your luxury house yet.

DB10: At least I'd clean away my soiled underwear before I did.

I LOVE MY NANA: So you're admitting that you soil your underwear?

As soon as he pressed the post button he knew that he had made a mistake. He didn't become the best at internet arguments by sinking to childish insults. Do your research, lay your trap and let the other posters fall into it; that's how you win. Whenever anyone replied to him with a childish insult he knew they were rattled, and it wasn't long before people picked up on his sign of weakness. The first reply was a picture of some handbags, it didn't get any better after that.

SIR STANLEY CUMMINS: Are they Dazza's handbags?

CURLY WATTS GEGS: He couldn't afford them, probably just uses Aldi carrier bags.

SIR STANLEY CUMMINS: He probably uses Aldi carrier bags as his underpants.

Darren had to let the thread go for now, he couldn't win this one. He scrolled through the other threads seeing if there was anything he could get his teeth into. One about someone losing their job looked interesting, there were bound to be opportunities for a wind up on there.

Darren heard the letter box go and whilst he couldn't be bothered to wander downstairs to check, there was always that sneaking little feeling of anticipation that it might be something interesting. A notification about a windfall he knew nothing about, a letter from a mystery admirer. Anything but the usual junk mail.

Eventually, his curiosity got the better of him and he edged down the stairs. He could see the Dominos leaflet with its money off coupons; always welcome. There were other takeaway menus along with two brown envelopes. He headed back upstairs to the flat, a little disappointed with his haul. He made himself a cuppa before examining the letters. They were official ones from HMRC. Maybe his benefits were being increased. He opened the first and didn't get much further than one word.

Sanctions.

He tried to focus on the letter, but only odd words and phrases caught his eye.

Benefits temporarily suspended.

Pending investigation.

It all started to blur after that. He felt dizzy, he started to sweat; more than usual. He stumbled to the sink and vomited into it over the unwashed dishes that were piled high.

"They can't stop my benefits," he thought, *"how am I supposed to survive?"*

He staggered back to the kitchen table and grabbed the second letter, tearing it open. It was an appointment for an interview in two days' time in which he was to explain why he had been fraudulently claiming Employment Support Allowance (ESA) for a disability he didn't have. This wasn't good, this wasn't good at all. He stood in the doorway of his bedroom and stared at his PC. "Have you not had your revenge yet?"

CHAPTER THREE

Darren was shaking. He couldn't remember being this nervous since school; maybe before his Nana's funeral but that was it. He'd spent the last two hours worrying about what to wear. He was being accused of fraudulently claiming benefits. Did he wear a suit and create a good impression or dress down to reinforce the impression that he wasn't fit for work? The trousers of his funeral suit no longer getting past his thighs took the decision away from him. The decision not to shower was his own.

The bus into town was packed and he was lucky to get a seat. The person sat next to him didn't feel so lucky and sniffed once before facing out of the window in disgust. Rain lashed down and drummed on the roof of the bus. Darren had already been caught in the downpour and it dripped off his coat onto the floor. His trainers were soaked through and his light grey jogging bottoms were now almost black.

He hoped the pathetic sight he presented would garner some sympathy in the interview. He got off the bus at the old Joplings department store and was surprised to find himself on time. Rather than head straight to the Job Centre he popped into Greggs, hoping that his ban wasn't city wide.

Filled with a corned beef pasty and with enough crumbs down his front to add to his dishevelled look, Darren headed to his interview. As he entered the Job Centre he produced some old safety glasses that he found on the bus once and put them on. The thick lenses helped with his claims that he could barely see. The crutch that he had stolen from the hospital aided the main part of his claim; the bad back that meant he couldn't stand or sit for prolonged periods. Satisfied that he looked suitably unemployable, he entered the Job Centre. He hated the place. The people who worked there, the scumbags who frequented the place trying to scam the government out of a few quid. He was doing exactly the same as them, but he was different.

He went to reception to announce his arrival where he was reminded that he was late. Of course he was late, he was unemployable. He thought that was a nice touch. Before he had a chance to sit he was called in for his interview. He'd had many of them over the years and he'd nailed them all but they were the usual run of the mill discussions.

He knew this one was going to be a little trickier. How tricky it would be became evident when the room was set out like a police interview room with a tape recorder at one end of the table. This was another level. He was officially cautioned as soon as he sat down which threw him again.

"I thought you would have at least offered me a coffee first." He tried to make light of it to hide his nerves.

Neither of his interviewers were in the mood for jokes. "It isn't that sort of interview, Mr Updike."

Darren realised that he was gripping the base of the chair and his knuckles had turned white. He tried to relax but his stomach was flipping more than a pan on pancake day. Only one interviewer had spoken so far. He was a thick set man who could have been anything between twenty-five and fifty-five years old. He didn't seem the type to appreciate Darren's sense of humour.

"As you've arrived late, we'll avoid the niceties and get straight to the point. Mr Updike, have you been fraudulently claiming Employment Support Allowance?"

—

"No, of course not and I find it very offensive for you to suggest that."

"May I remind you that you are under caution and it is in your interests to tell the truth from the beginning?" said the second interviewer, a small, mousey woman, again of indeterminate age, who looked as if she hadn't laughed since Jim Davidson was on television.

"I am telling the truth. Just because you have government targets to reach, doesn't mean you can bully the disabled. I have rights."

"You do have rights, Mr Updike," said the woman with the merest hint of a smile at one side of her mouth, "but we have the evidence."

"Evidence? Of what?"

Darren grew in confidence a little. He knew he hadn't done any work on the side, the one thing that normally caught out fraudulent claimants. He was too clever to be caught out like that; or too lazy. Whatever it was, they were mistaken.

"We have CCTV footage of you that shows that you aren't quite as disabled as you would like us to believe."

"CCTV footage. You've been trailing me? That's against my Human Rights."

"We haven't, and it isn't. Regardless, due to the good nature of a concerned member of the public who had access to these tapes, we now have a compilation of your greatest hits."

"Concerned member of the public?" thought Darren.

Darren knew he was defeated before he was shown the video. These people had really done a number on him. Attack his computer, ruin his reputation and now cut off his only source of income. They were destroying him bit by bit.

"All this for winding up a few call centre workers?"

"Come on then, let's see it."

The woman pressed play and there were hazy images of someone stood outside of what looked like a Greggs.

"That could be anyone, it's all blurred."

"Maybe if you removed those ridiculous glasses it would become a little clearer."

Darren removed the glasses, placing them on the table and it was clearly him standing outside of Greggs.

"Going to Greggs isn't a crime."

"Maybe not. But when you claim that you can't walk without the aid of a stick and you can't see without extra thick lensed glasses, one does wonder how you managed to find yourself outside of Greggs without either."

"That proves nothing, I'm resting against the wall. I'm not doing anything."

"Not until you make a dash for the butchers. You must have been hungry."

Darren shook his head in resignation. "Is that it?"

"We have much more, this one was a particular favourite of ours."

"You don't have anything, you are just trying to put the frighteners on me."

"The frighteners? We couldn't frighten you, Mr Updike. Anyone who is as disabled as you claim to be, anyone who can't take more than a couple of steps yet still lives in a first floor flat and isn't afraid of the staircase. Well, they don't sound like someone who could easily be frightened. We have more videos if you would like us to go on?"

"Don't bother."

Whilst Darren had been at the top of his game for a while, he knew when he was beaten.

"We'll be in touch soon with our decision. Is there anything you want to add before you go?"

"No." Darren pushed his chair back and headed for the door.

"Mr Updike?"

"Yes?"

"You've forgotten your glasses."

****

The CCTV footage had thrown Darren and he knew he hadn't performed in the interview. In the past, he would have been able to bluff his way through something like that, but the events of the past week had battered his confidence. He wished that he had asked about timescales or what happened next. Had his benefits been stopped? Was his rent still being paid? Would he need to find a job?

He cracked open a can of Coke, gulping half of it down in one go then started typing.

I LOVE MY NANA: Does anyone know the timescales for decisions on sanctions after an interview at the Job Centre? It's for my gardener. My privets are becoming a bit unruly whilst he sorts it out.

SIR STANLEY CUMMINS: They finally caught up with you Dazza? Looks like you'll have to join the rest of us in the workplace. It's not too bad, you'll still be playing on the internet all day, the difference is that you'll be getting paid for it.

ROKER REJECT: I've never been unemployed so wouldn't know but I think it depends on when a place in prison becomes available.

DB10: About time they caught up with you, you pathetic little scumbag. Hopefully they lock you up so we don't have to listen to your deluded fantasies anymore.

Darren should have known better than to ask. Whether he was asking on behalf his imaginary gardener or he really was in trouble, nobody was going to help him. His life was a soiled bed of his own making, and he had to lie in it. A sensible man would have switched off his PC and never returned to the message board. Darren wasn't that man.

I LOVE MY NANA: You'd know all about fantasies. Showing photos of yourself next to fancy cars means nothing. We all know that you work in one of those cash in hand car washes.

DB10: Whatever Dazza, you're the one in trouble with the dole. You'll be begging for a job in one of those car washes soon. And for the record, I've driven more top of the range motors than you've even seen. What do you drive, a mobility scooter?

Darren had once considered buying a mobility scooter as a way of getting around with minimum effort. He'd never stated it publicly but with a drink holder for his Coke, an extra soft cushion to ward off his haemorrhoids and a registration plate spelling out 'DAZZA'; it was his dream purchase. **DB10** knew him too well.

I LOVE MY NANA: Typical DB10, mocking the disabled. You should be ashamed. Mods, he should be banned for this.

It was a standard message board tactic. Start losing the argument, change the topic of discussion. It was a diversionary approach used long before message boards cropped up. Politicians, newspapers, almost everybody in the workplace; they all used it. The call for a ban was just as pathetic and Darren knew it. It was wishful thinking that **DB10** would give him a break.

He closed the forum tab and went onto the YouGov website to see if it gave him any information. Maybe he should have come here first. Whilst the information provided wasn't conclusive, Darren discovered that he'd be put out of his misery sooner rather than later. He prayed that the outcome would be in his favour but expected the worst. Maybe it was time to think about careers. It's not something Darren had ever done before, even when he was at school he had no desire for a career, his careers teacher finally snapping at his sarcasm and telling him that he needed to lose a few pounds if he wanted to fit into a Space Shuttle.

He made a list.

Journalist. Darren already spent all day typing on the internet, he had opinions, and nobody could argue that he didn't know how to do research. It was the first item on his list and it already felt like the perfect match. *"Why didn't I think of this sooner?"*

If the decision at the Job Centre didn't go his way, he would fire off a couple of emails. He would only consider working for the best newspapers, The Mail, The Sun, The Express, he had no time for the likes of The Guardian or The Observer; despite never having read them. He could point to the number of likes and replies he had to his posts on the forum as evidence of his suitability for the job. He was the top poster on the message board, it wasn't too big a leap for him to become a top journalist.

His mind was made up that he would become a journalist, but he jotted down some other options just in case journalism wasn't for him.

Train driver. Sitting down all day, very little effort involved as the trains run on tracks, so he could probably spend most of the day browsing the internet. For some time, he had argued that the role should be automated or that the jobs should be given to the unemployed whenever the train drivers went on strike. Whilst the rail companies were still paying top whack for one of the easiest jobs in the world, Darren was more than happy to drive this particular gravy train.

Postman. On the face of it, there was a lot of effort involved in walking about, but Darren didn't see why it couldn't be done on a mobility scooter. It meant getting up early but he would be finished by ten, so he could spend the day in bed or on the internet. Add in the Christmas tips and the number of bored housewives offering their services and it was worth considering.

Darren had only been thinking about it for five minutes and he already had three potential careers mapped out.

Anyone who thought he feared losing his dole was delusional.

****

It was nearly one in the afternoon when Darren heard the letterbox rattle. Whilst everyone knew that posties were finished their round by ten, his seemed to be late every day.

Darren had seen her once or twice and was surprised to find that they employed women now. That would explain the lateness, they were probably allowed to start late due to child care arrangements or some other politically correct nonsense. Maybe she liked a lie in.

He approached the stairs with a certain amount of trepidation. The Job Centre interview had knocked him sideways and whilst he had potential careers mapped out, this life on benefits was all that he knew.

He was both desperate for the decision and terrified of the outcome. The inevitable couldn't be delayed any longer as a single brown envelope lay on the mat at the front door. He edged down the stairs, gripping onto the bannister whilst his back slid down the wall. He reached the bottom step and stared at the envelope for a minute before attempting to pick it up.

The enormity of what could be in that envelope hit him and his legs began to shake. He took the final step and slumped onto the floor beside it. He considered taking the letter upstairs and making a cup of tea before opening it, but the decision had been made and he needed to know what it was. For once in his life, he wasn't sure he could stomach a cuppa anyway. This was the moment of truth. He tore open the envelope and read the contents.

The decision was brutal, his benefits had been stopped. Not only had his ESA been stopped but he needed to repay his overpayments unless he fancied a trip to court and a stay in prison. He banged his head against the door, rattling the letterbox once again. The staircase towered in front of him. The staircase that had been pivotal in the case against him now seemed as big a challenge as it would be if he were really disabled. His legs were now jelly and he had no desire to stand up. He curled into a ball and cried.

———

After five minutes on the floor, Darren knew he had to move but his legs still betrayed him. He crawled up the stairs, grasping the letter in his hand. Once he reached the top stair, he dragged himself to his feet, staggered into the bedroom and collapsed onto the bed. If he could lay here, maybe it would all go away. Maybe it was all just a bad dream. The letter gripped in his sweaty paw proved that it was very real and sooner or later he had to accept reality. But not yet. He rolled over, wrapped himself in his quilt and fell asleep.

Darren awoke confused, sweating and tangled in his quilt. The clock showed that it was 2pm. At first, he wasn't sure why he had been asleep and as he attempted to untangle himself he felt the crumpled paper beneath him. The decision from the Job Centre.

It all came rushing back. Nothing good came through that letter box these days. Maybe he should tape it up.

He dragged himself out of his pit and went to put the kettle on. Maybe a cup of tea and some Hob Nobs could help him come up with a solution. While the teabag steeped in the mug, Darren opened the fridge to get the milk, but the carton was empty. He had no idea why he had put an empty one back in the fridge but now he was left with two options; walk to the corner shop or drink black tea. Neither of them was acceptable to him so he dropped the carton onto the pile of rubbish overflowing from the bin, grabbed a can of Coke and the Hob Nobs and went back into his bedroom.

Deep down Darren knew that this situation was of his own making. He'd picked a fight with the wrong people and they had gone to town on him, but he wasn't beaten; not yet. When he was a journalist he would expose them for the pathetic hackers that they were. It wouldn't surprise him if they were working for the Russian government. Once he had the Daily Mail behind him, they wouldn't be so confident. It was time he started firing off some job applications, it was time for Darren to prove everybody wrong, it was time to prove that he was the best.

****

Darren checked his inbox again. Weeks had passed, and he couldn't understand why none of the editors of the national newspapers had responded when he had offered to work for them. He had a look at the careers page on their websites, but they all mentioned journalism degrees, internships and lots of other stuff he had no interest in. Why couldn't life be simple? He'd had follow up interviews at the Job Centre where he'd told them he was going to be a journalist for the Daily Mail. They used phrases like 'manage expectations' and told him that he was better off looking for factory work. He was on the most basic Job Seeker's allowance and his rent was no longer getting paid, he needed to look at his back up options.

They stopped being options as soon as he typed their description into Google. Train driving had a selection criterion stricter than the SAS and a lengthy training course and exams that you had to pass before you could even sit in the seat and press the buttons. Why did they make it so difficult for a job that was so easy?

Postman wasn't much better. Whilst it was possibly easier to get your foot through the door, the hours weren't quite what Darren was expecting. Apparently, finishing at ten in the morning was no longer standard practice. Surely there was a job out there that was easy to get and easy to do. Another rattle of the letterbox and another brown envelope gave him his answer.

Darren laughed out loud when he read it. Surely this was a wind up. Somebody was having a joke at his expense. Were they really sending him on a call centre training course? What sort of training could anyone need? You answer the phone, you argue with the customer, you hang up and move onto the next one. Easiest job in the world. Darren had spent the last few years tormenting call centre workers for this very reason. They had an easy job, so he set out to make it more difficult for them.

He resented being told that he had to attend the course, but he thought it might be a laugh.

****

Wiping the crumbs from his sweatshirt, Darren wandered into the training room. He knew he was late, but it wasn't his fault. The course was on a business park and the bus had taken longer than expected. He'd then spent ten minutes attempting to find the Greggs before he realised that he didn't know which building he was meant to be in. He'd wandered around aimlessly before a passing security guard noticed that he looked a bit lost and pointed him in the right direction. He was only half an hour late, it's not like he would have missed much.

"You must be Darren," said Rob, the trainer, "take a seat please."

Darren noticed that everybody else had a cuppa. "Can I get a cup of tea first?"

"No, we've already started. We'll have a break soon, you can get one then."

Darren scraped a chair across the floor and slumped down in it. He surveyed the room. A mix of ages, male and female and all of them eagerly taking notes and listening to Rob.

"Mugs," thought Darren.

A couple of the men even wore a shirt and tie. Who were they trying to impress? He was soon to find out. After another thirty minutes of drivel, the long-awaited break came. As Darren pushed his way to the front of the queue for tea, he noticed that everybody else was chatting. Not full on conversations but nervously finding their way with others in the room. Everybody ignored him.

He grabbed a handful of custard creams as Rob approached. "Can I have a word, Darren?"

"Suppose so," he said as he rammed a biscuit into his mouth.

"I'll make this easy for you. I'll assume that you have a perfectly valid reason for being late."

"The bus was late." Crumbs flew to the floor.

"Let me finish. I'll assume that you have a valid reason and I'll also assume that it won't happen again. I'll also assume that you will show the right attitude throughout the rest of the course."

"There's nothing wrong with my attitude."

"I never said there was however you are the only one in the room not taking notes. You are the only one browsing on your phone when you should be listening. I'm going to assume that is because you missed the beginning of the session where we discussed what standards we expect from you."

"Standards?"

"Yes, Darren. We expect everybody to arrive on time, we expect everybody to listen and we expect everybody to dress as if they haven't just crawled out of bed."

"Why? It's only a poxy training course." Darren slurped a mouthful of tea.

"It may only be a poxy training course, but it is one that you must pass, or your benefits get stopped."

"Stopped? You can't stop them, how am I meant to survive?"

"By getting a job. And believe it or not, I am here to help you do that, but I have more than just you in this class. I have nineteen other people to help pass this course and I need you to help me by doing what I ask."

"Why should I help you?"

"It's called respect, Darren."

"Respect. Why do I have to respect you?"

"You don't necessarily but if you want to succeed in the workplace, then you need to respect yourself."

Darren's face was bright red as he sat. He felt threatened and humiliated, but he knew he had no choice but to abide by the rules.

"Welcome back everybody," said Rob, "I think we are ready for some role play. Darren, come to the front please, you can go first."

"For fuck's sake."

****

—

Charlie sat in yet another Team Leader meeting considering her life choices. She had little to no interest in anything that was being said as everyone competed to be heard. She took a sip of her coffee as she stared into the car park below. A delivery van parked in the disabled bay. A latecomer dashed across the car park, no doubt thinking up their excuse on the move. In the distance stood Penshaw Monument, a landmark to anybody from Sunderland to let them know that they were home. A landmark to Charlie that let her know that she was trapped, and she had never been anywhere. She was brought out of her daydream by one word.

"Recruitment."

A groan went around the room.

"As you know," said Michelle, the Operations Manager, "staff turnover has been quite high recently so we're having another recruitment drive."

"Should we not be looking at why so many people are leaving?" said Charlie.

"We don't have time for that, we need bodies through the door. You've been lucky Charlie, none of your team have left recently."

"It's not luck, I work really hard to ensure that they are happy."

"Well, we're sharing that happiness. We're splitting your team up and spreading them around the call centre."

"You can't do that, I've got them all settled."

"The change will do them good, we don't want people getting complacent."

Charlie shook her head but knew it was a pointless argument. Nobody was interested in the work she put in to retain the staff on her team. Nobody cared that she took the time to get to know them and tried to be as flexible as possible given the restrictions imposed by Phonetix. Since she took over as Team Leader, the only people who had left her team had left due to promotion. None had left the company. She was very proud of this but now her team was going to be taken away from her.

"What sort of recruitment will it be?" said Charlie.

It was a loaded question and everybody in the room knew it.

"We will be recruiting via the normal channels, but we have a target to take twenty-five percent from the Job Centre call centre training courses."

Another groan.

"Why can't we employ the best people for the role?"

"If we take them from the Job Centre, their wages are subsidised for the first year which means more profit for Phonetix and more bonus for you."

"But it's a false economy, hardly any of them survive the first year."

"I'd rather you didn't use words like survive after the siege. It's going to be hard enough recruiting after that as it is. That's your target Charlie, unless you want to be joining them down the Job Centre."

She shook her head again and prepared herself for the next argument where the rest of the Team Leaders tried to cherry pick the best of her staff for their teams.

She needed to get out of this place. She needed to work on her exit plan. She jotted a list of the people on her team and a list of the Team Leaders and tried to formulate a strategy on how to protect the best of the former from the worst of the latter.

Charlie returned to her team with a dejected weariness. She was losing half of them to other Team Leaders and it felt like she was losing members of her family. Whilst the team had existed before she became a manager, she had brought some of them along from being new starters and she was proud of every one of them.

She was proud of herself for having the best performing team in the call centre. What the senior managers didn't understand was that she achieved this, not by using targets as a stick to beat them with but by giving them the support and the skills needed to do the job effectively. She knew they would be fine once they moved on, but she wasn't sure that she had the energy to start again with a new team.

—

"Team meeting in ten minutes."

There was a buzz of excitement, any excuse to get off the phones.

"Anything exciting?" said one.

"Some new opportunities," said Charlie.

She looked at her photo of Sydney Harbour again. "*New opportunities,*" she thought. Maybe the time was right.

There was silence in the meeting room after her announcement. "Thoughts anyone?"

"Do we have a choice?"

"I'm afraid not."

"Why are we being punished?"

"You aren't being punished, they are recognising your skills and they think others could benefit from working alongside you. You should take it as a compliment."

"But we're a team. We always stick together."

"You're only going three banks of desks away, it's not like we'll never see each other. We'll still be the number one team."

"Can we have a night out, a leaving do? "

"Yeah, I don't see why not. I think we've earned it," said Charlie.

"Are you sure there's nothing we can do, another armed siege maybe?"

This brought a laugh out of the team.

"Don't even joke about it, you've no idea how sensitive senior management are about such things. Come on, back on the phones. Let's show everybody why we're the best team at Phonetix Mobile."

They all trudged back to their desks, claiming every last second they could off the phones.

CHAPTER FOUR

Darren was on the last day of his call centre training and whilst he wouldn't say he enjoyed it, he doubted that anybody could enjoy role play, he had learned something. He'd learned that the job was a lot harder than he had imagined. For someone who spent half his life typing away on the internet, he found it almost impossible to type whilst talking, a crucial skill for working in a call centre. The way the tone of his voice had an impact on the customer was also a revelation. He knew that if he raised his voice it would more than likely end in an argument; but the idea that it would have a positive impact on the customer if he smiled when talking seemed insane. He didn't believe half of what he was told but he chose to hide his concerns. Some arguments are not worth having. Another vital lesson that he had learned.

"Morning everybody," said Rob, "we've covered a lot of ground in the past few days and I think you have all gained the basic skills to work in a call centre. For our final day, we're looking at a couple of things that could hinder you from getting a job in the first place. Can anybody think what they might be?"

"Bad breath?"

"I wasn't thinking quite so specific but yes, that could be one."

"Criminal convictions?" said a Scottish lad sporting a severe haircut and a neck tattoo that spelled out 'Made from girders.'

"Yes, any unspent convictions could be an issue."

"Even if they weren't my fault? I bought some skunk off this lad and it turned out to be all twigs, so I battered the twat. I can't be blamed for that."

"Probably best not to mention that in an interview," Rob tried to move on quickly. "Anything else?"

Someone else raised their hand. "Online presence?"

"Online presence, exactly. How many of you use social media?"

Everyone raised their hand.

"Do you ever give any thought about who can see what you post online? Potential employers perhaps?"

The colour drained from a lot of faces in the room when the penny dropped.

"They can't do that," said a girl in her twenties, "they've got no right."

"We can argue about the morals all day long," said Rob, "but the simple fact is that employers will do an online search against your name, whether officially or unofficially, and it could make the difference in you getting a job or not."

"Oh Jesus, I'm going to be unemployed forever."

"Do any of you have anything online that you wouldn't want a potential employer to see?"

Half the class put their hand up. The others, including Darren, were lying. His hands were firmly gripping the base of his seat as panic set in. *"What could they find?"*

"This is just a bit of fun," said Rob, "but for the next fifteen minutes I want you to go online and see what you can find out about your fellow trainees."

Darren should have been in his element, it is what he excelled at, however he couldn't help but focus on what everybody else could discover about him.

The results were shared with the group to laughter, gasps and general good spirits. A lot had been found out about them in a short time and Rob had got his point across well. A lot of people would be changing their privacy settings.

There was one notable exception. "Has nobody found out anything about Darren?"

Everyone shook their heads.

"I'm not on Facebook or Twitter or anything."

"What sort of freak doesn't have Facey?" said the Scottish lad.

"Probably the safest approach," said Rob. "So, you don't have an online presence at all Mystery Man?"

"I guess not," said Darren unable to hide the relief at them not finding his message board account and hoping that nobody ever did.

The rest of the day went quickly, and it ended with a small exam. There was an anxious wait whilst the papers were marked, and everyone stood around drinking tea and chatting. Whilst Darren hadn't made any friends, they at least included him in the conversations now.

They were called back in to get the results.

"I'm pleased to announce that everybody has passed. Well done, that's a massive achievement."

A cheer went up and everyone in the room applauded, even Darren. This wasn't like him, he had a broad grin on his face. They waited a bit longer for the certificates to be handed out and Darren hung back until everyone had gone.

This was another first.

"I just wanted to say thanks for all your help." He shuffled from foot to foot. "Especially after the first day."

"No problem Darren, good luck for the future."

Darren shook Rob's hand and walked out, the smile still on his face. Rob resisted the urge to wipe Darren's sweat from his hand until he was out of sight.

Darren got back to the flat, gripping the certificate tightly and wondering if he should put it on the wall. He was surprised to find somebody in his kitchen dressed in shorts, trainers and an anorak.

"You can't just let yourself in."

"I can do what I like, it's my flat. I can especially do what I like when you haven't paid your rent." It was Colin, his landlord.

"It's the dole, there was a mix up with my benefits. I'll have it for you next week." Darren had never bothered to read any of the correspondence properly. The DWP had informed the council of his change in circumstances and they had stopped his housing benefit.

"I'm not a charity, Darren. If I don't get that money by next week, or you miss another payment, you will be out on your rear."

"My rear? The saying is out on your ear."

"Not when I'm saying it, I'll put you on your arse."

"You'll get your money."

"And I'll have you out if you don't tidy this place up, it's disgusting." Colin adjusted himself in his shorts. "Look at the state of this place, it's like a pig's tie in here."

"A pig sty you mean?"

"I know what I mean, it's a bloody mess."

"The cleaner hasn't been." Darren's initial instinct was to lie.

"Cleaner? This place hasn't seen a cleaner since Jesus was a bairn. At least open a window, it smells like something has died in here." Colin stomped off down the stairs slamming the door on his way out.

Darren threw his certificate on the table amongst the empty takeaway cartons and slumped in the chair. One step forward, two steps back.

****

Darren lobbed a few cartons in a bin bag in a half-hearted attempt at tidying. He wasn't happy that Colin had been in the flat and he wasn't happy at the threat of eviction hanging over him. He dumped the black bag on the kitchen floor and logged onto his PC.

I LOVE MY NANA: Does the landlord have the right to come into your flat whenever he wants?

SIR STANLEY CUMMINS: Has he been making sexual advances towards you?

ROKER REJECT: Best check that he hasn't shit in your knicker drawer.

Darren knew that he wouldn't get serious answers straight away and he even left out any pretence about asking for his cleaner or saying it was a luxury holiday home he was renting. He just needed an answer so played along.

I LOVE MY NANA: Ha ha. I'll check. Does anybody know what my rights are here? It doesn't seem right that he can be sat in my kitchen when I come home.

SIR STANLEY CUMMINS: I'm no Legal Eagle but this link from the Citizens Advice Bureau might help.

Darren checked the link that had been posted and it was useful. He'd been on this message board under various guises for well over five years and this was the first time he could remember asking for advice and receiving it. He had previously asked for advice on top restaurants in Manhattan and the best place to get a bespoke suit and various other things that he had no intention of ever using other than to create the impression that he was successful. This was a first for him.

I LOVE MY NANA: Cheers, that's really helpful.

SIR STANLEY CUMMINS: No problem, don't let the landlord take the piss.

Spencer had just finished doctoring some more documents, adding his initials where Callum's should be to take his commission. Times were tough, and Callum would learn the hard way. The showroom was quiet, so he logged onto the message board to see what was happening. The post from Darren was an open goal to him.

DB10: The landlord has every right to be in the property when he has scumbag tenants like you. Why don't you try getting a job and paying your rent you absolute tramp?

ROKER REJECT: That's a bit harsh DB10.

DB10: Not harsh at all, he needs to learn that he can't live off other people's earnings. He's a parasite and he should be wiped out. I wouldn't have him living in any of my properties.

SIR STANLEY CUMMINS: Because you don't own any?

DB10: More than you ever will. Crawl back under your rock and let the grown ups speak.

SIR STANLEY CUMMINS: Grown ups? You're the biggest bairn on here. Always bragging about how much pocket money you get and how shiny your new Matchbox car is. Nobody is interested you dullard.

The argument raged on and Darren chose to stay out of it. He was beginning to understand the wisdom of not trying to win every argument. The truth of the matter was that **DB10** was right. He was the parasite that he always mocked on the message board. He was living off benefits and had no shame in doing so but that was slowly being taken away from him. For every one person like Rob trying to help him, there were two or three wanting to knock him down. He needed to do something about it.

Spencer sat at his desk in the showroom watching the argument unfold online. Everybody was wading in now, some siding with him, some with **I LOVE MY NANA,** but his main target had retreated from the field of battle. Spencer wasn't that bothered about continuing if the big game wasn't there, so he left them to it. He printed his doctored sales documents and took them into his manager, George, to countersign.

"Alright boss, mind sticking your moniker on the bottom of these?"

"Just put them down there, I'll have a look at them later."

"I've already double checked them, so you don't need to, everything's in order."

"Ok, leave them there, I'll sign them in a bit."

"No worries, you're the boss." Spencer dropped them into the in tray and headed back into the showroom.

"Spencer, before you go. How's the new lad getting on?"

"He's keen, I'll give him that, but he hasn't mastered the art of sealing the deal yet. I've been having to step in and rescue them. Don't worry though, if the master here can't teach him to sell, nobody can."

He didn't wait for a reply and he was already chatting up the receptionist when George muttered "Tosser" under his breath.

They didn't have much time for each other. Spencer resented George's position and George disliked his arrogance. You had to be arrogant to be a car salesman, but Spencer pushed the boundaries. It would trip him up one of these days and George was going to be there when it happened. Callum was walking past his office and George called him in.

"How's it going, son?"

"Really enjoying it, thanks. I'm learning loads, everyone here is willing to help."

"You sold many cars yet?"

"Quite a lot, more than I imagined I would in my first few weeks. Managed to shift that black Vogue with all the extras yesterday, it was my best deal yet."

"Good work, keep it up lad."

As Callum left the office, George looked through the papers in his in tray until he found the paperwork for the black Vogue.

Spencer watched from the receptionist's desk. He wandered over and put his arm around Callum's shoulder. "What did the boss man want to see you about?"

****

Darren farted as he woke and had a good scratch. After the highs of passing his course, he felt deflated. The visit from his landlord and the drubbing he got online had knocked the wind from his sails. He could quite happily lie in his pit all day, but he had yet another meeting at the Job Centre. They were making him jump through every hoop and for once, he wasn't intending on being late.

He wasn't going anywhere without some breakfast inside him though, he didn't have time to visit Greggs on the way. As he waited for the kettle to boil, he poured milk onto his Coco Pops and it splashed over the side of the bowl onto the table. "*I'll clean that up later,*" he thought.

He drank his tea without switching on the TV and stared at the peeling wallpaper. He didn't waste time with a shower but put on the cleanest pair of jogging bottoms and sweatshirt he could find.

He sat upstairs on the bus, in a spot furthest away from anyone, and watched the world go by. Everybody seemed happier than him. Whether it was the old man pottering about in the garden, the young lad walking his dog or the shopkeeper cleaning the shopfront of whatever was deposited there the night before. They were all going about it with a sense of something that Darren didn't possess. Then there were the couples, walking hand in hand or sitting chatting in their cars, comfortable being with one another. Even the other passengers seemed happy. The ones going to work, whilst they could be going to a job they hated, were using this trip as an opportunity to enjoy themselves. Listening to music, playing a game on their phones or reading a book. Why did they get to be happier than him?

He got to the Job Centre well ahead of schedule and resisted the temptation of a diversion to Greggs. He announced his arrival at reception, where he was sure they smirked when they saw how early he was, and he took a seat. He sat at the end of the aisle in the hope that nobody sat next to him. That hope was shattered as soon as a mobility scooter wheeled beside him. "Mind if I park this here, son?"

"Free country," said Darren.

"That's what they want you to think."

Darren sighed, he wasn't up for a conversation.

"The names Micky." The man on the scooter offered his hand.

"Darren."

"Pleased to meet you, Darren. Signing on?"

"Yeah and one of those meetings trying to force me into work."

"Force you into work eh? You not keen then?"

"They stopped my disability," said Darren.

"You're disabled?"

"Bad back but they don't believe me."

"Aye, there's a lot of it about," said Micky.

"Somebody grassed me up, CCTV, the lot."

"CCTV of you doing what?"

"Eating a saveloy dip, it's a long story." Darren didn't want to go into it.

"No amount of CCTV will help me out. This thing's buggered." Micky tapped his right leg with a walking stick.

"Buggered?"

"Aye, thing got shattered when someone reversed into me. Grafted my whole life and then one bad driver ruins it."

"I thought the scooter was a nice touch, make your story convincing."

"Not everyone is making it up, son. I'd give anything to be in your position. Young, fit, healthy. Well, you're maybe on the wrong side of fit but you know what I mean."

"Thanks a lot."

"What I mean is that you can do something about it. Nobody wants to know me, I'm on the scrap heap. I used to drive HGVs for a living. Loved being out on the open road, just me and my thoughts. It's a great job but now the only thing I can drive is this shit heap." Micky whacked the scooter with his stick, drawing attention from the security guards.

"Sorry," said Darren.

"Don't need to apologise to me, you didn't knock me over. Just make sure you're not apologising to yourself years down the line."

"Apologising to myself?"

"For wasting your life. You think you are the bollocks, beating the system by claiming when there's nowt wrong but they've got you exactly where they want you. They dictate what you can do, where and when you can go." Micky pointed towards the ceiling with his stick. "Can you hear that aeroplane flying off to foreign parts, I bet you've never been on one."

"No, don't want to, why would I want to go abroad?"

"How do you know until you've tried it son? I used to love my trips to Benidorm with the wife, only trips I get now are to the hospital."

"Sor—" Darren stopped himself from apologising again.

"There's a big world out there and there's more to life than trying to win battles with the jobsworths in here."

"Suppose so."

"There's no suppose about it. Get yourself a job. Graft hard enough and you can work your way up the ladder, earn the sort of money where you can do the things you want to do rather than what they tell you to."

"How long's that going to take?" Darren wasn't convinced.

"What does it matter? It will never happen whilst you're sat on your fat arse signing on. Get yourself in a position where you are in control, where you have money in the bank and can walk off and do whatever you want. That's what they are afraid of, not the people who come and sign on here every week."

"Sounds like hard work."

"It is, but at least you have the chance. Nobody will touch me, I'd love to work again but no amount of equal opportunities is going to get an old, disabled ex lorry driver a job." His raised voice had the attention of the whole waiting room.

"Sorry."

"I'll not tell you again, don't apologise to me. Just because my life is shit, doesn't mean that yours has to be." He poked his stick towards Darren's face.

Darren's number was called, saving him from Mental Micky.

"That's me," he said, more confused than ever.

Darren was still thinking about Micky's motivational talk when he was sat in his interview and he wasn't taking any notice of what was being said.

"Darren, are you listening? I asked how your call centre training course went."

"Sorry. Yeah it was alright, I passed."

"Well done. Did you enjoy it, did you learn much?"

"Not sure I enjoyed it but surprisingly I did learn some stuff."

"Surprisingly?"

66

"Well, you know, I just thought you sent us on these things to punish us."

The interviewer laughed. "I know it might seem like that and I suspect that a handful of my colleagues may do that from time to time, but you may also be surprised to know that most of us genuinely want to help you. We want to get you into work."

"I guess you have targets to meet."

"We do but that's not why I do it. Surely you want some options, you can't want to be on benefits all your life. What if you wanted a holiday or a car or to save for a wedding?"

"Have you been talking to Micky?"

"Who's Micky?"

"Never mind. Was there anything else?"

"As you enjoyed your course –"

"I never said I enjoyed it."

"Well, as you did so well on your course, how do you feel about attempting to get a job in a call centre?"

Darren felt his heart racing and his breath was getting shorter. "I don't know, it seemed difficult."

"There's nothing to be nervous about, Darren. Everything seems difficult at first but with a bit of practice it becomes easier."

The fear of failure gripped Darren and he wanted to say no but he kept thinking back to what Micky had said.

"Do you really think I could do it?"

"You won't know if you don't try. What's the worst that could happen?"

"Embarrassment, humiliation, ridicule," thought Darren. "I guess I could think about it."

"Good man. There's a few places recruiting at the minute. You'll need a CV, but we can help you with that. I'll look forward to setting up some interviews for you. This is the first step towards your new life."

Darren left the Job Centre in a daze. After the motivational talk from the mad man on a scooter to the interview where he wasn't quite sure what he had agreed to, it had been some morning. He treated himself to a pasty from Greggs and headed home. As he sat on the bus he watched the people around him again. Were they all happier than him? Was he happier than when he'd got the bus in? He'd agreed to look for work to silence his interviewer but maybe he could do it. Maybe it wasn't such a bad idea after all.

****

As Darren opened the front door he could hear voices upstairs. Maybe he'd left the TV on, but he was convinced that he hadn't watched if before leaving the house.

He edged up the stairs, looking for anything he could use as a weapon should he need it, the remaining bite size piece of his steak bake wasn't going to be of much use.

His eyes drew level with the top stair and he peeked into the sitting room where he was greeted with the sight of bare flesh.

Colin's calves.

"As you can see, it needs a bit of a tidy. We allowed some homeless veterans stay here free of charge, I'm all about helping the community, but it didn't work out and they left the place in a bit of a mess. Post dramatic dress or something, they need to create the feel of a war zone wherever they live apparently."

"Post-traumatic stress." The young couple seemed unconvinced as they edged along the wall looking for an escape route.

"Nothing a quick bust and polish won't sort out."

"Colin?" said Darren as he entered the sitting room.

"Darren," said Colin. He removed his hands from his shorts, briefly checking them before brushing unidentified hairs onto the carpet. "The cleaner I was just telling you about, you're here to give the place a good spring clean, aren't you?"

"I'm not..." said Darren but couldn't finish his sentence before he was ushered out of the room.

"Maybe you should start in the kitchen, where it is most needed." Colin pushed Darren through the kitchen door with some force.

Colin and Darren heard the front door slam as the young couple took this as their cue to make a run for it.

"What are you doing, Colin?"

"I warned you, Darren. This place smells like a bin lorry, I'm moving new tenants in."

"You can't do that."

"I can, they are a lovely professional couple, well-presented and they will pay their rent on time."

"They couldn't wait to get out of the place. They've run away."

"That was your fault, there'll be others. You're on burrowed time, Darren."

"Borrowed time."

"Exactly," said Colin missing Darren's correction. He put up his hood, ensured that his anorak zip was pulled up tight and jogged down the stairs. "Last chance, Darren, last chance."

Darren made himself a cuppa and took the last three Hob Nobs from the pack. He surveyed the sitting room. Dust covered every surface, Darren had convinced himself that to disturb it now would set off his hay fever. Crumbs littered the floor including the ones from the Hob Nob he was biting into. The windows hadn't been cleaned since the day he moved in and dirty plates peeked out from under the settee. The bedroom wasn't any better, the kitchen was worse, and he didn't even want to think how bad the bathroom was.

His life was a mess.

He couldn't be bothered to go on the internet because he would only be dragged into an argument that he didn't need. He didn't want to switch on the TV because it would only be other people arguing or people buying houses, holiday homes or antiques that he could only dream of. He didn't want to go out because there was nowhere to go. He had little spare cash and he would have even less very soon. He was confined to these four walls and the mess he had created. He was lucky that he didn't have any mirrors in the house as he'd see what a shambles he was. He could see his belly unfolding over the elasticated waist of his jogging bottoms. He could just about make out his swollen feet and his skin flaked off and drifted down to join the crumbs on the floor.

He'd brushed his teeth today, his only concession to the meeting at the Job Centre but he hadn't showered for a couple of days. Or was it three? He could use the grease from his hair to line his frying pan if it wasn't already covered in a thick layer of fat. The certificate from his course lay on the arm of the sofa, under a plate. Was this the sum-total of his achievements in life? One certificate and the promise of an interview that he would fail as soon as they took one look at him.

He was pathetic, and he knew it. Perhaps he had always known it. All the bravado on the internet was just to cover up his insecurities. He waddled into the bedroom and opened the drawer in his desk. The letter from his Nana sat on top of old leads and batteries. He didn't need to take it out of its folder to know what it said. His Nana said that he could be the best, but he was letting her down. He closed the drawer and stepped back, straight into an empty rice carton. He booted it across the floor.

"I'M SICK OF THIS!"

Something had to change. He was universally hated, his flat resembled a Bangalore rubbish tip and he dressed and smelled like the people who scavenged in one. He was penniless, friendless and about to get evicted. No amount of pep talks from Job Centre staff or motorised Yodas were going to help, he had to rely on the only person who could get him out of this mess. The man he feared most.

Himself.

He marched into the kitchen and snatched the bin bag that had been lying there since his last half-hearted attempt at tidying. He meant business now. Starting with the kitchen he binned every empty carton, used teabag and takeaway menu. He didn't care what was meant for the recycling bin, he didn't have time for that. He'd start with the rubbish, then the dishes, then the dirty clothes, general dusting and hoovering and then he would tackle himself.

Nothing was going to stop the new Darren.

CHAPTER FIVE

Darren's cleaning frenzy came to an abrupt halt as he only had one bin bag and little in the way of cleaning products. Old Darren would have been defeated but not the new one. He tied the bag that was full to the brim of cartons, wrappers and all sorts of random rubbish, dumping it into the wheelie bin on his way out of the door. On entering the mini supermarket, he wasn't sure what he was looking for, the cleaning aisle was one he normally skipped past on the way to the biscuits. He popped a pack of bin bags into his basket and gazed at the myriad of items on offer. This was just a mini supermarket, imagine what they had in a normal one. He must have been there quite a while as one of the shop assistants approached him.

"Are you alright there? Do you need any help?"

Social interactions were not his strong point and his face reddened. "Yes please, I've moved into a new flat and it's a bit of a mess. I need to give it a deep clean. I don't know where to start." As always, his initial instinct was to lie.

"No problem, we should have everything here to get you started. Just how messy are we talking?"

"On a scale of one to ten? An absolute shit tip."

She filled his basket with various industrial strength bleaches and cleaning products, advising him where to use them. "Do you need washing powder?" She gave him a quick look up and down and put a pack of washing tablets in his basket without waiting for a reply. Darren's face reddened again.

As they headed to the till she took a packet of chocolate biscuits and put them into his basket. "Well, you'll need to treat yourself to a cuppa after all that hard work."

She rang everything through the till and bagged them up. As Darren was paying he felt like he needed to confess.

"When I said earlier that it was a new flat, that wasn't strictly true. I've lived there ages but cleaning hasn't been a priority."

"We've all been there, I was a student once. Don't believe anyone who tells you that they've never lived in a messy house at one point in their lives."

Darren smiled, maybe honesty as a policy wasn't that bad.

"Thanks, guess I best get started."

"Happy to help, you're welcome to come and clean mine once you're finished."

"I think I could be some time." Darren headed home with a new determination.

Once the fifth bin bag was full and dumped in the wheelie bin, Darren had some space to work in. Washing up was next including dealing with some forms of growth that had not been seen outside a laboratory. He wasn't sure how long the plate had been under the settee, but he vowed never to let one go there again. He eyed the chocolate biscuits he had bought but he hadn't earned his treat yet, not until he had tackled the biggest job, the bathroom.

He went in armed with bleach, a pair of Marigolds and a new toilet brush. He took one look at the toilet, tipped some bleach into it and vowed to return to it later. He went through the whole house, dusting every surface. A dozen filthy dusters later and he still wasn't done. He went into the cupboard to attempt to retrieve the Hoover which was at the very back. He wrestled with the ironing board, which was also under-utilised, two suitcases he owned despite never going on holiday and various other pieces of junk he never used. Tidying the cupboard could go on his to do list.

After the hoovering, he decided that he had earned his cuppa. With the kettle boiling he put some washing in. Despite owning very few clothes, he had about three loads worth, including the ones on his back. He stripped to his pants and threw them in. He got his cuppa; the toilet cleaning could wait.

He logged into his PC. If he was going to look for a job, and it was a big if, he was going to need assistance. This was new territory to him. He'd been given advice at the Job Centre, but he had never looked for employment before, he needed to ask for help. He went to the only place he knew, the message board.

His other threads hovered about at the top of the board, but he chose to ignore them. He didn't want to know who was insulting him. He needed help and he knew that it would involve a fair amount of abuse, but he was going to give it a go. He put up a post asking for advice on writing a CV. Some of the suggestions were less helpful than others.

SIR STANLEY CUMMINS: In hobbies and interests put 'Jaffa Cakes and wanking' it shows that you have a sense of humour, they love that sort of stuff.

ROKER REJECT: In the personal statement I usually put 'I'll do owt for a bag of Quavers'. Shows my determination.

DB10: Don't bother writing one is the best advice I can give. Nobody is going to give you a job, you pathetic loser. You'd be better off writing a begging note on a piece of cardboard for when you are sleeping outside of the station.

—

Whilst most people on the forum had argued with Darren over the years, most recognised that he was in genuine need of help and it wasn't fair to kick a man when he was down. More than that, they universally hated Spencer and his **DB10** username so once he picked on Darren, they had his back.

SIR STANLEY CUMMINS: All joking aside, here's a couple of links to sites with good advice. They even have some CV templates. Once you're done, send it my way and I'll give it the once over for you.

ROKER REJECT: Ignore DB10, he's a sad lonely prick. His lass is probably reviewing a few other fella's CVs as we speak.

Darren had never had any mates, even at school, and most people on the board disliked him but this was the closest he had to having friends and he was going to make the most of it. He clicked on one of the links.

"Time to write a CV I think."

****

It had been two days since Darren's cleaning marathon. After delaying it as long as he could, he'd cleaned the bathroom and the suite was now something resembling white. He liked having a clean flat and washed up straight after eating now to keep on top of things. He hadn't bought a takeaway since then although his lack of cooking skills meant that he survived on microwave ready meals. It was a step in the right direction.

He'd created a CV as best he could, but his lack of any work experience whatsoever left it sparse. He'd taken advice from the lads on the forum and put a positive spin on his internet experience. He was also surprised to find how experienced he was with Microsoft Office although he didn't go as far as admitting to the Excel database that he used to own. He'd done the best job he could without fabricating anything, the common theme of the advice he was given was not to lie, and he sent it to a few call centres who were recruiting and some recruitment agencies. It was now a waiting game to see if anybody got back to him.

The one thing he did know that was that even if he got an interview, he had nothing to wear. The one suit he owned was no longer fit for purpose and despite having washed his jogging bottoms for the first time in months, they would never be appropriate. He headed into town. The likes of Debenhams were a bit rich for his wallet, so Primark became the only viable alternative. He surveyed their suits in a range of 'skinny fit' styles and surveyed his fat gut hanging over his pants. Primark wasn't viable after all.

One thing that Sunderland was blessed with, and one thing that he used to bring up on the message board when slagging the place off, was charity shops. He was spoilt for choice. He wouldn't get the most fashionable outfit, but he'd look ridiculous attempting to be fashionable anyway. After a couple of hours scouring the rails he came away with a navy pin stripe suit from the British Heart Foundation, two shirts from Scope and two ties from Barnardo's. All for the princely sum of £37.50. Not a bad day's shopping.

Next up was a haircut. Darren was never a fan of the barbers, and he suspected that the barber was never a fan of him. But needs must, and he had been going to the same place for years. He always asked for 'the usual' and he was in and out with the minimum of fuss. Conversation was almost non-existent, and he usually didn't return for another two months. It was a bit busier when he went in today and there was a new girl working. In all the years he had been visiting, the spare seat had remained empty. He wasn't expecting this added complication. He made a mental note of where he was in the queue and waited for his turn, praying that it would be with his normal barber. They might not like each other but at least he knew what to expect.

It was his turn next and he examined the head in each chair to see which was one finished first. It was neck and neck and he began to panic.

The panic subsided as soon as it came when his favoured barber was brushing down his elderly client whilst the new female barber was still applying the finishing touches to the young lad in the chair. Race over. He could relax.

"Would you like your eyebrows trimming?"

The curse of the old-fashioned barber, the old man was getting his furry caterpillars trimmed and whilst it only took seconds, it was long enough for the young lad beside him to jump out of his chair, admire himself in the mirror and exit the shop leaving Darren filled with dread. He had to speak to someone new.

"What are we having today then?"

"The usual ... sorry, number two on the back and sides and tidied up on the top please."

"No problem," she said as she applied the gown, "bought anything nice?" She nodded to the charity shopping bags.

"Just some clothes." Darren wasn't used to, nor comfortable with, this level of interaction.

"I love the charity shops. I can rake about for hours looking for a good bargain."

She never asked a direct question, so Darren remained silent, hoping that was the end of the conversation.

It wasn't.

"So, come on then, what have you been buying?"

"A suit and a couple of shirts."

"A suit? Lovely. A vintage one?"

Darren had no idea if it was vintage, but it looked pretty old. "I guess so."

"For a special occasion or just to impress the girls? Us girls love a man in a nice vintage suit."

"Interview, hopefully."

"Ooh great. Where are you going to work?"

"Not sure yet, I've applied to a few places."

"Well good luck, I'm sure they'll be impressed with your new suit."

Before he knew it, his haircut was over and even though he had struggled, the conversation hadn't been too painful. He paid, even leaving a small tip which he had never done before and picked up some toiletries from the pound shop before heading home. He chose not to buy the Alpha Male aftershave. At a pound, the risk of it taking his skin off was a price too high to pay.

He shut the door behind him and bounded up the stairs. He wanted to try on the outfit and check it out with his new haircut. He hadn't felt like this in a long time, Darren was positive about the future.

****

The rejections were coming thick and fast for Darren. He'd taken as much advice as he could on his CV but it was still threadbare. Most of the call centres he had applied to had rejected him. The others, he suspected, were not bothering to reply. On a positive note, two of the recruitment agencies had invited him in for interview, although they were based in Newcastle, so he was taken out of his comfort zone both mentally and physically.

He donned his suit, bought his Metro ticket and marched up and down the platform trying to calm his nerves. He realised that far from calming things down, his pacing up the platform was making the other passengers nervous, so he picked a spot and stuck to it.

He hadn't been to Newcastle since his Nana took him to see Fenwick's window one Christmas. An hour each way on the bus and the creepy automatons in the festive display had terrified him. He'd kept the tears at bay as he didn't want to upset his Nana, but he'd vowed never to return. Yet here he was, stepping off the train at Monument Station.

Once he had struggled through the ticket barrier he gambled on which exit to take, emerging into the light and the hustle and bustle of a busy city centre. Grey's Monument was behind him. From there he could get his bearings and find out where he needed to go. Learning from his previous mistakes he had given himself plenty of travelling time and had arrived with an hour to kill. He followed his map until he found the recruitment agency. He was far too early to go in but there was a coffee shop opposite. He'd inhabited such places many times in the imaginary life he lived on the message board, but this was his first real experience.

"How can we help you today?"

Surprised at finding himself at the front of the queue and yet to decipher the bewildering menu board he stuck to what he knew. "Tea."

"And what sort of tea would you like today? We have Earl Grey or breakfast, we have an extensive range of specials from around the globe, we have herbal teas, green teas and teas to please."

"White tea, three sugars."

"And was that a grandé?"

"A what?"

"What size would you like sir?" The perma-smile on the assistant dropped, just for a second.

"Big."

"One grandé, breakfast tea coming up sir. Would that be to sit in or takeaway?"

The interrogation was making Darren sweat. "I don't know." If he couldn't order a tea, how would he survive an interview?

"No worries, and the name sir?"

"The name of the tea?"

"Your name."

"Darren."

"Great name."

Beginning to appreciate how the East Germans felt after encountering the Stasi, Darren eventually staggered off holding a cardboard cup with **BARRON** scrawled on it, finding a seat by the window. There were a few people entering the recruitment agency looking full of hope. There were a number leaving looking crestfallen.

Ten minutes before his interview, he downed his tea and wandered into reception struggling to keep his shaking and sweating at bay. He was directed into a small office and wiped his hand on his trousers before shaking the interviewer's hand.

"I'm Nick. Nice suit," said the recruiter. Darren guessed it was sarcasm. "Let's see if we can get you to join us in the world of employment today."

Whilst the recruiter was brimming with confidence, he was fighting a losing battle with acne and Darren doubted that he was out of his teens. Darren didn't like Nick. After a couple of minutes, it was obvious that Nick didn't like him.

"So, you have no work experience whatsoever?"

"No, sorry."

"So how were you expecting to find work?"

"I was hoping that's where you might help," said Darren.

"Our clients expect people to have some work experience before applying for a job."

"I'm sorry, I don't have any, I do have a call centre training certificate," said Darren rifling about in his bag.

"Who hasn't? They give them away at the fairground now instead of goldfish."

"But I was told it would help."

"Little bit of a life lesson for you from someone who has been around the block, Darren, don't believe everything someone tells you. You can have that nugget for free."

Darren doubted that Nick had been around the block of his schoolyard, but it wasn't worth arguing.

"So why did you invite me in for interview?"

"You tell me, Darren, targets probably. Anyway, I've got people to see. Come back when you have some work experience and we'll see what we can do."

With that Darren found himself spat back outside into the hectic city centre wondering why he'd bothered. He had another two hours to kill before his next appointment and his stomach was rumbling. He didn't want to risk a visit to Greggs and the inevitable mess the pasty crumbs would make of his suit. He found the next agency and another convenient coffee shop. With the benefit of experience, he bought a tea and a sandwich and passed the time. Even Darren couldn't make one cup of tea last an hour, so he'd just finished his third when he headed for his second interview.

It was when he got into the reception that he realised that the tea had taken effect and he needed the toilet. Too embarrassed to ask he sat in pain, praying that the interview was as short as the last one.

"I'm Mick. Nice suit," said the recruiter.

Darren was having Deja-vu, the slim suit, the slicked back hair, this lad was a clone of the last one. He knew how it would go.

"Given your lack of experience there is very little we can offer you. There are some roles going plucking chickens in the poultry factory. It's a long shot but I'll see what I can do."

"What about my call centre certificate?"

"Worthless, everyone has one these days."

"Yeah, giving them out instead of goldfish I heard."

"What?"

"Thanks for your time, Mick."

Once again Darren was spewed back into the city centre, dejected. He switched on his phone and there was one voicemail message.

"Hi Darren, it's Rob the trainer from your call centre course. I've got some good news. I've got you an interview at Phonetix Mobile."

****

Of all the luck. The one place that Darren didn't want an interview at was the place he had been trolling for the last two years. As a Phonetix Mobile customer, he'd rung their free helpline on a daily basis to argue, bully, demand credits and be a general nuisance. The fact that the call centre had been in Sunderland had made it all the better. The people he was tormenting were close to home. Now they were a little too close.

He couldn't turn down the interview. How could he explain that he didn't want an interview because he had been a troll? What if he ended up getting interviewed by one of the people he'd targeted? They would recognise his name straight away. The main one had apparently left after the siege but there were others. The whole place would know who he was.

He was on the Metro back to Sunderland and his fellow passengers didn't seem to appreciate the flakes flying from his cheese pasty. He didn't care, he was upset, and he needed to eat. As the train passed through Brockley Whins then onto East Boldon, he tried to weigh up the pros and cons. Numerically, the cons easily outweighed the pros. Potential embarrassment, Job Centre finding out about his trolling, the people he had trolled getting to know his face, chance of a confrontation in the interview, they may even choose to investigate his account and the number of erroneous credits he had acquired.

There was only one pro, but it was a big one. He needed a job. He had to go for the interview.

Charlie scanned the CVs and shook her head. "Have you seen the calibre of people the Job Centre are sending us? Some of them don't even have work experience."

She hated recruitment, especially as she had lost all enthusiasm for the job herself. Half of the Job Centre applicants didn't turn up anyway which was a blessing. She was blocked out solid today. Eight hours of interviews, she'd need a drink after it. She got herself a coffee, nodded to Karen from HR. "Time to invite the first victim in?"

The first applicant was a young girl not long out of school. She was chewing gum. The day wasn't going to get any better. One by one they came into the room. One by one they disappointed her. She wondered why she bothered. Darren was the last interview of the day and working on the basis that first impressions matter, Charlie wasn't impressed. He was overweight, and his skin was so flaky that she was a little concerned that he had contracted scurvy. His suit was an obvious charity shop job, it was the only logical explanation. Nobody could have bought a suit like that new in the last twenty years. She read his CV as Karen went through the introductions. He had nothing. No experience, no qualifications to speak of. Not even anything in the hobbies and interests other than 'the internet'.

This was going to be hard work.

"Hello, Darren, could you tell me what you know about Phonetix Mobile?"

This was a standard question to get an idea of whether the applicant had bothered to do any homework on the company. The standard responses were 'not much' and 'you sell phones'. If anybody had bothered to even check the website, it was a bonus. She wasn't expecting much from Darren.

"I've been a customer for a number of years," he said, "and I have an extensive knowledge of your products. I regularly use your website and like to keep abreast of industry news. You could say it was a bit of a hobby of mine."

Darren was surprised at how comfortable he felt. He was telling the truth as well. Admittedly he left out the bit about why he had an extensive knowledge of their products; using them to troll the advisors when he phoned but nobody could argue that he didn't know what he was talking about.

Charlie was a little taken aback. "A hobby? I've never known us to be a hobby before."

"Maybe hobby is a bit strong, it is an interest. I like to know what is going on."

"No, no, it's a good thing. It's nice that someone has taken the time to find out who we are. I can't help but notice that you don't have any work experience. Why do you think Phonetix should give you a job?"

"I used to think working in a call centre was easy," he noticed Charlie's shoulders stiffen, "but after I attended the call centre training course I've realised that it will be a challenge. I know I wouldn't be your first choice based on my CV but all I want is a chance to prove that I can be the best at what I do."

With little to talk about from his CV, the rest of the interview passed quickly, and Darren left relieved that he didn't make a complete idiot of himself and even more relieved that they didn't seem to know his past.

"What did you think?" said Karen.

"He has no experience whatsoever, dresses like he has just come out of the army after the war and his hobby is looking at our website. He'd be eaten alive."

"He was keen."

"I'll give him that, he certainly wanted the job which is more than I can say for some."

"And we have a quota to fill from the Job Centre applicants. We've taken a grand total of none so far."

"I hate those bloody quotas. I'm sure the only human interaction he has is with the people in the Job Centre. How would he cope with our customers?"

"I hear you but if we don't employ someone soon, we'll be interviewing for the rest of our lives."

Charlie paused, she knew what the right thing to do was, but she also knew that she was sick of interviewing. "Bugger it. Let's give the lad a chance."

CHAPTER SIX

Darren once again found himself lying on his bed in shock. Shaking with the news he had been given. He had just come off the phone with Phonetix Mobile and they would like to offer him a job. He thought the interview had gone okay but he had nothing to judge it against other than his two failures with the recruitment agencies. His natural pessimism had led him to believe that the brevity of the interview meant that they didn't want him. It turned out that he was wrong. He was excited, he was scared, he was a lot of things but most of all he was happy. Something he hadn't been in a long time.

It was a few weeks until his induction, but he could now go to the Job Centre with his head held high. He could tell Colin that he'd get his rent on time. Things were looking up.

He half expected, hoped even, that he would receive confirmation that it all been a terrible mistake and he could retreat back into his comfort zone, but it never came and with his impending eviction, he really had no choice but to go through with it.

He owed it to his Nana and he was determined that he was going to be a success, so he used the weeks leading up to his start date to do more research on Phonetix and its rivals. He toured all the charity shops and got himself some more work clothes. Another suit, although the dress code only called for 'business casual'. He wasn't one hundred percent sure what that was so chose to play safe. He picked up more shirts, some dress trousers and even another pair of shoes. They were one size too big, but they were almost new, so he couldn't miss the bargain.

He set the alarm early for his first day, very early. He set it for 6am even though he didn't need to be there until ten. He was that nervous that he could barely manage a slice of toast, but he forced himself to eat. Showered, shaved and in his new suit, it was as smart as he had ever looked. He went for the bus at eight, with all the other commuters, he was now one of them. He was no longer a mere observer like the previous times he had used public transport. He was a fully paid up member of the employed.

He arrived at the business park with ninety minutes to kill. He didn't want to sit around in a coffee shop, so he went for a walk. Two big loops of the business park, watching his fellow workers go about their daily business. He felt something he hadn't felt before, he felt proud.

He got to Phonetix with plenty of time to spare and introduced himself at reception.

"Welcome to Phonetix and don't look so frightened, son," said Frank the security guard, "go and join the rest of your comrades." He pointed to the seating area.

There were already a handful of nervous looking individuals sat there; he nodded to Frank, unsure whether to thank him or run back out of the door. A few had entered into small talk, but they all wanted the day to start properly. To confirm that it wasn't all a terrible mistake and they did all have a job.

Walking across the highly polished floor Darren began to regret his decision of buying second hand shoes with leather soles. With almost no grip he walked with all the grace of a drunken giraffe. He flopped down on the nearest chair, relieved that he had survived the journey without humiliating himself totally. The smirks on the faces of his new colleagues suggested that his walking like he had soiled himself hadn't gone unnoticed.

Aiming for the nearest seat had also put him perilously close to a female colleague, an experience he was neither used to or ready for. His face reddened, and his palms began to sweat. He was perched with one cheek on the seat and one off, so he had no way of moving away from her. She took the dilemma from his sweaty hands and stood up, causing the chair to unbalance and Darren tumbled to the floor. Smirks turned to sniggers as the new starters bonded at his expense.

Quite the introduction to the world of employment.

Charlie looked down to reception from the balcony above. "Look at them, Sunderland's finest. Do they know what they are letting themselves in for?"

"We've all been there, Charlie. Remember the days when you were so full of hope and optimism?" said Lauren.

"Seems like a long time ago. Looks like our call centre hobbyist has been to the charity shop again. A brown suit and purple shirt? That's some combo."

"Give the lad a chance, it's his first job."

"It's alright for you, you don't have to manage him."

"You're managing him? How did that happen?"

"HR decided that he was going be the hardest work of all the new starters. Apparently, I'm the best at mentoring 'challenging' staff so I've got him. Serves me right for employing him, I shouldn't have let him through the door."

"You should take it as a compliment. If anybody can turn him into the perfect Phonetix employee, get him to live by the Phonetix values and have him recite the Phonetix mission statement before he goes to bed each night, it is you." Lauren nudged Charlie with her elbow.

"Behave yourself. I've been here long enough that I'm beginning to doubt that Phonetix has any values at all."

They finished their coffee and watched the new starters for another ten minutes. The length of the call queue was sneaking up on the board and neither of them wanted to be near the floor in case they got dragged onto the phones. This was a rare break for them.

"Do you think it's time?" said Lauren.

"Yes," said Charlie, "let's go and introduce them to the wonderful world that is Phonetix Mobile."

****

"Good morning. My name's Charlie and this is Lauren, I think I met some of you in the interviews. Welcome to your first day of which I hope will be a long and successful career at Phonetix Mobile."

Charlie was using all her customer service skills to smile while she was speaking to pretend that she meant what she was saying.

"We're going to give you a little tour of the building," said Lauren, "so you can get your bearings. Then we'll take you to the training room that will be your home for the next four weeks. If you have any questions as we are going around, please shout up."

"What time is lunch?" said one of the newcomers.

Charlie tried not to sigh. "All of that will be explained when we get in the training room."

She knew immediately that person wouldn't last. Everybody on the phones lived for their breaks and crawled towards lunchtime but asking about it before you'd even got in the training room wasn't a good sign.

"First things first, this is the most important person in the building. Meet Frank, our celebrity security guard who you may have seen in the news recently."

Frank gave them a wave from behind his desk. "Don't worry, armed sieges are very rare, but I would appreciate you trying to avoid annoying the customers too much."

Officially, Charlie had been told to pretend that the siege hadn't happened. It had been written out of Phonetix Mobile's history. Unfortunately, everybody knew about it and if she was to gain the trust of her new team, lying to them wouldn't help.

She was slightly concerned about those in the group who seemed surprised at talk of a siege, she had to wonder where they had been hiding for the past few months. They gave them the grand tour of the building, starting with the good bits, the canteen and the games room. The games room was the idea of senior management in an attempt to show that Phonetix was a fun place to work. It was modelled on those found in modern software houses with a games console and table football. The crucial difference being that in a software house, people were trusted to come and go as they pleased; have a break from what they were doing and use the relaxation to come up with innovative solutions to complex problems. In the call centre, the breaks were so rigid that by the time you had grabbed a cuppa and got to the games room, someone would be using the table football and you'd need to be back on the phones before they got a chance to finish their game. Instead of an atmosphere of fun and free thinking, it created one of bitterness and arguments.

The group were taken to the first floor. Two of them insisted on getting the lift which did not endear them to Charlie. This gave them their first sight of life on a call centre floor. Some of them had worked in other call centres so knew what to expect. They were hoping that Phonetix was a little less horrible than their last place of employment. For those that had never worked in one, like Darren, first impressions could be deceiving. Most teams' areas were decorated in banners, balloons and various other bits and pieces related to some new product. What wasn't obvious was that the decorating was done in the staff's own time in the interests of what Charlie called 'forced fun'.

There were a few people laughing but they were the ones heading for their break. Most were on calls and sounded professional, but the trained ear could pick up the frustration in their voices. The irritation at whoever was on the other end of the call.

"Stick it up your hoop, you snotty bitch!"

A headset was thrown at a monitor and a girl in her twenties fled in tears.

"Must be on her blob," said Darren.

Charlie glared at him whilst guiding the group away. She thought it best to adhere to the policy of pretending that the incident hadn't happened. She was more of a Phonetix corporate girl than she would like to let on.

There wasn't much more to see, just hundreds of people on the phone and a call queue on the wall rising steadily. Everybody on a call watched the new starters with a mix of envy, pity and a sense of knowing. Knowing what Phonetix had in store for them. Knowing for the next eighteen months or however long they lasted on the phones, they were going to hate their lives. They took the group to the training room, pleased that nobody had turned around and walked out during the tour. It had happened before.

"Help yourself to a cuppa," said Lauren, "I'll be back in five minutes."

Charlie and Lauren nipped for a chat before Charlie headed back to her team.

———

"Confident about this lot?" said Lauren.

"No more than usual. You?"

"There's a couple who aren't going to make it, that much is obvious. I hope they realise before we have to tell them."

"Then we've got suit guy," said Charlie, "I hope I won't be giving out fashion advice as well."

"Give him a chance. You said he was keen in the interview and I'm sure you've worked with worse in the past. You always get the best out of them."

"I'm not sure I've got the energy to deal with them anymore. I should be lying on Bondi Beach watching all the fit surfers, not babysitting a group of man babies who don't know how to dress themselves."

"Why aren't you lying on Bondi Beach? What's keeping you here?"

"I don't know, Lauren. I really don't know."

****

Nobody mentioned the girl who had the tearful outburst upstairs. All the new starters were sat in the training room as Lauren talked them through the basics.

"Some of you will have worked in call centres before, some of you won't so we'll try and bring everybody up to speed on what is expected. We'll teach you about our products, our systems and our policies and procedures. There will be role play and an opportunity to take real, live calls during training. Most of all, I hope we are going to have some fun."

People applauded. Darren wasn't sure why, maybe he had joined a cult by mistake, but thought he should join in regardless.

"As an ice breaker, we'll go around the room, so you can tell us a little bit about yourselves. Where you've worked before, what your hobbies are etcetera."

Darren started to panic. He had nothing to add to this conversation and had no idea what to say. Was King of the Internet and professional benefits cheat a previous job?

Luckily, they began at the other side of the room. There was a mix of recruits. Some with previous call centre experience, some who were straight out of college, one who had been a hairdresser and fancied a change and one older gentleman who clearly would rather be anywhere else but here.

He had previously had a managerial job for several years and had left for unspecified reasons. When pushed as to why he had joined Phonetix he answered, "Because the Job Centre told me I had to."

There was the single mother getting back into the workplace after bringing up two children, an ex-soldier and someone who claimed to be learning to fly. He was so enthusiastic about it Darren wondered whether he intended doing it without a plane.

And then there was Darren. It was his turn to speak.

"My name's Darren and this is my first ever job."

"And do you have any hobbies, Darren?"

"Not really, just the internet and stuff, you know."

There were a few sniggers.

"Well, welcome to Phonetix, Darren. Are you excited to be starting your first job?"

"I guess so."

The enthusiasm he had when he got up this morning was waning. Everybody had more experience than him and he was going to make a fool of himself. He knew it. His instinct was to run out and avoid the embarrassment, but he knew he couldn't. He had to go through with it no matter how painful it got.

The rest of the day was routine introductory stuff with a small test at the end. Darren passed comfortably as did everyone in the room. They were advised that this would be the format for the next four weeks, but the tests would get harder.

Darren boarded the bus with his arms full of folders and other reading material. A couple other recruits got on but sat apart, none of them comfortable in each other's company yet.

He spent the first night revising. Cementing the learning of the first day and he read ahead to the second day's material to give himself a bit of a head start. He needed this job and to be sure of keeping it, he needed to be the best.

The next day, he relaxed his dress a bit and didn't go for the full suit, just black dress trousers and a lime green shirt. His revision hadn't gone to waste as, when Lauren asked a question, he was first with his hand up. Same with the next question, and the one after that. If Lauren was impressed, she hid it well. His fellow trainees didn't seem overjoyed with his knowledge either. Nobody said anything directly, but he heard a couple of tuts and on the tea breaks he wasn't included in the little clique that seemed to be developing.

Darren was on a mission to be the best and if he alienated some of the group, then so be it. His mission became derailed when Lauren asked to have a word. "I know you are keen Darren and I like your enthusiasm, but you need to give a thought to the others in the room. Some of them might not find it so easy."

"But I'm just trying to do my best."

"I appreciate that but there's more to this job than answering questions. When you get out on the floor you will be part of a team and you will need to work together to succeed."

"Okay," Darren couldn't hide his disappointment, "I thought I was doing the right thing."

"There's nothing wrong with trying hard, maybe tone it down a bit and give others a chance to answer."

Darren agreed and went to get a cuppa. The rest of the class were chatting in a circle and they either didn't notice him or deliberately kept their backs to him when he tried to join in. He returned to the classroom alone.

The next two weeks were more classes, a couple dropouts including the older gentleman leading to rumours of an arrest. There were more tests, getting used to the system they would be using in their day to day jobs and role play. Darren hated role play. His classmates had lightened up a bit since his first few days but whenever they did role play, he always had someone being awkward with him and hoping to trip him up. Lauren explained it away by saying that they would encounter a lot of awkward customers, but he felt like he was being punished.

"Could I take your name please?" said Darren. He was wearing a headset and talking to a girl at the other side of the training room.

"Tharushi Vijayaraghavan," she replied.

Darren shook his head and looked at the girl whose real name was Angela Smith. "And how are you spelling that?"

"The same way I always do."

The rest of the class burst into laughter and Darren tried to keep his anger in check.

Lauren attempted to gain control. "Play nice, Angela, remember we are all one big team here."

Darren wasn't accepted by his classmates, he wasn't liked by his trainer and he was beginning to doubt if he would ever be accepted at Phonetix Mobile.

Maybe it was time to quit.
****

Darren sat on his bed looking at all his folders. He'd tried hard to succeed at Phonetix, but it didn't matter how much he revised and how much he learned, it was his inability to get on with other people that would be his downfall. Every time he attempted to make conversation he stumbled over his words, accidentally insulted someone or was ignored before he had opened his mouth.

The class was buzzing with nervous excitement. There was a lot of false bravado from people claiming that they couldn't wait to get on the phones but secretly they were all bricking it. Darren was no exception, he wanted to delay it as long as possible. They went through more role plays and at 11am they headed to the first floor.

As with the first time they got a tour, they were viewed with a mixture of pity, amusement and suspicion.

Lauren approached Charlie, "You sure you're okay with us taking a few calls?"

"No problem, they need to know what they are letting themselves in for."

"It'll mess up your team stats."

"I'm past caring to be honest, Lauren. I'll have a new team soon enough so I'm expecting my stats to be shot to bits anyway."

Half of the trainees, including Darren, joined Charlie's team and paired with someone. To everybody's surprise they were made welcome and their partner seemed only too happy to let them take calls even if it increased their call handling time. It soon became apparent that this was because they were grateful for five minutes off the phones, whatever the reason.

"Hi, I'm Emma," said Darren's partner, "don't worry, I'll be listening in so if it gets tricky I'll be able to help."

"Thanks." Darren put on his headset, plugged it in and, his hands dripping with sweat, his finger hovered over the 'Ready' button.

He pressed it, his headphones beeped, and he was on his first call.

"Good morning, you are through to Phonetix Mobile, my name is Darren. How can I help you?" He was surprised at how easily he slipped into the script.

"You can't. Get me your manager, now."

Darren looked at Emma for help, but she nodded towards the monitor and the script he should be following. He heard a voice in his headset.

"Hello, hello, are you still there?"

"Yes, I'm still here."

"I thought you'd gone to get your manager."

"No, my manager isn't available right now, if I could just take some details maybe I could help."

"I very much doubt it. I've spoken to you before Dean and you were useless."

"My name is Darren not Dean."

"Are you arguing with me?"

"No, that's what my name is," said Darren.

"Always the same with you lot, I phone wanting help and all you want to do is argue."

"I don't want to argue."

"You're doing it again, Dean."

"I'm not called Dean."

"You're doing it again. Can you stop bloody arguing and get me your manager?"

Darren looked towards Emma again, but she pointed at the screen.

"Could I take your name and mobile phone number please?"

"You know what they are, they are on the screen in front of you."

"If you could just confirm them for me please, sir." Darren's voice had gone up an octave or two.

"How many times do we need to have this discussion, Dean? I'm not confirming anything until you get your manager."

"I'm not called Dean." His voice was now getting louder.

"Don't start that nonsense again, son."

To Darren's relief another voice came across the headset. "Hello, my name is Emma, how may I help?"

"Are you Dean's manager?"

"I'm Darren's supervisor, how can I help?" Emma had corrected the caller without him realising and she was supervising Darren today, so she wasn't lying even though she wasn't his manager.

"Finally, I'm speaking to someone with a bit of common sense." The caller's tone had changed. Polite, friendly and even a sense of relief.

Darren was shaking. He was sweating from bits he didn't know he had, and he could feel that his blood pressure had risen. He watched in awe as Emma dealt with the caller's complaint. A straightforward query that had escalated due to misunderstandings on both sides. She brought the call to a close. "Is there anything else I can help you with?"

"No, thank you Emma. All I wanted was a simple explanation in plain English and I've got that now."

"Thank you for calling, hope you enjoy the rest of your day." She pressed the 'wrap' button, so she could talk to Darren before another call came through.

"What did I do wrong?" said Darren.

"Not a lot, some calls are like that. People get so angry after waiting in a queue and maybe being misinformed previously so they take it out on you. It's nothing personal. The trick is to stay calm, don't rise to the bait and let them think that you are giving them what they want."

"All I did was ask for his name. You'd think I'd asked him to sacrifice his first born."

"What you need to remember is that ninety-nine percent of customers are genuine. They just want help. Yes, we get the chancers and we get the trolls who only want to wind us up, but they are just pathetic individuals who have something missing in their lives."

Darren could feel his face redden as he remembered how many hours he had spent trolling Phonetix Mobile. "I guess so."

"Ready for another one?" said Emma with a smile as her finger went to press the 'Ready' button.

****

Darren's next call wasn't much better but he at least he saw it through to the end without Emma taking over. In total, he took six calls and Emma had to intervene on three. He hated this job and he hadn't even started.

"Don't worry," said Emma, "you get used to it. After a while you don't even notice the shouting."

"I'm sorry, I didn't have a clue what to do when they kicked off."

"Like I said, don't worry, we've all been there. It gets easier, I promise."

"I hope so, not sure I could deal with that every day."

He unplugged his headset and his hands were still shaking with nerves. "Thanks again."

The rest of the group were waiting for him with Lauren and Charlie.

"Enjoy that?" said Charlie as he joined them.

"Yes, thanks." His face betrayed the lie and Charlie laughed.

"You were unlucky, you can go weeks without a call like your first one." She hoped that he couldn't tell that she was also lying.

"You were listening in? Not the best start."

"Don't worry, you are still in training. You'll pick it up eventually."

Another team were returning from their break. Leading the group was Ryan. Swigging from a can of Red Bull and walking with the over confidence of someone who spends too long in the gym, his biceps straining the material in the shirt that was one size too small.

"More virgins to the slaughter," he said.

"Don't you mean lambs?" said his mate.

"Nah, definitely virgins. Look at the clip of him, man." He nodded in the direction of Darren. "Looks like he's had his hair cut with a bread knife."

"Playtime's over Ryan, get back on the phones," said Charlie.

Lauren guided the group back downstairs hoping that none of them had been too scarred by the experience.

Ryan watched them go then logged in to the phones, "Good morning you are through to Phonetix Mobile. Ryan speaking, how may I help?"

He dealt with the call with a level of confidence that made him perfect for the role. He may have been arrogant, he was undoubtedly a dickhead, but he knew how to charm and bullshit the customers. He breezed through call after call without once having a cross word. He spent most calls making offensive hand gestures at the monitor or trying to make colleagues laugh whilst they were on difficult calls. He made a paper aeroplane and sailed it across the room, ensuring that his head was down when a culprit was sought. He wheeled his chair over to his mate then kicked the lever on his friend's chair, so the seat dropped, and he nearly fell off it. He was the class clown and his team loved him. Or at least they gave the impression that they did.

His Team Leader, Ethan, looked on in dismay. Ryan was a nightmare to manage, he was disruptive and knew every underhand trick in the book. He undermined his line manager and everybody else in the call centre, but he got away with it.

Because his stats were good.

The one and only thing senior management cared about was call stats. They lived for them and expected everybody else to as well.

Ryan knew how to play the game and he played it well. Ethan suspected that Ryan was ending difficult calls prematurely. Not via the 'release' button which was monitored but by various other devious means that only the more experienced call centre worker knew.

Whenever the subject was raised with senior management they dismissed it because his stats were good, some of the best in the call centre. They didn't care that the customer inevitably called back due to being lied to or cut off. They didn't care that somebody else needed to deal with the mess Ryan had created. They only cared that his stats were good.

And Ryan knew it.

He took another swig of Red Bull, pressed the mute button and let out a loud belch before seamlessly un-muting the call and carrying on the conversation as if nothing had happened. It gained a few sniggers from his colleagues, but most carried on with their calls and pretended they hadn't noticed. Ethan made a mental note to have a word with him about it but knew that he never would.

He went through the daily stats with his yellow highlighter, picking out wherever one of his team had slightly gone under their target. Frustratingly, Ryan never did. He was the very worst kind of employee. Loud, opinionated, disruptive and perfectly suited to Phonetix Mobile. Ethan hated to admit it but Ryan was his star player and he had to keep him happy no matter how many corners he cut.

Charlie looked on from the next team and shook her head. Ryan wasn't only disrupting his own team, but he was now disrupting hers and she wouldn't put up with it for much longer.

But that would mean speaking to Ethan. A man who made the hairs on the back of her neck resemble a hedgehog. A man so odious that she would often pretend to take a call on her mobile rather than step out of her car and take the two-minute walk across the car park with him.

A man who took every opportunity to remind her of that one drunken encounter on their final day of initial training. An encounter that the whole call centre got to know about and she'd spent the majority of her Phonetix career trying to make people forget.

CHAPTER SEVEN

Emma watched Ryan's antics with barely disguised disgust. He was everything she hated in a man and couldn't see why Phonetix put up with him. Her approach was the polar opposite to Ryan, her only focus was the customer. If she did her job correctly, the customer never called back, and the call queues therefore came down. By treating them with respect, she usually got to help them and get them off the phones faster than someone who promised them the earth but didn't deal with their issue.

She worried about Darren. He had struggled with the calls and didn't react well to customers being rude to him. She saw him visibly shrink when Ryan mocked him. As difficult as it was, he needed to grow a thicker skin if he was to survive life in a call centre.

Emma wasn't the typical call centre worker, obsessed with fashion and holidays. She was in her mid-thirties, a little plump but not fat and she rarely bothered with make-up. She knew the lenses in her glasses were a bit thick, but she'd never been attracted to the more fashionable designs. Her hair was also a little on the frizzy side, but it was usually tied back in a pony-tail so she didn't think it mattered a great deal. She dressed in a smart white blouse and grey trousers. Business-like but not flashy.

It was lunchtime and she joined the rest of the team in the canteen. She would never be the life and soul of the party, but she seemed to get along with everyone. It was hit and miss if she joined in the conversation. If they were discussing a new club they had been to at the weekend, she was out of her depth. If they were discussing the latest episode of Coronation Street she was in her element.

They were discussing one of her new reality TV shows that aimed to shock. It wasn't her thing, so she sat picking at her salad and listened in. The things that some people were willing to do on TV to become famous shocked her, but she never let on. The conversation moved onto arranging a team night out.

"You up for it, Emma?" said one of the girls.

"Sounds good, what's the plans?"

"Just a cheap Italian then out on the lash afterwards."

"Great, count me in."

She knew that she'd only go for the meal and then slope off home when they headed into town; she wasn't a big drinker. The rest of the team knew that she wouldn't stay out long but they didn't mind. At least she was making the effort to be sociable and it probably suited all parties if she went home when she did. No sooner had they sat down for lunch then it was time to head back to work.

"No rest for the wicked," said Emma.

The rest of the team laughed, it had almost become her catchphrase after saying it a few times and she played up to it now. She hoped they were laughing with her rather than at her but didn't care a great deal either way. She was here to do a job, a job that she enjoyed and getting on with her colleagues was a bonus.

Charlie caught up with her on the stairs. "What did you think of Darren? He's joining our team when he comes out of training."

It wasn't in Emma's nature to be nasty, but she had her concerns. "He tried his best, but he was very nervous. I think we'll need to work on building his confidence."

"I was thinking of making you his mentor. How would you feel about that?"

"Okay I guess, he seemed nice enough."

"We'll talk about it closer to the time, he might not even pass his training."

Emma wasn't sure if there was maybe a little bit of wishful thinking on Charlie's part.

Emma had barely been in the house five minutes and she was already in her pyjamas and thick woolly socks and sitting under a blanket on the settee. She would think about making something to eat in a while, but the soaps were starting. Her cats jumped up beside her and snuggled in. Her chances of eating now depended on whether they were willing to move or not.

She'd been in the house six years now. It was a modest terraced cottage with a small garden out the back, but it suited her needs and she could afford the mortgage, even if the unthinkable happened and she had to leave Phonetix. She'd been careful in her financial planning and with no real outgoings apart from the house, she never worried about money. It's why she never chased promotions at Phonetix. She knew she was good at what she did, but she wasn't sure that she would be happy managing people. Dealing with their problems, pulling them up when they didn't hit their targets. It wasn't for her.

The cats purred, giving her a gentle reminder that they were the only thing that mattered in the house. She laughed. "We're happy here aren't we?"

She wasn't sure if it was a statement, a question or an attempt to convince herself.

"He's handsome, isn't he?" said Emma as she stroked Woody's fur. She'd convinced herself that she watched her favourite soap because of the gripping storylines, the witty dialogue and the well written characters but she knew that deep down, the reason that she watched it was that she was a little bit in love with Jon Radley, the actor who played Kyle Martins. His off-screen persona matching the cheeky, loveable but unreliable rogue on it.

Would she choose someone like that as a boyfriend in real life? Probably not, but then again, she'd never been in a position to choose. Social interactions with the opposite sex had been few and far between and she had somehow managed to reach the age of 36 without ever having a boyfriend or indeed any intimate relations since that first kiss in a school disco.

She just didn't attract the boys apart from a couple of drunken approaches at the Christmas Party and it wasn't something she gave much thought to. It occasionally crossed her mind that it would be nice to be part of a couple, but she'd conditioned herself to believe that she was happy with just the cats and her.

Friends had tried to persuade her to join dating websites or fix her up with inappropriate suitors but the more they tried, the more she dug her heels in and argued that she was happy being single.

They had given up trying.

But Jon Radley could change her mind, Jon Radley could change a lot of things.

****

George sat at his desk surveying the showroom. He'd done well for himself, running a dealership full of top end Jaguars and Range Rovers; making it one of the best performing showrooms in the country despite the apparent lack of high earners in the North East. He was a success and he enjoyed his job, he really did. But there were days when he wished he could be doing something else. Along with most of the country, he hated dealing with car salesmen. They were slimy, dishonest and told you whatever you wanted to hear to get what they wanted. Bit unfortunate then, that his job was managing a showroom full of them.

He checked the almost non-existent sales figures of Callum, figures that would usually have him shown the door. He then checked Spencer's. They'd been declining for months but had gained a bump recently; a bump that coincided with Callum's recruitment. Spencer was now selling a lot more second-hand cars. Cars that he had no business selling, he dealt with the high-end motors, the top customers. George was disappointed in Spencer. Not because he was trying to deceive him, although that was bad enough. It was because the deception was so pathetically obvious.

He called Spencer into the office.

"Have a seat, Spencer."

"What's up, boss?"

George hated it when he called him boss. It was dressed up as friendly banter, but he knew it was an attempt to undermine him. "I've been having a look at the sales figures across the dealership and I'm a little concerned."

"We all are boss, times are tough out there. There's a recession going on."

"That's not what concerns me, this market always does well no matter what the prevailing financial conditions, I'm more concerned about specifics."

"Specifics? Is that a new luxury competitor?" Even as he said it Spencer knew the joke didn't work but he was buying time until he could work out where the conversation was going.

"No, specifics as in the sales figures of our new junior salesman or the apparent lack of them."

Spencer was in no doubt where the conversation was heading now. "Yeah, he's struggling. Might be time to cut him loose."

"Spencer, we've both been in this game longer than I care to remember. Let's not waste any more time pretending that you don't know what I'm talking about."

"Yes, the young lad, he's shit. I thought we'd established that." He was going to front this out, there was no other alternative.

"Spencer, your sales have been declining for months now, you're losing your touch. We've all trimmed a few edges in the past to try and get ourselves back in the game but this? It's a little route one, isn't it?"

"I've no idea what you are talking about."

"Were you really going to ruin a young lad's career before it had begun just to make yourself a few quid? At least tell me you have financial issues that are forcing you into a corner. How much trouble are you in?"

"I'm not in any trouble." He didn't know whether he was lying for George's benefit or his own. It had become second nature to him recently with the amount of lies he'd been telling Rebecca about missing transfers and password mishaps.

"If you'd come to see me first, I could have helped but this, this is an insult to my intelligence."

"You've lost it, mate. I've no idea what you are on about. Sitting there all high and mighty like Mussolini on his lunch hour."

"I'm doing you a favour by giving you the heads up, Spencer. Giving you the chance to find something new before this gets unpleasant but be under no illusions, you are finished here. I'm giving you the opportunity to jump before you are pushed."

"I'm not listening to this, George. Trying to ruin my reputation with suggestion and innuendo. Are you jealous? Is that it? Come back with some evidence of whatever it is you are accusing me of. Until then I'll be out there selling cars and being the best salesman you've ever had. It's what I do." He stormed out, slamming the door on the way.

———

He headed out past the service department and collared one of the mechanics who was having a sly smoke out back. "Lend us a tab, mate?"

"Didn't know you smoked."

"Gave up years ago but fancy one today."

It was also against policy for the salesforce to smoke, it was unprofessional to smell of it whilst dealing with customers.

He took two long drags, reminding himself of why he enjoyed smoking in the first place, and why he packed in when he coughed up a lung full of phlegm. He dropped the cigarette to the floor and stubbed it out with his shoe.

"Cheers mate, I needed that."

He wandered around the side of the showroom, so he didn't have to face George again and he needed some time to think.

For all his bravado indoors, this was bad. If he lost this job, he wouldn't get another one anywhere near as well paid. Then there was Rebecca, how would he tell her? Despite her mounting suspicions, she had no real idea of his financial problems but if he lost his job he couldn't hide them much longer and they couldn't survive on her wage, no matter how good she thought her job was.

He watched from afar as Callum nabbed himself another customer. The lad was actually very good but needs must and Spencer would have no hesitation in throwing him under the bus if he had to. That avenue seemed closed to him now.

There was a growl to Spencer's right and he watched George drive a nearly new F-Type off the forecourt. Taking a luxury car for a spin was a perk of the job even if it wasn't strictly in the rules. It gave Spencer an idea. A risky one and one that needed some planning, but it was maybe his only option.

He selected the number in his phone of someone he hoped he would never need to call.

****

Charlie watched as the trainees filed in once again to take some calls, a mixture of fear, misplaced confidence and hapless oblivion. Thankfully they weren't joining her today.

She examined the call stats for her team. Most of the top performers were leaving for other teams and she was left with this new bunch. If she didn't get them up to speed quickly she could be out of a job, you were only as good as your last set of call stats.

The picture of Sydney Harbour was calling her again; the bright blue water, the sun beating down. She could see herself sitting by the Opera House sipping on a glass of Chardonnay and people watching. She could meet new people from all corners of the globe and with different backgrounds, different stories to tell. Whilst Phonetix prided itself on being a diverse employer, the workforce barely stretched to all corners of Sunderland.

She wandered over to the window and looked out over the car park. Row after row of cars packed in, some on the verges, their drivers desperate to get as close to the door as possible, desperate to achieve one perceived victory in a day of failure and disappointment. The sky grey and sullen offering none of the charm that the Sydney one offered. It may have been the same sky, but it was literally worlds apart.

Lauren was busy supervising the trainees and Charlie went over for a chat. Anything to break the monotony of what she was meant to be doing.

"How are they getting on?" said Charlie.

"Not bad, some better than others."

"And my lot?"

"They're not a bad bunch, they'll do okay after a few months of your expert guidance."

"Not sure I've got it in me anymore."

"Course you have, you love the challenge even if you don't admit it."

"I'm not sure I do anymore. How's Darren doing?" said Charlie.

"He's passing all the tests, some of the best results in the class."

"But?"

"Well, he's Darren."

Lauren had a point. They looked over at him trying to be professional and take a call, but Ryan and his mates were flicking bits of rolled up paper at him. It was like being back at school. Ethan seemed oblivious to Ryan's behaviour or chose to ignore it. Charlie felt like she should intervene but didn't want to cause a scene.

"He needs to learn how to deal with these people or they will eat him alive," said Charlie.

"I'll try my best with him," said Lauren, "but there's not much we can do in training. It's only when he's out in the big wide world with you that he'll learn about the reality of working in a place like this."

"Anything you can do will be appreciated. Fancy a drink on Friday? I'm meant to be saving but I need a night out."

"How's your Sydney fund going?"

"It's going well, in fact I've already reached my target."

"So why are you still here? Get yourself away, lass," said Lauren.

"It's complicated."

"Your parents?"

"They think I'm saving for a deposit on a flat. Or a wedding but God knows who they think I'm getting married to."

"You need to tell them."

"I know, I'm waiting for the right moment."

Charlie closed the front door behind her. "Hi, Mam."

"Was the traffic bad, was there an accident?"

"An accident? Not that I know of, why do you ask?"

"You're ten minutes late, we were worried," said her mother, drying her hands on a tea towel that seemed to be permanently in place.

"Ten minutes late for what?"

"From when you normally come in."

"We've discussed this hundreds of times, I don't have a normal time. I get in when I get in."

"But we worry about you. If you are going to be late you should phone."

"I'm twenty-five years old, Mam. Do you not trust me to get to and from work on my own?" said Charlie.

"I'm your mother, Charlie. I'm allowed to worry."

"I'm not having this discussion again."

Her mother headed back into the kitchen. "We're watching the turn down the club with Clive and Rita on Friday, you should come along."

"I'm meeting Lauren for a drink on Friday."

"But we've already told them you would go."

"Without asking me?" said Charlie.

"You never do anything on a Friday, we thought it would be nice."

"Well, I am doing something this Friday so thanks for the offer, but I'm sorted."

"They'll be disappointed, they haven't seen you in ages," said her mother.

"You shouldn't have promised them without checking first."

"But Julian will be home from the army, he's been promoted."

And with that, Charlie's mother revealed her true motives. Julian was an arrogant prick and had been since childhood. His time in the army had only made him worse. Her parents couldn't see it though and were always attempting to match make.

"I've already promised Lauren, sorry. I'm sure you'll have a great night without me."

"But it's Feat Loaf."

"What is?"

"The turn, he's like Meat Loaf but he doesn't just do his hits. Your Dad loves his Billy Ocean."

"Sounds extraordinary."

"He once got Barbara from down the road up to do Islands In The Stream. She shouldn't have been up on stage though, far too much on show after her operation."

"Sounds like I'm missing out, but I've got plans."

"But what will we tell Clive and Rita?"

"Tell them I've run off to join the circus, I don't care. You shouldn't make arrangements for me without checking first."

"There's no need to be like that, Charlie. We're only trying to help, you can't spend your whole life on your own, you'll need to settle down one day."

And therein lay the problem with her parents. They couldn't see any future for Charlie other than living at home or being married. But Charlie could, and she needed to do it sooner rather than later.

****

The Dudley branch of the Premier Inn was never going to be the most romantic of locations, but Rebecca was on expenses and her company had a budget. She wasn't even sure it was romance that she wanted, or sex; maybe just a change from Spencer. Whatever it was she was after, here she was flirting with a colleague five years her junior. As HR manager, she was breaking all sorts of rules, but she needed some excitement in her life.

Thomas was cute and whilst Rebecca could put it down to too much drink after the conference, they both knew that this had been brewing for some time. The rest of their workmates had gone to bed an hour ago, they barely noticed that they had left.

"One for the road?" asked Thomas shaking his glass.

Rebecca hesitated; she was already tipsy, another one would take her into the realms of being drunk and who knew where that might lead. "No, best not. I'll not get up in the morning."

She gathered her bag and jacket, gave him a hug, a second longer than necessary, pecked him on the cheek and squeezed his hand. "Goodnight, Thomas. See you in the morning."

She waited for the ping of the lift; the descending floor numbers a countdown as to whether Thomas followed her.

****

Rebecca thought about phoning Spencer before she went for breakfast, so they could talk like normal couples did. But she didn't have anything to say and doubted that he did either. She still hadn't confronted him about how he had accidentally changed her banking password and accidentally transferred cash out of the same account without telling her. It wasn't that she was afraid to challenge him, she was tired of his lies and couldn't be bothered to watch him try and create some more. Maybe Thomas was a reaction to that but who was she trying to kid, the flirting had begun before the money problems. The problems in her marriage existed long before that.

She sent some work emails and headed down for breakfast. Thomas was already there along with a couple other colleagues.

"Morning, everyone."

"Morning, Rebecca. Sleep well?"

It was an innocent enough question and she doubted that her colleague suspected anything but she still blushed. "Like a baby."

There were two seats free, one next to Thomas, one on the far end of the table. She chose to sit next to Thomas, to do otherwise appeared suspicious, everyone knew that they were friends.

"Sleep well?" she asked.

"Like a baby." His knuckles brushed hers under the table.

She hoped that nobody else noticed the smiles passing between them but part of her enjoyed the risk. She ordered some coffee then helped herself to some fruit and yoghurt from the buffet. She couldn't face a cooked breakfast. It was going to be a long day and she was a little hungover, but she'd grab a croissant for later.

As expected the day was a tiring one and she was ready for a nap when she boarded the train home. Her colleagues had stocked up with wine and cans and she was relieved that she couldn't get a seat with them. Thomas hinted that he would sit with her, but she was happy to be alone. She logged onto the train's intermittent Wi-Fi and tried to catch up on emails but didn't have the interest. Instead she checked her bank account; her log in details now working again after Spencer had 'accidentally' changed them.

The joint account balance was a lot less than it should have been. Both her and Spencer had been paid but it seemed that only her standing order had been transferred. This was basic stuff, they both transferred a set amount each month to cover bills, save for holidays etc. and whatever else they earned was their own. If Spencer hadn't contributed their Direct Debits would fail.

He'd been making a big deal about how well sales were going recently, maybe it was a genuine mistake. It wasn't a conversation she could have on the train, so she sent him a text.
Your wages haven't transferred into the joint account. Is there a problem?

She didn't expect a response and she didn't get one. She sat for the rest of the journey stewing about it. It was one thing that he was lying to her, he always had. But now this was causing problems for her financially. If Direct Debits failed it would impact her credit score; she had plans for the future and a bad credit rating wasn't going to help. She needed to have it out with him when she got home. Tired, hungover and a little bit guilty after her liaison with Thomas, the timing wasn't ideal, but it was now or never.

Rebecca left her suitcase in the hall and looked in the sitting room. Spencer wasn't there. He wasn't in the kitchen either and she eventually found him in the bedroom on the phone. He was shocked to see her.

"So, your phone does work?" said Rebecca.

"Not now," said Spencer with his hand over the mouthpiece, "this is an important call."

"Phoning the bank to transfer your wages into the joint account?"

"Seriously, Rebecca, I haven't got time for this." He pushed her out of the room, her own bedroom, and slammed the door behind him, putting his back against it so she couldn't get back in.

Not only was he hiding money issues from her, he was now making secret phone calls. She tried to listen, but the door muffled his voice.

"Yes, I'm serious." Was all she could make out. She went downstairs and poured herself a glass of wine. Five minutes later, Spencer joined her.

"What's with all the secrecy?" said Rebecca.

"It's work stuff, you wouldn't understand."

"You sell cars, what is there to understand?"

"I don't ask what you get up to on your conferences down in Birmingham."

"Maybe you should."

Part of her wanted him to ask about her colleagues, ask about Thomas but it was pointless, he had already grabbed a beer and was back in the sitting room with the football on.

****

Another day, another meeting, Charlie wasn't sure how many more of these she could take. Michelle hadn't said what it was about, but it was more than likely pointless, much like all the others.

She grabbed a coffee on the way and trudged towards the meeting room, not wanting to spend any longer in there than she needed to.

Lauren was already there so Charlie grabbed the spare seat next to her, tactically placed far enough away from where Michelle would sit and not directly in her line of vision. All of the Team Leaders were present but none of them had a clue what the meeting was about with the calendar invite they had received offering up no more than a time and a place.

Michelle arrived five minutes after the meeting starting time. "Why isn't the video conferencing on?"

"Nobody said it was a video conference." The newest Team Leader still hadn't learned when it was best to remain silent.

"It was on the invite," said Michelle, looking flustered as she attempted to operate the remote control. "Why isn't this thing working?"

"There's nothing on the invite." The Team Leader wasn't giving up, but Charlie gave him a shake of the head to show that it wasn't an argument he could win.

Lauren had retrieved the remote control from Michelle. "Which meeting room are we calling?"

"London boardroom, did you not read the invite?"

Lauren knew better than to argue and dialled in the London Office. Finally connecting, an unfamiliar face filled the screen. A man in his thirties, dark hair and bright blue eyes.

Except it wasn't unfamiliar to Charlie, she'd seen that face before. And that wasn't all she'd seen.

She slid down in her seat.

"Nice of you to finally join us," said the face on the screen.

"Sorry, a few technical difficulties at this end," said Michelle, "you can't get the staff these days." She let out a pathetic whimper of a laugh. All the eyes in the room stared daggers at the back of her head.

"I assume Michelle has already filled you in on who I am. My name is Henry Towns and I am the new Chief Operating Officer. Michelle's boss."

"Yes, I've given them all the update as you requested."

A number of shaking heads around the room showed this to be a blatant lie.

"I'm based in the London office, but I plan to spend a lot of time in Sunderland, so I can get to know you better."

He winked which would have been unsettling in normal circumstances, but it was especially weird when his face filled a giant TV screen.

"I feel sick," whispered Charlie.

Lauren stifled a giggle. "Stop it, you'll make me laugh."

"No, I really feel sick." Charlie had gone pale.

"Did you have something to add, Charlie?" said Michelle. Her face red with anger at the interruption.

"No, sorry," said Charlie whilst covering her face and sliding so far down in her chair that she was almost under the table.

The meeting lasted for another twenty minutes until Henry had to dash off to something far more important.

"He's great, isn't he?" said Michelle, beaming at her team.

Nobody agreed but they chose not to disagree either.

As Michelle left the room Lauren nudged Charlie. "What's up? You looked like you were about to hurl your breakfast all over the table. He was creepy, but did he really make you want to vomit?"

"Worse than that, much, much worse."

"Wow, that's some first impression he's made on you."

"That's not my first impression Lauren, I've seen his dick."

"You've seen the new boss's dick?"

"Even worse," said Charlie.

"How can it be worse?"

"It's what he's seen that's the problem."

"You didn't?"

"Not everything. Oh God I feel sick. Just in my underwear; not even my best pants."

"Why on earth did you send photos to him?"

"It was just a bit of fun on a dating app. I was drunk, I didn't think it would lead to anything. I didn't know he was going to be our boss, did I?" Charlie banged her head on the table.

"He might not remember you."

"Thanks for the vote of confidence."

"That's not what I meant, he's probably the type who speaks to hundreds of girls online, it's just a terrible coincidence."

"It's not though is it? He said himself on that call that he's going to be spending a lot more time in Sunderland. He was obviously looking to hook up with girls from here. He asked me where I worked. He knows, he bloody knows."

Lauren put her arm around Charlie's shoulder. "It might not be as bad as it seems."

"My life is over."

"Come on now, we haven't got time for group hugs." They hadn't noticed Michelle stood behind them. "Let's get back to our teams and let our new boss see us in all our glory." Her false grin was sickening.

Charlie and Lauren headed back to their desks. "Do you think she heard?" said Charlie.

"No, I don't think so." Lauren didn't sound convinced.

"Could this get any worse? I've seen boss man's dick, he's seen me in my pants and to top it all, the most indiscrete gobshite in the whole call centre knows all about it. She's going to have this hanging over me forever."

"There's only one thing you can do," said Lauren.

"What's that?"

"Move as far away as you possibly can; Australia for instance." She gave Charlie a playful punch on the arm.

"Looks like you may finally get your wish, Lauren, I can't live like this."

It didn't seem like five minutes since Darren had set foot in the classroom and here he was passing his final exam. The rest of the group had gone to the pub for lunch, as was tradition, but he didn't want to join them, and nobody had offered him a lift anyway.

What should have been one of the happiest days of his life was tinged with the realisation that whilst he may have a career ahead of him, it was going to be a lonely one.

He needed some help on how to he could improve his situation so headed to the message board.

He tried various titles for his thread.

How to make friends.

How to make your colleagues like you.

Surviving in the workplace.

He deleted them all and went with something a bit more generic in the hope he could tease the answers out of people.

Just passed training at work.

I LOVE MY NANA: Just passed my initial training. Any tips for success when I finally start working in the call centre for real on Monday?

SIR STANLEY CUMMINS: Get out now while you still can.

ROKER REJECT: Lie, cheat, be rude, hang up on customers and never call them back. At least that's what happens every time I ring a call centre. Must be the way. Good luck!

VITO MINTO: All joking aside, it's a tough job. Keep your head down, try and meet your targets no matter how daft they seem and get another role off the phones at the earliest opportunity.

SIR STANLEY CUMMINS: Finger some lasses at the Xmas Party.

TROTSKYREDANDWHITE: Have a laugh with your mates, it's the only way of keeping yourself sane.

VITO MINTO: Agreed, the crack on is the only thing that will get you through the day. Hopefully you get to be on the same team as your mates from training.

I LOVE MY NANA: What if I didn't make any mates during training?

TROTSKYREDANDWHITE: Fuck's sake, are you some sort of social leper? If you didn't make any mates during training, you've got no chance.

It may have gone unnoticed by the others on the board but there was one significant development on the thread. His initial post about passing training had received a number of likes but one user in particular had clicked the like button. **DAZZLED,** his old account. The hackers were still watching, and they seemed to approve of his progress.

CHAPTER EIGHT

The sun streaked through the blinds and Emma thought that she should probably be doing more with her Sunday. A gloriously sunny day with a light breeze, it was what her mother would call a 'good drying day'. Which was a stroke of luck considering that she'd just taken a load of washing out.

She took the washing basket into the back garden. It wasn't much, a small patch of grass, a few potted plants and some paving slabs which at a stretch could be called a patio. She really should make more use of it.

"Morning." A voice from over the fence.

"Oh hi, Leanne. Your hair looks lovely."

"You think so? I've just had it done, do you like the colour?"

"Yeah, it really matches your skin." Emma didn't like Leanne's hair, but it was a charade they went through. Leanne changed her hair colour as often as most people changed their bedding and it was a well-worn conversation piece that meant the neighbours could get on without ever really saying anything.

"Fancy joining me?" Leanne raised a glass of wine towards Emma.

"Oh, I'd love to, but I've got loads of housework to do." Emma nodded towards the washing basket.

"Live a little, Emma. It's the weekend, the sun's out and the wine is chilled. The housework can wait for another day." Leanne was sat with her feet up on a chair, her flip flops lying on the floor, her denim skirt hitched up and the straps down on her vest top. A massive pair of sunglasses covered half her face, she was certainly making the most of the weather.

Emma didn't want to waste the day making small talk with Leanne, despite being neighbours they had nothing in common, but somehow, she didn't feel like she could say no to Leanne. It was a lovely day, and should she really be spending it inside doing housework? "I guess one glass won't hurt, I'll just finish pegging these out and I'll join you."

Emma wasn't sure if it was her third or fourth glass, but she was feeling light headed. A combination of wine, sun and a lack of food left her far drunker than she had intended. She wasn't sure if her face was reddened from the sun or from listening to Leanne's tales of her sexual exploits via Tinder.

"You should join and get yourself some action," said Leanne.

The thought horrified Emma. "I don't think it's for me."

"But you might have to upgrade those first." Leanne shrieked with laughter whilst pointing at Emma's underwear on the washing line. She'd definitely gone for comfort over sexiness.

Emma wanted out of the conversation but wasn't sure she could stand. "I'm going to have to go soon."

"I'm only joking with you," said Leanne as she touched Emma's arm, "come on, who was the last bad boy to get inside them pants?" She howled again.

"That's none..." Emma was really struggling here, "nobody, you'd know."

"Okay, sorry, I understand no names. Without naming them, what was your best shag?"

"I've really got to go."

"Come on, we've all got one. The one that even the slightest thought of it gets your clout trotting."

"I don't, there isn't one." Emma tried to stand.

"Wait, what?" Leanne placed her hand on Emma's arm again. "There isn't one as in there isn't a best one or there isn't one at all?"

"There just isn't." Emma was drunk, confused and wanted to be anywhere but here right now.

Leanne poured more wine into Emma's glass. "Come on, tell your Aunty Leanne all about it."

"I'm going to have to move, it's the only option," thought Emma.

She'd woken hungover, sunburnt and with a deep sense of regret. Why had she agreed to have a drink with Leanne? Why had she opened her big mouth?

Before long the whole street would know what she'd told her, she'd be a laughing stock. This is why she didn't drink. She couldn't even remember exactly what she'd told Leanne, but she remembered running out of the garden embarrassed and crying herself to sleep. How was she going to face her again?

Emma liked where she lived but she couldn't stay if she was going to be humiliated every time she stepped out of the door.

Not only was she ill, bright red and filled with fear, she had to get herself ready for work. The cats, normally a welcome addition to her bed were swept away with one hand as she used the other to prop herself up and force herself out of bed.

****

Darren approached his first day on the phones the same way he did his first day of training. He was used to the public transport system now but wasn't taking any chances and got the earlier bus to ensure he arrived in plenty of time. When he arrived at the business park he went for a walk to calm his nerves. He'd been walking for about thirty minutes and was surprised at how refreshed, calm and confident he was.

That was until the seagull shat on him.

How were they even this far inland, why didn't they stick to the sea? He panicked and raked in his bag looking for a tissue, but he came up short. The seagull must have had a big breakfast because it had covered his hair, his face and the sleeve of his suit. He needed to improvise.

He grabbed a handful of leaves and scrubbed at his face. He thought he'd made good progress until he wiped the leaves down his suit and they left a green streak, far more noticeable than the seagull droppings had been. He made a run for the call centre, bursting through the doors much to the surprise of Frank the security guard.

"Morning, son. Do you realise you've got a little bit greenery on your face?"

"Yes, Frank, a seagull shat on me. I need to get it washed off before my shift starts."

"A seagull? The bugger's been eating a lot of seaweed by the looks of things."

"Sorry Frank, I'm in a rush, I need to get to the toilet."

"Well, as long as it's an accident, I get a bit twitchy when people come running in here dressed as Rambo."

Darren rushed to the toilets and cleaned himself as best he could. With five minutes to spare, he arrived at his desk to be greeted by Charlie.

"Morning Darren, welcome to the team. Do you realise that you've got..." she picked some leaves from his hair, "half a bush on your head?"

"Yeah, sorry. Had a bit of an accident on the way here."

"Not to worry, get yourself settled in and I'll introduce you to the rest of the team. Your desk is just there next to Emma."

Emma waved over. At least he would be sitting next to someone he vaguely knew. The rest of the new starters from training arrived and were allocated their desks. The team opposite eyed them as they always did with new starters. Either looking for potential sexual conquests, new mates or more often than not, new targets. Darren immediately became Ryan's target.

"Looks like we've employed David Attenborough over there. You spend the night sleeping in the jungle, mate?"

Darren tried to think of an amusing response but had nothing. He went red.

"Pipe down and take some calls, Ryan," said Charlie, "Wasn't that long ago that you were new. Try and remember what it was like."

Ryan saluted Charlie and returned to the phones. Charlie hated him; yet another reason why she needed to get out of this place.

She introduced the new recruits to the team, what was left of it after most of them had moved on. "I've paired you all with a mentor, make sure you use them. Anything you are unsure of, make sure you ask. We've all been new ourselves, so we'll be happy to help. Good luck."

Charlie sat back and watched, there were always a few tell-tale signs. The first new starter to get logged in and take a call was probably over confident and would cut corners. The last one would be nervous and always second guess themselves. She also worried about those who never asked for help. They could be either over confident or too nervous to ask and she needed to work out which one very quickly. She didn't mind people making mistakes but not trusting those who have been in the job a lot longer than you was criminal. Charlie was confident that by the end of the day she'd have a good idea of what sort of team she had.

Darren was first to log on, she listened in. It was a straightforward billing enquiry and he handled it well. A good start. The next two were similar, not difficult but in the wrong hands they could easily upset the customer. She was interested to see how he handled a difficult call so listened to a couple more.

The next one seemed easy and he was breezing through it but then he stumbled over his words, he became confused, distracted. The customer hadn't said anything to prompt this change of mood. She looked towards Darren and he was flustered; bright red and shaking.

He'd possibly clicked into the wrong screen and didn't know how to get back. Worryingly he didn't seem to be looking to Emma or any of his other colleagues for help. She removed her headset and went to help him. He hadn't clicked into the wrong screen. An instant message was open in front of him with a picture of David Bellamy peering through a bush. She didn't need to look at who it had come from. Ryan and his little gang were all howling with laughter. She would deal with him later.

Charlie pressed the mute button on Darren's console and took the mouse from him to close the message. "You're doing well, Darren. Take a deep breath and go back to the customer, apologise to them. Blame a slight system hiccup, a little white lie won't hurt and go back to explaining as you were before."

Darren did as he was told, and Charlie went to deal with Ryan. She stood behind him with her arms folded until his call was finished and stopped him from taking the next one. "I know you think you are untouchable because of your stats but if you mess with my team again I will make it my mission to make sure every dodgy call gets transferred your way. Do you understand me?"

"Yes, Miss, anything you say, Miss."

"Grow up, Ryan. You're pathetic."

She knew he was laughing at her as she walked away but she was in the mood to destroy him.

****

Darren went through several emotions when he logged off at the end of his first day, but the overall feeling was one of relief. After the encounter with Ryan, his day had gone smoothly. He'd had a couple of difficult customers, but he dealt with them with a bit of support from Emma. He found the pace of the calls a bit of a struggle. No time to relax after one call or even to write up sufficient notes, they were relentless. One after the other and you never knew what type of call was coming next. In some ways, he found it exciting, but he could see why people lived for their breaks.

Day two was much the same. He ignored the quips coming from Ryan and his friends and got on with getting through the calls. He was due a break but got stuck on a complicated international roaming related call.

"No, you don't need to be able to speak Spanish to use your phone in Spain," said Darren.

"Eee, but how does it know what you are saying?"

"It works exactly the same as it does in the UK."

"I'm too old to be learning new languages, son. That's why I stick to the British bars out there, I don't want to be dealing with foreign nonsense."

"Well, you won't need to worry about your phone, it will work fine."

"And they have better turns on."

"Turns?"

"In the British bars, I saw a lovely Neil Diamond last year. Could even have been him if it wasn't for the ginger beard."

"Sounds great. Hope you have a lovely time." Darren tried to hurry the call along to some form of conclusion.

"So, will my daughter need to learn Spanish if she is phoning me from home?"

"No, there's no need for anyone to learn Spanish."

"I mean, she's the brains in the family, even went to college after she was kicked out of school, but the only Spanish word she knows is pizza. Are you sure the phone will understand?"

"Yes, one hundred percent."

Darren couldn't quite believe what he was hearing but he was glad that the call was coming to an end. The caller finally rang off as the rest of the team were coming back from their break.

With only a couple of minutes until lunch, Darren was relieved to get an easy call. This would take him up to lunchtime and he could go for dinner with the rest of the team.

"Are you heading to the canteen?" he said to the assembled group, mainly made up of the new starters from his training group.

Most pretended not to hear him and only one answered. "No, we're heading out."

"Where to?"

"Out."

They left without offering an invitation to join them. He wasn't sure that the invitation was implied, and he was to follow them or whether they didn't want him with them. He suspected the latter. Regardless, he had hesitated so long that he had missed his chance, they were gone. He headed to the canteen, alone.

He got himself a burger and chips and looked for somewhere to sit. He spotted Emma sitting alone and went to join her, but her head was buried in a book. He didn't know whether to speak or not so hovered for a while unsure what to do next.

Emma raised her head. "Hi, Darren, didn't notice you there."

"What are you reading?"

"The latest Harry Potter." She showed him the book cover. "Have you read it?"

"No, not that one."

"Have you read the other Harry Potters?"

"No, I'm not a big fan."

"What sort of books do you read?"

"I'm not a big fan of books, I find them boring." Truth was that apart from textbooks, he hadn't read a book since school.

"That's a shame, you're missing out. I'm getting to a really exciting bit here."

"Sorry, didn't mean to disturb you. I'll leave you to it."

"It's okay, I wasn't chasing you, I can read it on the bus home."

But Darren had already shuffled off. Annoyed at his awkwardness. Annoyed at his ignorance at not reading books. How could he ever make friends if he had nothing of interest to say?

He needed a different approach.

Next morning Darren got an earlier bus as he had an idea that would endear himself to the team. He nipped into the Greggs on the business park and got two boxes of doughnuts. He couldn't afford the extravagance, but it should be a good ice breaker with the team. There were enough for everyone including him and Charlie and he got a selection, so he would hopefully please everyone.

"Morning, Darren," said Charlie, "bright and early, that's what I like to see."

"Morning." He produced a box from his Greggs bag. "Would you like a doughnut?"

"I'm watching my weight," she said then had second thoughts, "but I guess one doughnut won't harm me."

Darren had a big smile on his face as he handed her the box. "I got a selection."

"You bought these for the team? That's very kind." Truth was that she didn't even like doughnuts but thought she should be polite if he had made the effort.

He went to get a coffee and as he returned he saw the team tucking into the doughnuts. His plan had worked.

"Thanks, Charlie."

"Cheers, Charlie, you know how to make the mornings more bearable."

"You're too kind, Charlie."

"They aren't from me," said Charlie, "Darren brought them in."

But nobody was listening.

There was one jam doughnut left when he got to his desk, his favourite. As he was about to grab it a hand came over his shoulder and snatched it.

Ryan.

"Hey, they were for our team."

"What?" said Ryan through a mouthful of jam and sugar-coated lips.

"Never mind."

Emma noticed what had happened. "Here, you can have mine."

"It's okay, I bought them for the team, I don't like jam ones anyway."

"That's really kind of you. Don't worry about the others, they'll come around eventually."

"Think it's going to take more than a few doughnuts."

Darren put on his headphones and logged in.

****

Rebecca nibbled on her sandwich and checked her watch. "We'll have to get back soon."

"You're allowed a lunch hour," said Thomas.

"I know, but we've got a lot on and it's a long walk back." They'd chosen a pub far enough away from the office so that they wouldn't be disturbed by colleagues. Not that them having lunch together was unusual, they regularly nipped out for a sandwich, but being sat down in a pub together felt different, like it signified something.

"We've got plenty of time, what were you saying about your bank account?" It was Thomas who had suggested lunch as he'd picked up the signals that Rebecca wanted to chat about something she couldn't discuss in the office.

"It's probably nothing. No, it's not nothing, I know Spencer is lying to me. He's hiding something."

"We're all hiding something." Thomas regretted it as soon as he said it, it was a cheap dig. They'd not spoken about that night in the Premier Inn, skirting around it whenever it came up, and he didn't want to waste whatever time he had with Rebecca talking about her feckless husband.

"Maybe we are. I can't go on like this." She pushed her sandwich away and grabbed her coat. "Come on, let's make a move before somebody misses us."

****

Lunchtime came around and Darren eyed the selection in the canteen, curry, mince and dumplings, a variety of pies and salads for those a little more self-conscious about what they ate. Whilst he was queueing a thought struck him. He searched his pockets.

"Shit."

He left the queue. When he'd bought the doughnuts, he hadn't considered how much they cost and the money he had on him only just covered them, he had nothing left to buy lunch. Not even enough to buy a bag of crisps. He helped himself to a free coffee from the vending machine and joined the rest of his team.

"Not eating?" said Adam.

"No, not hungry."

"Probably stuffed his face on those doughnuts Charlie bought. Greedy bastard."

Everyone laughed but he didn't bother explaining. Just sat watching others eat and trying to keep the sound of his rumbling stomach from reaching them. Emma joined them and pulled up a chair next to Darren, taking out her Tupperware box containing sandwiches, crisps and a Twix. He was jealous.

"Not eating?" she said.

"He pigged out on the free doughnuts earlier."

"He didn't get one," said Emma, "which was a shame considering that he bought them."

But once again nobody was listening, and they shared a private joke.

"Come on, are we going for a tab?"

The group stood as one even though most of them didn't smoke. Darren knew the invitation wasn't extended to him. He watched them leave and his stomach betrayed him by letting out a huge growl.

"Not hungry eh?" said Emma whilst raising an eyebrow.

He decided honesty was the best policy. "Left myself a bit short after buying the doughnuts. Never thought it through properly."

"You should have said; how much do you need?" Emma reached into her bag for her purse.

"No, it's okay. I'll wait until I get home for my tea. The queue's massive now and by the time I get something I'll have to be back on the phones."

"We can't have you starving. Here, have one of my sandwiches."

"I can't eat your dinner."

"You'll be doing me a favour."

"Doing you a favour?"

"If you don't eat something soon I'll not be able to hear the customers this afternoon over your rumbling belly."

Darren laughed and accepted the sandwich. "Thank you." It was gone in two bites, he was hungrier than he thought.

"Here, you best have some of these as well." She offered him some crisps.

"Thanks, but I've already eaten half of your dinner."

"Go on, I've been thinking of going on a diet."

"You don't need to go on a diet," Darren wasn't used to giving compliments, "you're not half as fat as some of the girls who work here."

"Wow, you really know how to charm the ladies."

"Sorry, that came out wrong." He was blushing and started to shake again. "I'm sorry." Darren pushed his chair back, almost knocking it over, "I've got to go."

He loitered in the car park until it was time to go back. "*Idiot,*" he thought, "*why can't I do anything right?*"

He noticed the rest of his team returning from wherever they had been, but they spotted him before he could get away.

"What are you doing out here, Darren? Come out for a sly fart?"

They all laughed at him again.

"Just getting some fresh air."

"Won't be fresh for long if you've been dumping your guts after scoffing those doughnuts."

He could still hear them laughing as they entered via the double doors. He was tempted to cross the car park, get the bus home and never return.

He knew that wasn't an option so swallowed his pride and headed back inside.

Emma was already on a call, so he couldn't tell whether she was annoyed with him or not. He logged on and got on with his job.

Apart from Charlie, Emma was the only person who had shown any kindness to him and he's spoilt it by sticking his big foot in his gob. *"Why do I always make a fool of myself?"*

"Hello?"

"Shit." Darren was in a world of his own and hadn't noticed the call coming through.

"Good afternoon, you are through to Darren at Phonetix Mobile, how may -"

"Manager, now."

"If I could—"

"Manager, now."

"My manager's not—"

"Manager, now." The caller followed up with an exaggerated sigh.

Charlie wasn't at her desk and Emma was on a call. Nobody else was likely to help him, he was on his own.

"I really need—"

"Are you backward? Did your mother drop you on your head as a baby? I don't want to speak to the office simpleton, I want to speak to your manager."

"I'll try and—"

"Are you not listening? I don't want you to try anything, I expect you to do as I say and get your manager."

Darren stood to see if any other Team Leaders were around, but they must have all been in a meeting. "Could I just-"

"My God, you are the thickest fuckwit ever to dribble down a phone. Don't worry, I'll call back and speak to someone who isn't on day release from the special school."

The call ended

Darren felt physically drained. He prayed that this call wasn't being monitored, it could bring his probation period crashing to a halt.

He tried to write the notes, but another call came through. Again, he was unprepared and was on the back foot. Again, this led to confusion and a dissatisfied customer. He had a quick look at his call stats and he was well over his target call time, there was no way he would recover them by the end of his shift.

CHAPTER NINE

Darren woke with the smell of chicken vindaloo stinking out the flat. He'd cut out the takeaways since starting at Phonetix, but his bad day yesterday had broken his new regime and he was annoyed at how easily he crumbled. He went for a shower and realised that it wasn't just the flat that stunk of Indian curry. It was never a problem before when he was sat in the flat in his pants but now he had to go to work. He scrubbed himself in the shower and drenched himself in Lynx before getting dressed. Hopefully this kept the smell at bay.

Emma was at her desk when he arrived. "Morning, Darren."

At least she still seemed to be speaking to him. He was tempted to apologise for yesterday but thought better of it. "Morning."

"Darren, could I have a quick word before you log in please?" said Charlie.

"What's up?" He already knew.

"I'm having a look at yesterday's stats and you seem to be way off target. Was there a problem?"

"Just a couple of bad calls." The nerves were making him sweat, the last thing he needed after last night's southern Asian cuisine.

"Do you want us to listen to them together, see if there's any training needs there?"

He dreaded Charlie hearing that car crash of a call. "I know where I went wrong, thanks. Hope I can bring my stats back up today."

"Okay but remember that you are new and if you need help, ask. I'm not going to get hung up on stats in your first week, but I will be unhappy if you don't ask for help when you need it."

"Okay."

Darren wasn't sure if that was friendly advice or a shot across the bows. He desperately wanted to do a good job, but he realised that he had underestimated the task in hand. Maybe he wasn't cut out for call centre work after all; it certainly wasn't as easy as he had imagined. He returned to his desk.

"Just ask if you need anything," said Emma, "even if I'm on a call, give me a nudge."

"Thanks." Darren wondered why Emma was so nice to him after yesterday. He understood why the others were horrible to him, that's the way people were but Emma was nice to everyone. He wasn't sure he could ever be like Emma.

As per usual, as break time was coming around, he got stuck on a nightmare call. He watched the team file off one by one for their break whilst he struggled to convince a customer that paying his bill was the only way he would get his phone line reconnected. It was a nightmare call where Darren knew the customer was lying, the customer knew she was lying and whatever sob story she was giving, Darren had to stay firm.

One of the team hadn't gone for their break yet; Emma. She sat by him, giving him encouragement and guided him thought it.

"Well done," she said as Darren ended the call after securing payment from the customer.

"Thanks, I'd have struggled without your help. Should you not have been on your break five minutes ago?"

"I couldn't leave you on your own."

"Oh." Darren didn't like the idea of being babysat.

"I meant that I didn't want to leave you to have your break on your own again, not that I thought you needed supervision. Come on, let's get a cuppa."

"I'm paying," said Darren.

"It's a deal."

"That was a joke, the vending machines are free," said Darren, slightly flushed, "but I would pay, if they weren't free."

Emma smiled. "I know Darren, I got the joke."

"What did you get up to last night?" asked Emma. They'd sat in the comfy seats near reception rather than go in the canteen with the rest of the team.

"Not much, just got a takeaway."

"Indian?"

Darren felt a little self-conscious. "That obvious?"

"I think it's impossible to eat something like that without it being obvious. Not that I eat Indian takeaways, I wish I was a bit more adventurous. I'm a bit boring."

"You're not boring."

"Not half as boring as half the dullards in here?" She smirked as she said it.

"That's not what I meant."

"I know, I'm joking with you. You shouldn't take everything so seriously."

"Sorry, I don't like talking to people."

"Am I boring you?" said Emma.

"No, you're not boring. I'm just not good at talking to people."

"You're probably in the wrong job then."

"I'm beginning to realise that," said Darren

"I was joking again." She shook her head. "What part do you find difficult?"

136

"All of it," he looked to the floor, "I guess I haven't had much practice."

"You can practice on me. Go on, ask me a question," said Emma.

"Like what?"

"Anything you like."

"What did you do last night?"

"Not much, watched the soaps with the cats. Told you I was boring."

"Okay."

"This is where you come in with a follow-up question."

"Like what?" said Darren.

"Ask which soaps I watched or what my cats are called."

"What are your cats called?"

"Buzz and Woody," said Emma.

"Buzz and Woody? Sounds like nicknames for dildos." He regretted it as soon as he blurted it out, his cheeks glowed scarlet.

"Oh my God, no; from Toy Story." It was Emma's turn to blush. "Have you never seen Toy Story?"

"Never seen it, I don't watch films. Strange names for cats though."

"There's no rules on naming cats as far as I am aware. Nothing wrong with having a bit of fun. Maybe I'm not as boring as you think."

"I never said you were boring."

"Do you have any pets?" said Emma.

"No, I don't like them."

"All pets or just cats?"

"All, especially cats."

"Have you ever owned a pet?"

"No, never. Sorry, that's a lie, I had a snail I found in the garden once. It died."

"A snail? How did it die."

"Fed it some lettuce but I didn't know they didn't like salt on their lettuce."

"Eeuggh. If you haven't owned a proper pet, then how do you know you don't like them?"

"I just, I don't know." He didn't have an answer.

"You don't watch films, you don't like pets, I'm sure we'll find something we have in common before we retire. Come on, we'd better get back," said Emma shaking her head "you'll be getting me into trouble."

****

Charlie reviewed her teams call stats yet again. Her trusty highlighter coming out to put a splash of fluorescence on anything that wasn't quite up to scratch.

"That's a lot of yellow." Lauren had wandered to her desk.

"Yeah, mainly Darren. I'm concerned."

"Will he make it through probation?"

"He's borderline." He had good days and bad days, but his overall stats hovered just above the cut-off point. The call centre had very strict rules and anyone under the line come the end of their probation was shown the door. No second chances.

"What's the quality of his calls like?" said Lauren.

"Not much better, he's hit and miss but if he gets one bad call, he spirals downwards."

"I'm not being funny Charlie, but is it not time to cut him loose? Anybody else would be jumping at the chance of getting rid of someone high maintenance."

"I can't do that to him, he's desperate for this job."

"It's not you doing it to him, the stats speak for themselves."

"No, it's not him failing, it's me. I've never had someone not get through probation before and it's not happening now."

"You're mad."

"No, I owe it to him. I brought him into the company, I've got to make sure he stays."

"And how are you going to do that?"

Charlie worried that by drawing attention to how perilous his position was, that he would crumble. But she couldn't ignore it. "It's time for a pep talk."

She took both Darren and Emma into a small meeting room. "This isn't anything to get worried about, Darren, but as you know, you only have a couple days left of your probation. You are on target, but only just."

"Okay?"

"We need to ensure that everything you do over the next two days is perfect. Emma and I will do whatever we can to help but you must ask if you are struggling. Are you okay with that?"

Darren was gripping his chair. This shouldn't have been a surprise as Charlie had spent a lot of time with him discussing his stats and his calls, but the timeframe brought it into sharp focus. "Yes."

"You don't sound sure."

"I've tried, I really have, maybe I'm not good enough."

"Nobody is questioning your effort. You've come this far, Darren, we need to get over the final hurdle. A lot of it is down to confidence. You get one bad call and let it affect the rest of your day, you need to forget them."

"I try but some of the stuff they say," he looked to Emma then to the floor, "it's not nice."

"We've all had them in the past, once you realise that the customer doesn't know you and it's nothing personal, it becomes easier to move on. You need to have the confidence in yourself that we have in you." She wasn't sure if she did have that confidence in him, but she was going to try.

"I'll do whatever it takes," said Emma, "I won't go on a break if you are on a call. If I'm on a call myself, interrupt me if you need help. If there's anything you want to talk about, just ask."

"But it'll ruin your stats if I keep on interrupting you."

"Who cares? I was new once and I had help from my mentor, it's my turn to return the favour."

"Thank you. I'm sorry that you have been dragged into this."

"I haven't been dragged into anything, I'm happy to help."

"Thanks, Emma," said Charlie, "so that's the three of us agreed? For the next two days, our only focus is Darren passing his probation?"

"Agreed."

"Agreed."

"One last thing Darren," said Charlie, "you do realise that anyone who passes their probation has to get the doughnuts in?"

The rain was bouncing off the pavement as he walked to the bus stop. He'd never invested in an umbrella and he discovered just how water repellent his twenty-pound coat from Sports Direct was. He was soaked through by the time the bus came but he managed to get a seat. The windows were steamed up and previous artistic endeavours that had been drawn into the mist revealed themselves. The obligatory cock and balls and an in-depth explanation as to what Kevin's mam did with a toilet seat.

Any other day he may have laughed, today his mood matched the weather. Today could be his last day at Phonetix. No matter how hard he tried, if the Gods were against him he was finished. He knew that it had nothing to do with the Gods, he'd had a month to prove he was capable, and he hadn't convinced anyone. Nobody had put more effort in, but he allowed himself to get upset when customers abused him, and it was likely to be his downfall. Ironic considering how much time he spent abusing call centre workers in the past.

He was drenched when he arrived at work and had to make a detour to the toilets to use the hand dryer to dry out a little bit. He used paper towels to dry his hair and did the best he could, but he was still soaked and dishevelled when he arrived at his desk.

"Must be a big day, Darren's had a shower," said Ryan.

Darren tried to ignore him.

A post it note was in the middle of his screen and he wasn't sure that he could take more abuse. He removed it and read the message.

Good luck today.

It also had a little smiley face drawn on it. It could only have been from Emma.

She arrived at his desk with a coffee. "Thought you might need this, it's horrible out there."

"Thank you."

"You ready to seize the day?"

Darren pointed towards his sodden clothes. "Not the best of starts."

"That means that you've got all your bad luck out of the way early."

"Guess I'm as ready as I'm ever going to be."

"Just treat it like any other day. You've done well up to now, you know you can do the job, stay calm and let me know if you need anything. We'll get through the day together."

"It's not your job on the line," said Darren.

"I know, but I don't want you to leave. We're a team and we're going to succeed. Are you ready?"

"I'm ready."

"Let's do this."

The sky had got darker and the rain heavier since he arrived and the rain lashing against the windows provided a dramatic background to his last afternoon of probation. As thunder rumbled in the distance, the first call after lunch provided more drama than he had hoped for.

"I want a new phone."

"Okay sir, I'll pop you through to our upgrade department."

"I don't want an upgrade, I want a replacement for the one you broke, and you are going to give it to me."

"The one we broke?"

"Yes."

"I'm not sure I understand," said Darren, "how did we break it?"

"I dropped it in a puddle."

"Okay, I see. Did you have phone insurance?"

"No, I didn't, why would I have phone insurance?"

"In case of accidents like the one you described."

"This wasn't an accident, this was your fault."

"I don't follow, you dropped your phone in a puddle and you think it is our fault?" His voice had got louder and slightly higher pitched, alerting both Emma and Charlie. Emma put her customer on hold and Charlie plugged in her headset to listen in.

"Of course it's your fault, if you hadn't sent me a promotional text I wouldn't have taken my phone out of my pocket."

"You do have the option to opt out of promotional texts."

"I shouldn't have to opt out."

"I can change your preferences for you now."

"I don't want my preferences changing, I want a new phone."

"We can't offer a new phone I'm afraid." Darren looked to Charlie and Emma for help.

"For Christ's sake. You're probably the same idiot who sent the message. It was asking me if I was going for a holiday in the sunshine, why the bloody hell would I want a sunshine holiday?"

"Because there'd be fewer puddles for you to drop your phone into?"

Emma let out a gasp, Charlie put her head in her hands and Darren knew that he had ruined his chances of a career at Phonetix mobile.

Charlie took over the call before the customer even got a chance to ask to speak to his manager. She tried to talk him down, but it took over thirty minutes, all on Darren's log in. All on Darren's stats.

His averages were screwed, he was screwed, he was out of a job.

****

Spencer had been biding his time, waiting for the right moment; that moment had come.

George had been monitoring him closely since he'd given him his warning and time was running out for him finding another job. He'd tried to convince other dealerships that he wanted to leave for a bigger challenge, but everyone knew that he worked for the best dealership in the city. If he was leaving, then something must be up, and nobody wanted to touch him.

Rebecca didn't want to touch him either. They weren't quite at the separate beds stage, but they were barely communicating. He couldn't explain why there was no money going into the joint account and she had got tired of listening to his excuses. Rebecca covered the household bills and he kept himself and the credit card bills out of her way but there was no way he could hide losing his job.

George was leaving in the F-Type again. Whilst he had hauled Spencer over the coals about his conduct, he wasn't squeaky clean himself. Spencer knew that he was having an affair and knew that he took the F-Type to impress his young female friend. He nipped into the office where the keys were kept.

"Just taking that old XF out to a customer, shouldn't be long." He signed for the car and took the keys from the key box. Each car came with two sets of keys. He took both sets.

He made a call as he got in the car. Once that call was made, there was no way back.

Spencer waited in the car park at Durham services. The place was crawling with CCTV, but he hoped to be innocuous. He felt safer than meeting in a secluded lane given who he was meeting.

A black Range Rover pulled in behind him and wound its window down. Spencer got out of the car, walked past and threw a set of keys through the open window without saying a word to the occupants.

After using the toilet in the services, he returned to the showroom, signed to say he had retuned the car. "They never showed, bloody time wasters," then put one set of keys back in the key box.

The young girl working in the office ignored him. She may have been young, but she was wise enough to avoid conversation with the creepy older salesman.

George got out of the shower and wandered back into the bedroom, still feeling the need to breathe in and hide his beer belly. "You can stop here if you like, I've paid for bed and breakfast."

"And do what?"

"I don't know, a round of golf or something."

"Golf, are you taking the piss?"

"I don't know, watch a film, get some room service. I'll try and get back later after I've finished in the showroom, but I can't stop all night, the wife will get suspicious. I've already had three sales trips in the last fortnight."

"I thought you said you were separated?"

"We are, sort of. It's complicated but she's the jealous type. If she knew about you it would make the divorce settlement a lot harder."

He changed back into his suit, grabbed the car keys and gave her a kiss. "I'll see you later."

He left reception trying not to catch the eye of the staff. Whilst they were used to this sort of behaviour, they always made him feel guilty.

When he got to the car park something wasn't right. He doubted himself for a moment, but things weren't right at all.

The F-Type was gone.

Panic set in. Strictly speaking he shouldn't have had the F-Type. Strictly speaking he shouldn't have been spending the afternoon at the Ramside Hall Hotel with an eighteen-year-old barmaid. He was in deep shit. How was he going to explain this?

He ran back into reception. "My car, my car has gone."

"I'm sorry sir, your car?"

"Yes, my Jaguar. It was parked outside and now it's gone."

"And you're sure you remember where you parked it?"

"Yes, I'm bloody sure."

"And nobody else has the keys for it? Your wife for instance?"

He wasn't sure if the receptionist was being sarcastic. "No, the wife doesn't have keys."

"Okay sir, I'll call the police straight away."

"No, not the police. Not yet. Do you have CCTV?"

"Yes, sir but I do think we should call the police as soon as possible."

George prayed it was someone from the garage playing a prank. He didn't know how they knew but involving the police would ruin everything for him. "I agree but one quick look before we make the call."

The hotel manager arrived and took him into the office where they viewed the CCTV. The theft was blatant. Someone walked up, his face obscured by a baseball cap, and got into the car without any fuss and drove off. Maybe they had intercepted the signal from his remote when locking the car. No car was fully secure, no matter how expensive.

The thief was six foot five and all muscle, definitely nobody from the garage. This wasn't a prank, this was real.

"Guess we'd better make that call."

He slumped into the armchair and thought about all the excuses he needed to make. None of them would work, especially with his wife.

His career was over as well.

"My whole life is finished."

****

"Try not to worry," said Emma as they took their final break of the day, "you might be able to pull back some time."

"There's no chance. It wasn't only that thirty-minute call, every call after that was a nightmare, my stats just got worse."

Emma knew he was right, even if the calls for the rest of the day were straightforward, he was unlikely to get that time back and if that call had been monitored he had no chance. "You've got to try, anything could happen."

"I'll do my best, at the very least I'll try and go out with a scrap of dignity," said Darren knowing that him and dignity had rarely been acquainted.

The sky had turned pitch black and the thunder was crashing overhead as they returned to their desks. Lightning flashed and illuminated the whole floor. They were now in the eye of the storm.

"Do your best," said Emma, "and everything will be okay." She didn't believe it but felt that it needed to be said.

Two more hours and Darren's career at Phonetix would be over.

His next call was a standard billing enquiry and as he was explaining the cost of voicemail there was another flash of lightning.

Then darkness.

All the lights went off as did Darren's PC and monitor. He looked around the floor and everyone was having the same problem.

"Hello, are you still there?" said the customer.

"Sorry, sir. Yes, I'm still here but we appear to have had a power cut and our systems have gone down. I think we may have been struck by lightning. Would you mind phoning back later please?"

"I guess so." The customer hung up and the emergency lighting came on.

Team Leaders rushed about frantically and whilst the power was off, the calls were still coming through on another circuit.

There was a very simple process when such a situation occurred.

"I'm sorry, we're experiencing system problems due to a power cut, would you mind calling back later please?"

Call after call dismissed in seconds. The mood lifted on the floor, there was nothing like system downtime to rally the troops.

And as the callers hung up, the call stats rose. Call stats didn't care whether you resolved a customer's query, they only cared how long a call took and they were only taking seconds. Darren watched his stats rise, maybe there was a way out of this after all.

He'd never been happier to hear a customer's voice. Every one of them bringing him a step closer to reach his target. If the systems stayed down for the rest of the shift, he was in with a chance.

Emma winked at him as they both watched his stats climb.

Charlie arrived at his desk with the news he had been waiting for. "I've been talking to the IT guys and we're on the emergency generator. That's enough for the basics but it'll take some time to get the systems back up and running. I don't think we're getting them back today."

Darren and Emma grinned at each other. He was going to do it.

By the end of the shift he had the best stats he'd ever had in one day. He didn't care how he got them, he deserved some luck.

"Well done, Darren," said Charlie, "you got there in the end." She was genuinely pleased that he had hit his targets. "We'll need to catch up in the morning."

As he walked out of the building with Emma he didn't look as happy as she expected. "What's up?"

"I'm not out of the woods yet. If anyone was monitoring that call, I'm finished anyway."

The storm had moved on, but the thunder still rumbled in the distance. Darren knew that he could well be walking into another storm in the morning.

Darren didn't sleep and took the bus to work with a sense of foreboding. He knew he had dodged a bullet with the call stats, but the call monitoring would catch him out. He knew that what he had said to the customer was out of order, but he was asking for it. Demanding a new phone because he had dropped it in a puddle, that was the sort of nonsense Darren came out with when he was trolling call centres.

If the worst happened, as he expected, and he was finished; he hoped he could walk out without crying. He didn't want to give Ryan and his gang the satisfaction.

Charlie wasn't looking forward to the conversation with Darren. These things were never easy, and he had at least tried. When people were sacked, they were normally lazy or wouldn't listen, Darren had at least put the effort in. He was odd, awkward and dressed like a jumble sale, but he had done his best.

"Morning, Darren. Can I have a word before you sit down please?"

"Okay," he removed his jacket.

"Bring your things with you." The implication was clear.

They sat in the small meeting room again. "Bad news I take it?" He wanted to make it easy for Charlie, she had been kind to him. It wasn't her fault that he wasn't up to scratch.

"As you know," said Charlie, "your call averages were just above the cut-off point, so you reached the target you were aiming for. The power cut also wiped out any call recordings from yesterday, so the call monitoring team won't be able to mark your calls."

"Really?" Maybe there was some hope.

"Unfortunately, Darren, as your manager I have to decide based on all the evidence available to me. I know that you scraped through your call stats due to a power cut and whilst it wasn't recorded, I heard that call. I can't ignore it. We can't talk to customers like that."

"I'm sorry." Darren's voice was wavering.

"So, on balance, from everything I know..." Charlie's voice was wavering as well.

"I understand," said Darren picking up his bag.

Charlie looked out of the glass door towards the call centre floor, so Darren couldn't see her welling up. Ryan walked past making a wanker sign at Darren "... I'm giving you a second chance."

"What?"

She wasn't sure where it came from, that wasn't what she intended to say. "Don't let me down, Darren."

Darren put his head on the table. "I won't, I promise."

CHAPTER TEN

Darren shared his good news with the message board.

I LOVE MY NANA: Passed my probation at work. I'm chuffed, first job I've ever had.

SIR STANLEY CUMMINS: Well done, hope you are going out to get pissed to celebrate.

I LOVE MY NANA: Not really a drinker, might get a takeaway though.

ROKER REJECT: You don't drink? How do you get through the working day?

CHEESY QUAVER: I passed mine twenty years ago. This place has been slowly eating my soul since then. Escape now while you still can.

LAST KING OF SUDDICK: Don't drink? Last time I worked in a call centre I kept a bottle hidden in the ceiling tile above trap five to get me through the day. Lad in the next cubicle got a hell of a shock when I dropped it. He thought my piles had burst.

The rest of the messages were in a similar vein, gently mocking him but all good natured. That was until **DB10** arrived on the scene.

Spencer was sat awaiting another interview with the Police about the stolen F-Type and he was calming his nerves by posting abuse on the message board.

DB10: Getting to your age and this is your first job? Pathetic, you should be ashamed of yourself. You might as well celebrate now as you'll not last five minutes in the real world.

Darren had vowed never to get into any more fights on the forum, but Spencer knew how to push his buttons.

I LOVE MY NANA: Only pathetic person here is you. Someone trying to improve themselves and all you do is mock. You should be ashamed.

DB10: Who are you trying to kid Darren, everybody knows who you used to post as. You were pathetic then and you are pathetic now.

Darren didn't reply and while Spencer was waiting for a response that he could argue with, he was called into the manager's office where two detectives sat alongside George.

"This isn't a formal interview, Spencer, we're still trying to establish the facts. Tell us again why you had access to the key cabinet."

"I was taking the XF out to show a customer as I explained earlier. I signed the keys in and out as I am supposed to do. It's all written down."

"And where did you meet this customer."

"I was meant to meet them at Durham Services, but they never showed. A wasted trip."

"And you never went anywhere near Ramside Hall? Can anybody vouch for your whereabouts?"

"Don't know, CCTV I guess, I imagine there are cameras all over the services." He was confident that when he threw the keys into the Range Rover that it wasn't spotted on camera.

"Okay, we'll check that out."

"What about the Sat-Nav?" said George. "The memory in it will show where he was. Bet you hadn't thought of that, Spencer?" George was convinced that Spencer was to blame for his predicament.

"No, guess I hadn't. Is that all gentlemen, these cars won't sell themselves?" He got up without waiting for a reply. A smirk spread across his face as he left. The Sat-Nav provided the alibi he needed, and it was George who suggested it, not him. Just like he always knew he would.

The showroom was still quiet when Spencer came out of the interview. After his Oscar worthy performance, he'd earned himself a treat. He browsed the sites of his favourite clothing retailers, looking at £500 coats and £300 shoes, things that he could pass off as legitimate workwear to Rebecca. She wouldn't know the difference. An email pinged into his inbox, a promotional one for 50% off Titleist golf clubs. He considered the slump he'd been in sales wise, and the fact that he'd hardly been on the golf course recently. He wasn't a great player but allowing potential clients to win was all part of the game. Maybe new clubs were the inspiration he needed to get himself back out there. They were an investment.

He flicked through the ones in the half price offer, but they weren't that much better than what he had. The next range up only had 25% off but it still amounted to a few hundred quid; they were virtually giving them away. By the time he'd added a bag, balls, shoes and a couple of new outfits it was itching close to £1500 but it was only going on his card, it wasn't like it was real money. He took the shiny new credit card from his wallet, yet another company foolish enough to allow him to get into more debt. It seemed that the more debt you had, the more attractive you were to the credit companies.

He'd struck lucky when ordering it as the card arrived when Rebecca was away on a conference. It wasn't worth the aggravation of telling her about it. He took no such chances with his purchases and as always, he made the showroom his default address for all deliveries. The clubs stayed in the boot of his car and she would never see them. Even if she did she couldn't tell the difference between the new ones and the cobweb covered clubs in the cupboard under the stairs.

With the police off his back, he'd soon be able to collect his cut of the F-Type deal. That would cover the golf gear, the clothes and more. Rebecca never needed to find out. He might even consider treating her to a night out if she ever cheered up. He completed his order as the policemen were leaving.

"Nice clubs," one of them said looking over Spencer's shoulder at the screen.

"Do you play?" said Spencer.

"On a copper's wage? No, I'll stick to the crazy golf with the bairns."

That's where Spencer differed from the detectives. He knew that the money he was spending could only further his career. If the coppers knew how many senior policemen were members of his golf club they may consider making a similar investment.

"Well, if you ever fancy a quick nine holes, you know where I am."

"We certainly do."

****

Darren arrived for work carrying another box of doughnuts and sporting a new suit from the Debenhams Blue Cross sale. Ryan had mocked his brown one and his pinstriped navy one, so he went for a lighter blue this time. Sensible, non-controversial and remarkably cheap. The trousers were a little snug and the suit a little shiny, but he felt great in it.

"Morning, Frank."

"Morning son, new suit?"

"It is Frank, thanks for noticing."

"I couldn't help but notice, it's a bobby dazzler."

Talk amongst the team was of the night out they had on Friday to celebrate passing their probation. A night out that he hadn't been invited to. He didn't drink so wouldn't have gone but it would have been nice to have been included.

"Cheers, Darren."

At least they acknowledged that the doughnuts were from him. None of the other probation passers had bothered.

"Ooh, Darren's come dressed as a bottle of Blue Wkd," said Ryan as he helped himself to a doughnut.

Darren begrudged him it but had bought extra knowing that Ryan would take one to goad him.

"Ignore him," said Emma, "I think it's a lovely suit."

Darren assumed that everyone would have liked it. Maybe it was a little shiny, it was in the sale for a reason.

Charlie gathered everyone together for a quick team brief.

"Congratulations to everyone who passed their probation, I hope this is the beginning of a long and successful career with Phonetix."

A smattering of applause rang around.

"With perfect timing, Phonetix have announced that we're going to have a Star Employee Award. The rules are simple. Everybody is given five stars that they can give out to colleagues who they think have gone above and beyond. Any stars you receive can be kept to try and become Star Employee yourself or you can donate them to whoever you see fit if you believe they deserve them. The catch is that you need to write up justification of why you are donating them, you can't just give them to your mates. There will be a big cash prize for the winner, so it is worth aiming for."

Darren was determined to repay Charlie's faith in him and this seemed like the ideal opportunity. If he could win this, it would show that she was right to give him a second chance. His Nana always said that he could be the best if he put his mind to it. He was going to prove her right.

"Are you going for the Star Awards then?" said Lauren as she met Charlie for a coffee.

"Are you joking?" said Charlie, "I have to use all my strength to be polite to people."

"Nothing like an incentive scheme to motivate the staff, eh?" said Lauren.

"I'll be honest, I'd happily give the award to whoever can make this coffee taste like anything but muck." She poured the remainder of the vending machine coffee away. "Best get back up there and watch our stars shine."

Over the coming days, the office got decorated in stars to publicise the awards. As well as the official posters, each team was expected to design their own display; in their own time, of course. Nobody was too keen, but Darren volunteered. He made an early start after a visit to the pound shop to get supplies. Glitter, glue, fluorescent cards, he had the lot. He had approached Valerie, the woman in charge of the stationery cupboard but she wasn't forthcoming with any help. It appeared that Star Awards, and being anything but officious, weren't her thing.

"Thought you might need a hand." Emma had arrived early to help him.

"Thanks."

"Looks like you could do with it." She removed a silver star from his cheek.

Glitter covered his desk, the stars he had cut out weren't very star shaped and he had glue everywhere.

"I'm not very practical when it comes to this sort of stuff."

"You don't say? When was the last time you attempted anything like this?"

"Infant school."

"Doesn't look like you've improved much."

She had a point. He lifted his hands and they were covered in glitter. "It's going to take ages to get this off."

Under Emma's instruction, they cobbled together some half decent posters and put them up around the walls, carefully following both Health and Safety rules and those of the facilities manager about using blu tac on certain surfaces. They didn't want to upset anyone.

They stood back and admired their work as the rest of the team arrived.

"Good effort, Darren," said Charlie, "you've done a great job."

"It was mainly Emma, I was just making a mess."

"That's what I like to see. The Star Awards are already promoting team work. Thanks, both of you."

"Charlie, is it okay if I give one of my stars to Emma for helping me?"

"No problem. As long as you write the justification you don't need to ask my permission."

"Great, I'll do it now."

With a big smile on his face Darren typed his report and fired a star Emma's way.

"Thank you," said Emma, "you didn't have to do that, it was a team effort."

"You didn't have to help me, I was just getting into a mess."

"On that subject, do you not think you should get cleaned up?"

"Good point." Darren took a quick look at the clock and realised that he didn't have time. "I'll do it at break."

He regretted it instantly as Ryan came in. "Ha ha, look at Gary Glitter there."

"Prick," thought Charlie. She started typing and a couple minutes later Darren heard the ping of an email.

Charlie had awarded him his first Star Award for teamwork.

****

Darren placed the tray of drinks on his desk and dished them out. It was only a small thing, but it was another step towards being accepted by the team. He'd learned everybody's order and even brought extra sachets of sugar for those who liked their tea sweet. He didn't mind that nobody else offered, he quite liked the responsibility; he knew that he wouldn't get any stars for walking to the vending machine, but it all helped. He checked his emails before logging into the phones and was surprised to find one from the Star Awards. He'd received another one. This time from somebody on the call monitoring team who was rewarding him for the way he had remained calm and helped a customer who was abusive. He had no recollection of the call and suspected that it was meant for somebody else.

He clicked on the link to listen in and it was indeed him and the customer definitely was abusive; with the language of a docker. Darren vaguely remembered the call but hadn't considered it abusive. The customer sounded drunk, had run out of credit and in her drunken state she struggled to apply her new voucher. It showed how Darren had become institutionalised as he'd filtered out the swearing without even thinking. It wasn't aimed at him, just a customer with a potty mouth, so he dealt with what was an easy query.

His headset pinged as another call came through. It was one of the calls everyone dreaded, a pensioner who had received a text message from a wrong number.

"It's a text message," said Darren.

"I don't have any of that fancy stuff."

"Everyone has it on their phones even if they don't use it."

"But why is there an envelope on my screen? Is it from the post office?"

"No, it's probably a wrong number."

"Why does the post office have my number?"

"It's not the post office."

"How do you know? Do you think there is a letter waiting for me at the sorting office?"

"It's not the Royal Mail. Open the message and you'll see who it is from."

"What if it is one of those scams that I've seen in the Daily Mail?"

"There's nothing to worry about, it could be a wrong number."

"Why has somebody I don't know got my number?"

This would take all the skills that Darren had learned recently. He needed to remain calm and patient and attempt to explain in the simplest terms so that his customer clearly understood. A couple of colleagues picked up on what was happening and laughed. They'd all been there and knew how frustrating it could be. If Darren negotiated this call, he could be on his way to another star.

Ryan also noticed what was happening. "Glitter got a senile on the line there? I thought he preferred them young."

He said it loud enough for Darren to hear. Loud enough to put Darren off.

"It could have been fat fingers," said Darren.

"Fat fingers, how do you know I have fat fingers?" said the customer.

"Not you, the person who dialled the number. They may have accidentally dialled an incorrect digit."

"It's a medical condition I'll have you know. I've been to the doctors, but he is worse than useless."

Darren nipped the bridge of his nose. This call wasn't going in the direction he wanted it to. "So, if you open the message, you'll be able to see who it is from and the mystery will be over."

"The mystery?"

Darren felt a presence behind him and wasn't impressed to find that it was Ryan.

"You seem to be struggling there big man," said Ryan, "need a hand from Phonetix' number one star holder?"

Darren pressed the mute button, so the customer couldn't hear him. "It's okay, Ryan, I've got this."

"You sure? I'm always happy to help."

Darren un-muted the phone. "The mystery of who is sending you text messages. Everything will become clear if you open it up."

Ryan laughed. "And this joker doesn't think he needs my help." He leaned in to look at the screen.

The call went dead.

Ryan removed his hand from the console.

"Sorry Darren, looks like I've accidentally released your call."

Releasing a call was the worst crime you could commit in a call centre. Every released call showed on the stats and needed to be reviewed and explained. This one didn't look good. A call was getting increasingly difficult and as far as the stats would show, Darren had released it. Ryan had now returned to his desk, laughing as he went.

Darren looked around his team for support. "Did you see what he did there?"

But nobody had, not even Emma. Whilst most of them had been on calls at the time, they also knew better than to get involved in a dispute that wasn't theirs, especially with Ryan.

He was on his own.

The calls came thick and fast and he stressed through every one until break time came. Instead of going to the canteen he went to see Charlie to explain.

"Do you think he did it deliberately?" Part of her wanted to tackle Ryan's behaviour but she also knew it was hard to prove and not worth the effort.

Darren was thinking the same. "It could have been an accident."

"Could have been?"

"I'm not sure." He was one hundred percent sure that it wasn't an accident, but he'd begun working on becoming more popular, it would be a bad time to make an enemy of the most influential man on the floor.

"Okay, Darren. I'll let the call monitoring team know what happened, so they don't flag it up. Don't worry about it but be careful about who you let in and around your desk in future."

"Thanks, Charlie."

Relieved that he wasn't in trouble but with no time for a proper break, Darren went to the vending machine for a cuppa. As he passed Ryan's team, Ryan blew him a kiss.

"I hate that man," thought Darren.

The rest of the day improved to the point where not only had Darren recovered the time for the text message call, but he recorded his best daily stats yet.

****

"You're pathetic, Ryan," said Caitlin, "we've been together nearly two years and you're still working in call centres. You're not even a Team Leader."

"I've been at Phonetix less than a year. They don't promote you until you've been there for twelve months."

"You're always saying how much they love you, how you're the best at your job, why don't you demand that they change the rules and promote you now?"

"That's not how it works."

"Like I said, pathetic." Caitlin wandered into the sitting room and picked up the remote.

Ryan finished making up his protein shake and tried to calm himself. He didn't like being shouted at but he couldn't argue back, Caitlin had left him in no doubt that if he ever questioned her again she would leave him. Or to be more precise, she would kick him out onto the street.

He wouldn't have anywhere to go, and he didn't have the deposit for a flat himself. They were saving for a deposit for a new build, but all the money was in Caitlin's account. They didn't have a joint account yet, Caitlin didn't trust him to have access to her money.

In theory he had loads of friends, over one thousand on Facebook and there were at least twenty lads who went out every weekend. But he knew where he stood if he needed a real favour. If he needed a couch to sleep on, or a new flatmate. They would all disappear.

The lads who were in relationships would take Caitlin's side, it wasn't worth the hassle to do otherwise. The single lads wouldn't want him moping about pining for Caitlin. It had happened once before; their breakup being played out over social media and his so-called friends soon got sick of him.

Ryan followed Caitlin into the sitting room and started massaging her shoulders. "I'm sorry, love, you're right, I'll have a word and see what they say. I'm in the lead for the Employee Star Award and there's a five-grand prize. That can go towards our deposit."

"You'd better make sure you win it then as I'm not hanging around with anyone who can't even beat the pathetic call centre freaks you work with."

"I will, don't worry. I've got it all worked out. I'm off to the gym, see you in an hour."

"Straight there and straight back and no talking to any of those sluts who hang around the gym pretending to work out."

"See you soon." He kissed her on the top of the head as she flicked through the channels on the TV.

"Don't forget to switch your app on this time. I want to see that you're putting the effort in. There's no point in us getting married if you're going to look fat on the wedding photos."

"Switching it on now, love. See you soon."

"Pathetic."

Darren bounded into work as if he was on springs, eager to find out how his stats compared to the rest of the team. For the first time, he was top of the list. He did a small fist pump as Charlie read out the stats.

"Well done, Darren," said Charlie, "but remember, we're a team. We're not in competition with each other."

She was right but that didn't stop him from feeling proud of his achievement. His smugness soared when an email came from the customer admin team. A follow-up call to a customer he had dealt with had resulted in them singing his praises. It was from one of the rare good days he had before passing his probation and before the Star Awards started but they still saw fit to award him a gold star.

He'd now received three. Maybe he had a chance.

Darren spent the next few days looking for opportunities to add to his star haul. If anybody was struggling on a call and he thought he could assist, he would hold his own call and try and help. He did the coffee run each day, extending it to the Team Leaders of the neighbouring teams. He volunteered for the social team despite having no experience of organising events or even having been to one. When they asked for volunteers to give up their Saturday morning to collect for the food bank, he was first with his hand up. He tried to get involved in everything, even discussions about football; something that he knew nothing about. He'd read the message board to try and pick up the basics and he'd heard enough football conversations to assume he could carry it off.

"Looking forward to the match on Saturday?" he said to the group of lads stood at the coffee machine.

Most ignored him but one replied. "You going?"

"Yeah, can't wait."

"To Croatia? That's a canny trip."

"Croatia?" Darren was suddenly less confident.

"For the England match."

"No, I meant Sunderland. The Lads."

"Sunderland aren't playing, it's an international weekend."

"Yeah, I knew that. I meant next weekend."

"Southampton away? I'm not travelling all the way down there to watch us get thumped again."

"Yeah, me as well. Sick of it, rubbish, aren't they?" He was getting out of his depth despite not even being up to his ankles football wise.

"Do you go to the matches?"

"Yeah, every week." He wasn't sure why he was lying; old habits maybe.

"Where's your season ticket for?"

It seemed like a strange question. "Sunderland?"

"Obviously, but whereabouts in the Stadium?"

Darren was struggling now. "The seats."

"The seats? Wow, that's posh. Which stand?"

"The big one," said Darren, floundering, "on the right."

The lad turned his back on him and re-joined the group. "Dickhead."

Darren wasn't one hundred percent sure where he had gone wrong in the conversation, but he was sure that he would never try and discuss football again. Dejected, he returned to his desk as the group walked away laughing and pointing at him. As hard as he tried, Darren just wasn't popular. Emma was nice, probably because she felt sorry for him, but he was largely ignored by the rest of the team. It was time for a new approach. He wouldn't become popular by joining conversations where he didn't have a clue what was being discussed. He needed to know his subjects, know who he was talking to.

There was only one way he was going to do this, he needed to go back to his old ways. He had to build a new database.

****

Darren fired up his PC and went to work. This was something that he excelled at. He'd spent years building a database on members of the message board and knew a ridiculous amount of detail about everyone on there. He'd been warned not to try recreating it but this time it would be a force for good.

Despite previously vowing never to join it, Darren decided that it was time that he had a Facebook account. Once he'd created his account it asked if he would like any help locating his friends? He didn't need any help, he didn't have any. He didn't have anybody in his contacts that he wanted to connect with and old school friends were the last people he wanted to speak to. He started with the one person he hoped would accept his friend request, Emma.

There weren't that many Emma Bennets on Facebook and certainly not in the Sunderland area, so she was easy to find despite her profile picture being of her cats. He sent the request and waited. People discussed social media as if they were on 24/7 so he'd hoped for an immediate response, but none was forthcoming.

He searched for the rest of the team and once he found one, the rest were easy to locate because they were all friends. He seemed to be the only one on the team who wasn't. Emma was friends with them all which surprised him as she didn't appear to socialise much. He tried to look at a couple of profiles, but their privacy settings were set so only friends could view anything more than their profile picture and their friend list.

He Googled each of their names in the hope of finding something useful. There wasn't much apart from a few sporting achievements, a charity day at work and bizarre tale in the Echo about a missing parrot. He made a note of that.

He knew that the trick to finding out about people wasn't necessarily what they showed on accounts like Facebook, as helpful as it was but what they posted with anonymous usernames on forums and message boards. He tested his theory and went to the message board, typing 'lost parrot' into the search field. A couple of threads appeared the most recent entitled **My mate has lost his parrot.**

A quick check of the date showed that it matched the story in the Echo about his colleague. The poster who posted the thread wasn't a regular that Darren could remember but he was sure that he'd be on the old spreadsheet. He added his name to the new one and then searched his posts to see if there was anything of use.

He hit upon one thread discussing a Stag Party in Stuttgart. Whilst it didn't state explicitly that Darren's colleague was on the trip, there was a good chance. There were twenty lads going to a beer festival, this was something Darren needed to read up on. He had a look at various other popular message boards to see what he could find. There wasn't much but what he had was a start.

His PC pinged with an email. He didn't receive many.

Emma Bennet has accepted your friend request.

He went back onto Facebook to view her profile. There wasn't a great deal to show. More photos of her feline friends and various YouTube videos of cats. A few photos of Emma with her cats and a handful with friends on a night out. She had 63 Facebook friends, he didn't know if that was a lot but with ten of them being people on her immediate team, he guessed not. Facebook showed a notification waiting for him and he clicked on it.

Emma Bennet has accepted your friend request. Would you like to send her a message?

He was unsure of the protocol. Should he send one? What would she think? Was it normal?

His PC pinged again, and it showed a message waiting. From Emma.

Hi Darren, never had you down as a Facebook user. Hope you are having a good night. Honoured to be your first friend. Emma.

She ended it with a winking emoji.

He sat for a while with a grin on his face. She wasn't just his first friend on Facebook, she was his first ever adult friend. He thought it best not to share that piece of information.

Hi Emma, thought it was about time I joined the twenty-first century and signed up. Darren.

He was about to press send but read her message again and decided to add a line.

Hope you are having a good night as well.

It felt a little unnatural talking to a woman online. Nearly as unnatural as he found it in real life, but Emma was okay, she made it feel easy. He hoped she kept the conversation going and now that she was on board, it wouldn't be so bad adding the rest of the team. He went through each one, in order of preference and sent the requests. He wasn't expecting much of a response but was pleasantly surprised to hear his PC ping a couple of times with people accepting his requests. A quick look at their account showed that they had hundreds of friends so probably accepted anyone. He didn't care, this gave him the insight he needed on the likes and loves of his colleagues.

It was going to be a long night of researching.

Before Darren knew it, it was two in the morning and he needed sleep. He hadn't received any more messages from Emma, but he had received a couple more acceptances to his requests. More importantly he'd found out a lot more about his colleagues. Facebook was a mine of information and his spreadsheet was filling up.

He should have thought of it sooner but one of the most popular threads on the message board was about the Phonetix siege. The thread that was the beginning of his online downfall. He cringed as he read it again, embarrassed at how obvious his lies were. Putting the pieces together on the thread he discovered that at least one of his teammates posted on the board and from his posts, he found out a lot about the others.

CHAPTER ELEVEN

"It'll be great," said Ryan, "we've got live music, a disco, a magician, loads of great prizes for the raffle. It'll be a cracking night."

He had a decent audience as he laid out his plans for the charity evening he was organising. Darren listened in from the back. As much as he hated Ryan, he couldn't deny that the lad knew how to have a good night out. Everyone was enthused, and it was obvious that they would raise a lot of cash for the company's chosen charity. And more importantly for Ryan, it was bound to earn him a couple more precious stars.

"I need some volunteers to help out with the organisation and getting stuff set up on the night. Anybody here?"

A few hands went up and despite himself, Darren put his own arm in the air. Ryan spoke to each volunteer individually thanking them and saying he'd be in touch with more information. When he saw Darren's hand up he sneered and ignored him.

The meeting dissolved, and Darren returned to his desk, once again dejected. He didn't seek acceptance from Ryan but saw the charity night as a way in to being part of the social scene in the office that he was excluded from.

Over the next few days posters were created, raffle prizes collected, and excitement was building. Tickets for the night went on sale and had to be purchased directly from Ryan. Darren didn't have any proof, but he was convinced that a fair chunk of the takings would be filtered off to fund Ryan's beer for the night.

Darren approached Ryan. "Can I have a ticket for the charity night please?"

"Sorry mate, I haven't got any on me, you'll need to come back later."

Darren could see an envelope full of them next to his keyboard. "What about them?"

"Pre-orders, pal. They're all spoken for."

For the next two hours Darren watched as various people went to Ryan's desk and purchased tickets with no problem. None of them seemed to be pre-ordered. He tried again the next day to be told they were sold out. Hours before an email went around from Ryan saying tickets were still available. He was taking the hint. He wasn't welcome.

"Why do you want to go so much?" said Emma.

"I just want to fit in like everybody else."

"Fitting in isn't all it's cracked up to be. Do you really want to be like Ryan's disciples?"

The problem was that Darren did want to be like them. He wanted to be popular, he wanted to be laughing and joking every day, he wanted to be part of something.

That night he scrolled through Facebook and saw the few teammates he had as friends on there discussing the charity night. They must have forgotten that he could see this. Or forgotten that he existed.

The next morning, he was surprised to find a ticket for the charity evening on his desk.

"You owe me a fiver," said Emma, "although I still don't see why you want to go."

"Thank you." He fumbled in his pocket and produced a crumpled five-pound note. "I owe you one."

"Well, I hope you have a good night. I'll be sat at home watching the soaps with the cats."

Spencer's alibi for the car theft was standing up for now but the atmosphere was poisonous at work. George was in danger of losing his job for taking the F-Type on an unauthorised trip and he was in more danger of losing his wife due to his unauthorised hotel stay with a young barmaid. He blamed Spencer but had no proof. He had to let Callum go due to poor sales despite knowing that Spencer had stitched him up, but he couldn't challenge him as it would look like he was creating a diversion from his own problems.

He passed the time browsing the forum looking for people to annoy and it didn't take long before he settled on his old foe. He clicked on Darren's **I LOVE MY NANA** profile to see what he had been up to.

Last seen viewing thread 'Armed siege at Phonetix' at 2:12am.

"Going back to the scene of the crime Dazza? " he thought.

Everybody had realised that **I LOVE MY NANA** was a reincarnation of Darren's old **DAZZLED** account. He was wondering what he would pick on today then it became obvious. He scrolled through recent threads posted by Darren and they were all about his new job. His new job in a call centre. His new job at Phonetix.

"Why hasn't anyone noticed this before?"

He had Darren by the balls now and he was going to squeeze them until the pips squeaked.

The armed siege thread had been locked long ago as it had got out of hand but there was nothing stopping Spencer from posting another one. He had to be careful that the moderators didn't pull the thread, so he worded it carefully.

Phonetix Mobile - Anybody work there? I have a query.

And he waited. He knew that Darren wouldn't reply but he'd let the thread gather some momentum before going in for the kill.

Darren saw the thread title and was surprised at the coincidence. Just as he was researching who worked at Phonetix, somebody asked that very question, it could save him a lot of time. Then he noticed the poster. **DB10.** His stomach plummeted like a dropped pint glass. This was no coincidence.

He waited for the responses, frantically pressing F5 on his keyboard for the screen to refresh. This wouldn't end well for him. A few replies came in, a couple of people worked there, more suggested people who may do. He didn't know who any of these people were but added them to the list for further research. His appetite for researching his colleagues had waned since **DB10's** post. He was quite happy to poke about and look into other people's lives, he was far less comfortable with other people doing it to him.

He waited for the inevitable punchline and Spencer delivered it.

DB10: How about you I LOVE MY NANA? Don't you work there now?

Darren wouldn't respond, and Spencer knew this, but he didn't need to. It only needed one other person to make the connection that Spencer had.

It took twenty minutes, but it eventually came.

CRAYON EATER: Isn't he the absolute bell whlff who got destroyed on the siege thread? Is he claiming to work there?

DB10: That's him but I think he does actually work there now. From pretending to be their biggest customer to begging them for a job. How the mighty have fallen. Pathetic.

It then became open season with poster after poster joining in to ridicule him. What was worse was that they were right, **DB10** was right. He was pathetic.

———

Spencer leaned back in his chair. *"I've got you where I want you Dazza, but I think I'll leave you dangling for a little bit longer until I decide what to do with you."*

****

Darren didn't sleep much. He'd shown his hand and given too much information away on the forum and he was going to get punished. He didn't know what **DB10** had in store for him and he wasn't keen to find out. He arrived in the office a little dishevelled and Charlie asked to speak to him before he sat down.

"Are you okay? You look a little tired."

"Yes, thanks, didn't sleep much. Next door's dog was barking all night." He tucked in his shirt and fastened a button that was exposing his belly.

"I wanted to have a word with you, Darren. I know that you are very keen on winning the Star Employee Award and you are doing well in that respect."

"Thank you."

"But, the award is dependent on your stats being up to scratch and yours have dipped severely since you started chasing the prize."

"I'm sorry. It's hard to balance helping people and keeping my stats up."

"I know you want to win but the customers are your bread and butter. You need to focus on your calls."

"I can do both."

"Darren, I haven't seen a dip this scary since the last time I was at Alton Towers."

"But I promised my Nana."

Charlie was a little confused by that admission but carried on. "Darren, I put my neck on the line by passing your probation. I need you to do this for me. I am getting a lot of grief from above about call stats."

"I thought I was doing the right thing."

"From now on, your stats are your number one priority."

"Okay, if you say so."

"Thank you, Darren. Let's have a good day today," she nodded downwards, "and you possibly want to fasten your flies."

Darren returned to his desk dejected and fiddling with his zip. Even a smile from Emma couldn't cheer him up.

There was cheering from the next bank of desks and everybody was high-fiving Ryan. Darren knew what this meant. He had a quick look at the league tables for the Star Awards and Ryan had received another. It was from one of his mates and Darren knew that he wouldn't have deserved it, but he couldn't prove anything. It wasn't his problem anymore anyway. He wasn't in the running.

It was break time, but he took another call, so he could go down late. He didn't want to spend any time with Emma or the rest of the team. Didn't want to let on what he was beginning to realise, that he wasn't up to the job. Darren sat alone in the canteen with his coffee as the doors crashed open and he realised what a mistake he had made. He may have avoided having his break with his team, but it now coincided with Ryan's team.

"Alright, Glitter," said Ryan, "how are you doing in the Star Awards?"

"I haven't looked recently."

"Of course you haven't. Just so you know, I'm well ahead. Almost unassailable, I'd probably give up if I was you."

"It's all yours, Ryan, I wasn't even going for it."

"Yeah, whatever. If you come for the King, you're going to have to kill him." With that, Ryan swaggered off with his little gang following him.

As he approached his desk Darren eyed his team, he wasn't part of it. The camaraderie, the in jokes, the nights out, he wasn't part of any of it. At best, he was a reluctant last pick, harking back to his school days when he was forced to make up the numbers on the football field. He would never belong, and he didn't know why he ever thought he would.

He only had one mission now, to keep on the right side of Charlie. He would never be the best, he needed to concentrate on not being the worst. He needed to keep himself in a job. The strategy from now on was to keep his head down and his stats up. It was the only way he was going to survive.

When he got home he thought about messaging Emma but what was the point? She probably thought he was as pathetic as the rest of them did. He had a scroll through her Facebook account. It was her birthday in a couple of days. Maybe he should get her a card. Even if she was pretending to like him, she had at least made an effort.

The microwave pinged, and Darren removed the lasagne. It was piping hot on the outside, burning his tongue, but the middle was still frozen. He couldn't even cook a basic microwave ready meal. He put it back in for another two minutes. He logged onto the forum and the thread taking the piss out of him was still going strong. He didn't bother clicking into it to find out what was being said. He had a fairly good idea.

"Why is my life so shit?"

He no longer wanted his lasagne and tossed it in the bin. He made himself a cuppa and took a pack of Hob Nobs into his bedroom where he stared at the monitor hoping for inspiration.

****

Rebecca looked at the bank account again. It didn't look good. She didn't want the argument with Spencer, she didn't want him to have the opportunity to concoct another story to get him out of the mess. Last time he claimed he'd accidentally changed her password to the account. Anybody who has ever attempted to use online banking and its laborious security procedure knew that there was nothing accidental about it.

There would be no excuses this time, she was leaving.

It was going to be tricky. In an ideal world, Spencer would do the decent thing and move out, but Spencer wasn't a decent man. She had to do this the hard way. She'd found a house to rent, a lot smaller than she was used to and not in an area she was keen on, but it would do for now.

The deposit was an issue with Spencer not paying his wages into the joint account, but she knew work would help her out. As HR manager, it was a bit embarrassing asking, but it was five minutes of embarrassment or a lifetime of putting up with Spencer's crap.

She needed to wait for the right moment to tell Spencer. There was something going on at his work that he wasn't telling her the whole truth about. His boss, George was in trouble due to a car being stolen but that was all he'd said. She hoped Spencer wasn't involved but if she was honest, she didn't care.

She needed to speak to Thomas as well. She didn't want him misreading the situation, didn't want him to think that he was the reason she was leaving. It was an easy conclusion for him to come to, but he was another symptom of Rebecca's unhappy marriage, not the cause. What they had together was fun, they were friends, very close friends, but Thomas wasn't ready for the reality of life with two kids even if he thought he was.

Worst of all, she had to tell the kids. There's no easy way to tell your kids that their Dad is a lying shithead without them turning against him. As much as she hated Spencer, she didn't want the kids to. Hopefully he would eventually see sense and move out, letting them have their house back. Making him an enemy for the sake of it wasn't worth the hassle.

All this grief because her husband couldn't bring himself to tell the truth about anything.

Spencer watched the police in George's office. The F-Type had disappeared without trace as he knew it would; probably on its way to the Middle East in a shipping container by now. He was dealing with professionals, very dangerous professionals. He was getting paid well, or he would do when it was safe to collect his payment. As much as he needed the money, it was safer to wait for the drama to die down before he had a sudden influx of cash.

There's no way they could link the theft to George either, as he had nothing to do with it. He'd been stupid, but the police could tell that he was fundamentally honest. Despite his years as a car salesman, he wasn't good at lying and he owned up to the affair as soon as he was challenged.

Taking the car without good reason was reckless but it was something they all did from time to time. Maybe not an F-Type but George was the boss, the higher the role, the bigger the perks. The rest of the staff were so keen to distance themselves from the crime that they owned up to all sorts of other minor misdemeanours from dishonest overtime claims to stealing somebody's yoghurt from the fridge. Issues that George would deal with any other time, but he was hardly in a position to pull people up on their dishonesty right now.

The police left without acknowledging Spencer, he didn't know if that was a good sign or not. He popped his head around the door of George's office.

"Okay, boss? Everything alright with the police there? Any luck in finding the car?" His matey tone did nothing to disguise the fact that he was fishing for information and George wasn't giving anything away.

"Yes, thanks. You had any luck on the sales front, our numbers are right down, and we need to buck our ideas up. Seem to have got worse since Callum left. Any idea on why that is?"

****

Ryan removed his sports bag from the boot of his car and checked his reflection one last time before sauntering the short distance to the gym entrance.

He'd parked on the pavement again despite numerous warnings from the gym staff. There were ample car parking spaces however he didn't see why he should waste energy walking across the whole car park when there was space on the pavement. Any energy expended would be done on the weights, in front of the mirrors where people could see him. What was the point otherwise?

Had he bothered to park properly, he may have spotted the familiar black Range Rover parked in a regular space. He may have had time to turn around and head home again before it was too late. Before the muscled tattooed arm clamped around his shoulder.

"Evening, Ryan. A quick word, mate?" Two men led Ryan past the entrance, towards the bushes and crucially, out of sight of the CCTV cameras.

"I was just about to call you," said Ryan.

"I guess we've saved you the bother. So, you've got our money then?"

"Yes, well not exactly but I will."

"We discussed this."

"I know, I know but I've got a plan."

"We're not interested in plans, we're interested in the money you owe us." He grabbed Ryan by the arm. "You're turning into quite the strapping young gentleman, aren't you?"

"I guess so." Ryan was previously proud of his gym work but stood next to these two hulks, he wasn't sure if they were being sarcastic.

"So, our steroids work then?"

"Yes, I guess they do."

"But you guess they aren't worth paying for?"

"I never said that."

"You didn't have to." He compared his forearm to Ryan's. "You've still got some way to go. You'll be needing some more injections."

"I was thinking of trying to do it naturally."

"Not only do you insult us by not paying what you owe, now you say our roids aren't any good."

"I didn't say that."

"You didn't have to." The second man handed Ryan the metal box he was carrying and flexed his pectoral muscles one at a time. "Can you do that?"

Ryan was thrown off guard by the bizarre question and the weight of the box. "No, I don't think I can."

"Thought not."

"Look, I've got a plan to get your money." He tried to hand the box back, but it wasn't taken.

"You had a plan when you took our gear and said you could shift it in the call centre. I'm guessing the demand for steroids for lifting cups of tea isn't as high as you thought."

"It is, it's just getting people used to the idea, and getting people to pay up. It's nearly pay day." The box was getting heavy and he went to put it on the ground but the glare he was met with suggested that it was bad idea.

"Pay day is your plan?"

"No, that's just to get the money off the lads who owe me. I have another plan." He wondered what the hell could be in the box that was making it so heavy.

"We have plans as well and none of them involve us waiting until you deem it worthy to pay what you owe us."

"End of the month, honest. It's the Star Employee Award, I'm going to win. It's a five-grand prize." His arms were burning now. He tried to lower them, but the glare prevented him again.

"Five grand at the end of the month? That should do it I suppose."

"Five, but I only owe you three."

"Bless, he thinks that's how it works." They both laughed. "We'll be back at the end of the month for our five grand and the box."

"The box?"

"Don't look inside it or you'll end up in there as well."

They disappeared and only when Ryan was confident that they had gone did he dare put the box down. His arms were shaking, and his fingers had turned white.

He was relieved to have parked so close to the entrance as he dragged the box to his car.

"Morning," Rebecca sat herself down opposite Chris Hopwood, Stratosphere's Managing Director, "you wanted to see me?"

"Yes, keep this between us for now but we're very close to signing a major new contract."

"That's fantastic news, will it mean more recruitment?"

"I'm afraid so, the HR team are going to be very busy over the next few months."

"We don't mind, we've got the structure in place to deal with any expansion. We're ready for it," said Rebecca.

"I didn't expect anything less. Sorry to do this when I'm already ramping up the pressure on your team but there's something a bit more sensitive I need you to look into."

"Go on." Being HR manager, Rebecca had dealt with everything from someone needing compassionate leave due to their hamster dying to one of the development team transitioning from a woman to a man. Not much phased her.

"Shouldn't be a major issue but the new company we're bringing on board are a major financial institution. They are bound by financial regulations and after a number of recent scandals, they've tightened up their procedures somewhat."

"How does that impact us?"

"Like I say, it's hopefully not a big deal but they've asked if we can credit check all of our employees."

"Credit check them?"

"Just to see that they're not financially compromised. Could be a conflict of interest if somebody was working on financial software and was in a lot of debt."

"I'm not sure that's any of our business."

"Maybe, maybe not but it's one of the conditions to them signing the contract."

"Who are we checking?"

"Everyone," said Chris, "you know how much we move people around between projects and clients. We can't have this as a barrier to getting the right people on the job."

"So just the development and testing teams who could work on the contract?"

"No, in the interests of fairness, I think it has to be everyone. Me, you, even the receptionist, we all have to be squeaky clean financially."

Rebecca thought about her own financial predicament. The missing money from the joint account, the bounced cheque to the childminder, the secrets that Spencer was clearly keeping from her. "And what if the credit check shows that one of our employees is in financial difficulty?"

"That's what I need you to look into, Rebecca. We can't have somebody's financial situation being the difference between us getting this contract and not getting it. If they don't sign, we could all be failing credit checks soon."

"I thought the company was doing well."

"We are if this contract gets signed, it could be another story if it doesn't."

"We would consider sacking someone who has money problems? That can't be right."

"That's what I need you to look into Rebecca. Where do we stand legally if we have to get rid?"

"Legally, what about morally?"

"Needs must, Rebecca, needs must."

****

Darren didn't know what to wear for a charity evening and there were no instructions on the ticket. He'd lost all enthusiasm for it since his chat with Charlie but as Emma had gone to the trouble of buying it, he felt obliged. He hadn't ventured onto the message board much since he was outed by Spencer but decided to ask for their help.

What should I wear to a charity do?

ROKER REJECT: Fancy dress is the only way forward. Go as Pudsey the Bear.

SIR STANLEY CUMMINS: Why not turn up in a bath full of beans?

The answers continued in the usual jocular style until a couple of sensible answers appeared.

ANDY REID'S FRUIT BOWL: Every charity do I've been to has been black-tie.

BLUNDERBALL: If it's black-tie, it could be costly. Matalan usually has offers on, you can pick the full outfit up for about £50. Not the best quality but it's not like you will be wearing it every day.

Darren had a look on the Matalan website and he was right. He didn't want to spend £50 on an outfit but he wanted to look his best.

The night of the party came around and Darren got himself dressed. He didn't have a full-length mirror at home, so he had to check his reflection at the bus stop. He thought he looked a little like James Bond. He couldn't help assuming the pose with pretend gun, much to the amusement of the passengers as the bus pulled up.

"Who let that dickhead in?"

Ryan said it within earshot of Darren, but he pretended not to hear. Looking around the social club it quickly became apparent that it wasn't a black-tie event; he was the only one in a dinner suit. Whilst he felt self-conscious, he knew that he looked smarter than everyone in their shirts and jeans, so he tried to portray an air of confidence.

He approached the bar where his teammates stood.

"Oh, hi Darren. We didn't know you were coming."

They didn't know because they didn't invite him, but he let that go. "Yeah, last minute decision."

"And you had that penguin suit lying around? You must attend a lot of these events."

"One or two, you know how it is."

The conversation was already over as his colleagues returned to chatting and sniggering amongst themselves. He'd come prepared with a card including information that he'd picked up from the internet about his teammates. He intended to sneak to the toilet to read it then use it to strike up conversation, but it wasn't much use to him if they wouldn't speak to him in the first place.

"Lemonade, please," said Darren.

"Pint or a half?"

"Pint, please."

"Ice and lemon?"

"Does it cost extra?"

The barman laughed. "No, I'll throw them in for free seeing as you've made an effort."

This was the first time Darren had ordered any sort of drink at a bar, he wasn't expecting so many questions. "Thank you."

"Shaken not stirred," said the barman as he placed the drink down, "that'll be two pounds please."

Darren paid him not having a clue what he was referring to. He intended to make this drink last. Excluded from the crowd of his teammates and with nobody else he knew well enough to talk to, Darren took up position at the end of the bar; alone.

He watched as others, especially Ryan, breezed through the crowds, chatting and joking without any problems. As if it was the easiest thing in the world. Darren would never be that confident no matter what his online persona used to be. He was going to give it half an hour then drift off, this had all been a terrible mistake.

And then he spotted a kindred spirit. Somebody else who had misunderstood the dress code and had arrived in a dinner suit. He too was trying to integrate himself with various groups but was being rebuffed despite what seemed like a very confident introduction. Darren didn't recognise him from the call centre, maybe he was new. It wasn't long before he made his way across to Darren and shook his hand.

"The name's Carl. Nice to see that it's not just me who has dressed up."

"I'm Darren. I wasn't sure what to wear, I don't get out as much as I'd like."

"Nice to meet you, Darren. Do you have the right time on you?"

"Yeah, it's..." Darren looked to his left wrist where his watch should be, but it was missing. He'd had the Casio Digital watch for over ten years, the strap must have broken. He panicked. He didn't know why, it was only worth a tenner, but it was always there, one of the few things in life he could rely upon. "Sorry, my watch, I had it on earlier."

"Not to worry. That's a nice earring you are wearing."

"Earring, I don't wear earrings."

A small crowd had gathered and laughed as Carl produced Darren's watch from behind his ear.

"Sorry about that, can't help myself sometimes." He produced a pack of cards. "Pick a card, Darren, any card."

"I don't like magic." Darren didn't know whether he liked magic or not but the idea of being tricked in front of a big group of people didn't appeal. He put his watch back on.

"We all like magic, Darren. Go on, pick a card and don't show it to me, show it to the crowd."

The crowd had grown bigger with Ryan right at the front. Darren reluctantly picked one, the eight of hearts, and showed it to everyone. "What next?"

"Put it back in the pack. Anywhere you like."

Darren did as he was told then Carl got one of the girls in the crowd to shuffle the pack.

"Now," said Carl, "you've got a card in your pocket haven't you Darren?"

"How does he know about my info card?"

"Do you want to take it out and show it to the audience?" said Carl.

Darren realised that he was talking about the playing card he had chosen earlier. He fumbled in his pocket and pulled out the eight of hearts much to everybody's amazement. As he did so, his info card fluttered to the ground.

The crowd was too engrossed in the magic to notice and Darren didn't want to draw attention to it by picking it up.

"Thanks for being such a good sport Darren," said Carl, "any chance you could tell me the time now?"

Darren looked to his watch, but it was gone.

"You've taken my watch again."

"You've lost your watch Darren? I wonder where your hands have been?"

Carl then produced the watch from the cleavage of one of the young girls in the crowd.

"Eee, you dirty bugger." She was giggling and didn't seem to mind the intrusion.

"Should always take good care of your wrist, Darren? Bet you'll be putting it to good use later."

The audience howled in laughter at his discomfort. He needed to pick up his info card and head home.

But the card was no longer on the floor.

"Don't rush off anywhere just yet ladies and gentlemen," said Ryan, "it appears that the entertainment is just beginning."

Darren made a grab for the card, but Ryan swiped it away. Darren didn't wait for the humiliation and stormed out.

CHAPTER TWELVE

Darren considered not going to work on Monday morning and phoning in sick. He'd been humiliated by the magician and he could only imagine what Ryan had said after he had gone. Of the handful of workmates who were friends with him on Facebook, two had already deleted him so it was clear that they weren't happy, but he had to face them sooner or later.

He took his Nana's letter from the drawer and read it again despite being able to quote it word for word. He was letting her down, there was no way he was going to be the best at anything apart from being a failure. He placed it in his jacket pocket. Maybe if she was with him each day it would bring him strength, or luck, or anything at all that made his life more bearable.

He got a coffee and logged straight into the phones without speaking to anyone. An information card had been left on his keyboard.

Darren Updike

Likes: Babestation, wanking dogs for bingo money, stalking colleagues, hanging about outside of schools, Fred West and Josef Fritzl.

Dislikes: Fashion, spending money on haircuts, basic hygiene and other people's privacy.

He could see Ryan laughing as he read it. He tore it up and threw it in the bin. If he'd held onto it and took it to HR he could have got Ryan into a lot of trouble, but he knew it would backfire. He had to pretend that it didn't bother him.

Easier said than done.

Starting the day in a bad mood was never going to be good for call handling and so it proved as he managed to argue with the first two callers about quite trivial matters. It was unlikely to get any better as the day went on. Before another call came through he noticed that someone from a different team was trying to ring him.

"Hello, this is Darren. How can I help?"

"Hi, Darren, it's Sarah from Team 204. Sorry to do this to you but I've got a customer who is insisting on speaking to you. He's convinced that he's spoken to you previously but there's no notes on the account. I would deal with him myself but he's refusing to speak to anyone but you."

"Okay, have you got his account number?"

Sarah gave it to him and he looked at the account. He recognised the name Spencer Proctor but wasn't sure where from and as she said, there were no notes on the account from him. He was however, a prolific complainer.

"Thanks, Sarah, I don't have any idea who he is but put him through. I'll see what he wants."

"Thanks, Darren, and be careful, the bloke's very difficult." She put the call through.

"Hello, Mr Proctor, you are speaking to Darren, how may I help?"

"Hello, Darren, it's been a while."

The Mackem accent caught Darren off guard, a quick look at his address showed he also lived in Sunderland. A quick look at the password field confirmed what Darren feared. He'd never spoken to this man before, or at least he'd never heard his voice. He'd spoken to him plenty online. His password was **DB10.**

"What can I do for you, Mr Proctor?" Darren wasn't sure if transferred calls were monitored but he had to be extra careful.

"It's about that credit you were going to apply the other day. It doesn't seem to be on my account yet."

"I'm sorry, I don't recall discussing any credit."

"You do, Darren, it was in relation to lack of service when I was desperately trying to contact my Gran. You were saying how much you loved your Nana. Surely you remember now?"

Darren was in no doubt that this wouldn't end well for him. **DB10** knew loads about Darren's past. His controversial views online, even if they were made up just to annoy people, weren't something that he would like shared with his employers. "Aah yes, I seem to remember now, ten pounds, wasn't it?"

"No, no, no. It was far more than that. It was a very important call, I had lots of important information I had to pass on."

"Twenty?" Twenty pounds was the limit Darren had for applying credits.

"Surely you remember, it was fifty pounds."

"But I don't have authority to give fifty-pound credits."

"That's probably why it has taken so long, you must have been getting authorisation for it. Don't worry, you can put me on hold while you sort it."

Darren was in a panic. He pressed the hold button and tried to catch his breath. This was blackmail, it was fraud. It was his worst nightmare, someone using the tactics he always used himself back in the day.

"Emma, do you have authorisation to apply a fifty-pound credit to an account?"

"Fifty pounds? What for?"

"It's a long story, can you do it?"

"I have the authorisation, but I need to know why first."

"I'll explain afterwards but I really need to get this customer off the phone. My stats are already screwed for the day."

"I'll do it just this once, but I'll need more information next time, what's the account number?"

Emma applied the credit and gave Darren the thumbs up. He returned to the call.

"The fifty-pound credit has now been applied to your account, Mr Proctor. Was there anything else I could help you with?"

"Not at the moment Darren but I'm sure I'll be in touch as soon as there is."

His hands were shaking as he came off the call. His stats were already ruined so he went for a glass of water to compose himself before his next call.

He owed Emma a big favour, she had got him out of a dodgy moment, but he didn't think it was the last he would hear from Spencer Proctor.

"What was all that about?" asked Emma as they headed for a break.

"Can I trust you?"

"Of course you can."

"No, I mean really trust you?"

"Yes, Darren."

"He's someone who knows me from my past, he's blackmailing me."

"And you included me in this?"

"I'm sorry, I panicked."

"We need to report this, Darren."

"I can't Emma, I wish I could, but I can't. This job is all I have."

****

"All the evidence is there," said Chris Hopwood.

"You've got to be joking," said Rebecca.

"No, Thomas has been fiddling his expenses for months. He was clever but it's obvious once you realise what he's been up to. The accounts team have the proof, I asked them to go through the expenses before you started on the credit check stuff."

"But, but Thomas isn't like that."

"I know the girls in HR all like Thomas..."

"It's more than that."

"More?"

"He's not like that, he wouldn't, there's been a mistake."

"Like I say, I know all the girls in HR like Thomas, we all do, but the evidence is irrefutable."

"I can't believe I'm hearing this."

"I know it's come as a shock, Rebecca but we don't know what's happening in people's private lives. He could have a fancy woman or anything."

"A fancy woman?"

"Anything, it doesn't matter what it is, he's been defrauding the company and we need to deal with it."

"There must be some explanation."

"I'm sure there is, and we'll find out what he says once you've set up his disciplinary meeting."

"Me?"

"You are Head of HR, Rebecca. It's part of the job no matter how unpleasant."

"But..." A million thoughts were racing through her head at this point, but she had to remain professional. "Okay, I'll sort it out."

The door to her office closed and Rebecca sat in shock. Yet again, a man she thought she knew had betrayed her trust.

If he revealed the truth about them then her job could be on the line as well. No job, no income, no prospect of being able to escape Spencer. She was lurching from one crisis to another and she was losing control.

Darren needed to thank Emma for getting him out of trouble. He'd never bought a present for anyone other than his Nana and he didn't have the first idea on what women wanted so he did what he did best; research.

Emma didn't leave much of an online footprint. Her Facebook profile was sparse, and Googling brought up very little. He did however manage to find her address. That along with a couple of photos she was tagged in on Facebook led to a bit of a plan. It wasn't very original, and it wasn't much but he hoped she appreciated the effort and remain the closest thing he had to being a friend.

Charlie was called into a Team Leader's meeting as soon as she walked through the door. There wasn't even time to grab a coffee. Her grumpiness at the lack of caffeine was amplified when she realised that she was the target of the meeting.

"Charlie, your team's stats are some of the worst in the call centre," said Michelle, "what has gone wrong?"

There were so many different answers to this question that she didn't know where to begin. She started on the defensive. "As you know, most of my team, the consistently top performing team in the call centre, were moved on. I've been left with a group of new starters and a handful of experienced staff who are trying to assist them. It was always going to have an impact."

"They aren't new anymore, they've all passed their probation. Probation periods that were signed off by you."

"They've been here a couple of months, it takes at least six months to a year for someone to be fully up to speed."

"We don't have six months, Charlie. Have you seen the call queues?"

She had seen the call queues and they were rocketing. Mainly because of shocking network coverage, a billing system that didn't work and a staff turnover rate so high that it was a wonder that anyone hung around long enough to learn how to say their own name. "I'm doing what I can."

"It isn't good enough. Look at this."

A pile of stats was thrown onto the table. She didn't need to look to know that it was Darren's name that was highlighted.

"If you want to discuss individual members of my team, can we do it in private please?"

"No, I want everybody to see this. Can you explain why we even employed this fool in the first place?"

A few sniggers went around the meeting room.

"We were under pressure to fill a quota of recruits from the Job Centre. Darren was the best of a bad bunch."

"I don't know where you were getting that pressure from, but it certainly wasn't me; the man's an idiot." Michelle folded her arms.

"That's unfair. He may be a little odd, but he was top of his class throughout training, doing far better than recruits from traditional avenues. He has struggled with the pace a little, but he is determined to do well as is shown by the number of gold stars he has received."

"Who gives a shit about gold stars?"

Charlie pointed to one of the promotional posters on the wall. "Phonetix Mobile apparently."

"The Star Awards are a sideshow to make the staff think they are valued. I would have thought that you had been around long enough to know that. If I discover that people have been wasting their time helping others in the hope of getting stars instead of taking calls then they will be out of the door," Michelle threw the stats across the table, "and so will you."

Charlie wasn't given the chance to respond as Michelle stormed out.

Officially Rebecca wasn't allowed to speak to Thomas, officially she couldn't have any contact at all. But she needed to speak to him, she had to speak to him.

She had to find out whether it was true, whether it was all a horrible mistake. She didn't believe it, she didn't want to believe it.

That's why she found herself sat outside his home in the car waiting for him to leave the house. She didn't know why she didn't knock on the door, it just felt wrong somehow.

She'd only been waiting for ten minutes when she saw the door open. Expecting to see Thomas' six-foot frame, she was shocked when a petite blonde, no more than twenty-one leaving. She gave Thomas a kiss and skipped down the drive.

The dress that she was barely wearing suggested that she wasn't a permanent resident of the household and that she'd met Thomas on a night out.

Rebecca felt sick. It appeared that she didn't know any of the men in her life.

She thought about confronting the girl but didn't know what that would achieve. She thought about confronting Thomas but came to the same conclusion.

He wasn't her property, they weren't an item and he owed her nothing. What he had or hadn't done no longer mattered. The only thing that mattered was what he was going to say in the disciplinary meeting and whether he would reveal their relationship.

It was in the lap of the gods now, she would have to wait and see how it played out. A dishonest husband, a dishonest and more than likely fraudulent boyfriend, she knew how to pick them.

Rebecca started the car and went to work. See if the world could throw anything more at her.

Despite the terrible day, Darren had yesterday he was excited to get into work and see Emma. He wanted to see her reaction.

"Morning Darren," she said, "did you pay for a pizza to be delivered to my house last night?"

"Yes, did you like it? Anchovies and olives, your favourite." He stood like an expectant puppy waiting to have its fur ruffled.

"It was a little, unexpected. Sixteen inches was a bit much as well."

She chose just the wrong moment to say that as Ryan walked past. "Darren giving you sixteen inches last night? You are a lucky girl."

"Shut your mouth, Ryan. Before someone shuts it for you."

He walked away pretending to hold a handbag, knowing it wise not to start an argument.

Darren had never seen Emma lose her temper before.

"Over here, Darren, I need a word." She pushed him towards the coffee machine, but Charlie cut them off.

"Sorry, Emma but I need to talk to Darren."

Emma walked off without speaking. As Charlie led Darren to the meeting room they passed Frank carrying a bouquet of flowers. Darren would miss Emma's response when she received them.

****

Charlie should have left some time between her meeting with Michelle and her meeting with Darren. She was angry at being humiliated in front of everyone. Angry at having to take responsibility for decisions that were outside of her control whilst the person responsible claimed they knew nothing about it. Angry at being in a job she once loved but now hated. Angry at still living at home when she could be living on the other side of the world because she couldn't face up to her parents. Angry at everything and that was going to manifest itself as anger towards Darren and he didn't deserve it.

He was frustrating at times, to the point of being annoying. Whenever he had a chance to fit in, he made the wrong decision and made himself a figure of ridicule. In his desperation to be liked he focussed on gaining those pointless gold bloody stars instead of concentrating on doing his job properly. But she knew it wasn't his fault. It was hers for taking him on in the first place. For letting her standards slip and not sticking to her principles. She shouldn't have let him through the door.

She couldn't help but think that Darren may have been happier if he'd never got the job in the first place and had found something more suited to his personality. Not that she could think what that would be, she hadn't seen such a combination of bad dress sense and lack of self-awareness since she was once dragged to a performance poetry evening. But here they were again, discussing his under-par performance. And this time it was serious. She had to take the emotion out of it, she couldn't foist her anger onto Darren, but she couldn't sugar coat it either. He had to know that this was his last chance.

She took a deep breath and placed Darren's stats in front of him.

"Darren, I know we've had similar conversations in the past, but it has become apparent that your call stats have been slipping. In fact, they slipped so far yesterday I thought you were on ice skates. Is there anything I should know about?"

Darren thought back to the call from **DB10** but couldn't bring himself to mention it. "I just had a couple of bad calls at the start of the day."

"I'm not only talking about yesterday, Darren. You've been struggling with your targets for weeks now. It can't go on."

"Sorry."

"You don't need to apologise to me, but it needs to improve. It's been noticed by people further up the food chain and they want to see an improvement."

What they wanted was blood, but she didn't want to share that with him.

"Sorry."

"Like I said, you don't need to apologise but we need to take this seriously. I'm afraid there's no other option, I need to put you onto a recovery plan."

It shouldn't have been a surprise to Darren, but the shock hit him, and he felt sick. Everybody in the call centre knew what a recovery plan meant. It was a holding pattern until you got sacked. Nobody ever recovered from a recovery plan.

"How long have I got left?"

Charlie couldn't help smiling, the first thing that made her smile that today. "I'm not a doctor, Darren. A recovery plan is exactly what it says. It is a plan to get you back on track, it's not signalling the end."

"But nobody survives a recovery plan."

"There's loads that do, you'd be surprised. They don't make it public because they don't want anybody to know they've been on one. I've got faith in you Darren, if I didn't I wouldn't have taken the risk in passing your probation."

"I was a risk?"

She realised that she shouldn't have said it but she couldn't back out now. "My job is all about managing risks. I make an assessment on whether I think the risk is worth it and I think you are."

"I want to be the best at what I do, and I do try really hard."

"I know you do but this plan will give us some focus. Focus on what is important and at this moment in time, it is your call stats. No Star Awards, no charity nights, only stats."

Darren felt dejected. He'd worked hard and tried his best, but it wasn't good enough. He wasn't cut out for the world of work. Most of his colleagues hated him and if they didn't hate him, they laughed at him. Most behind his back but loads to his face. He'd been humiliated on the night out and he had **DB10** on his case. Now he had the embarrassment of a recovery plan to deal with.

"Would it be easier if I resigned now rather than getting sacked? I don't want to cause you any more problems."

"Nobody is getting sacked. Not if we follow the plan. I've done this hundreds of times Darren and I haven't lost anyone yet."

"It won't look good on my CV if I get sacked."

"And it won't look good if you walk away when the going gets tough. You need to have some faith in yourself."

Darren returned to his desk with hundreds of thoughts racing through his head. He'd really messed up this time, even by his standards.

He'd almost forgot about the flowers. They lay on Emma's desk separating where the two of them sat. He hoped she liked them.

He looked for recognition from her, but she didn't look happy, she didn't look happy at all.

****

Darren logged into the phones and tried to block out the conversation he'd had with Charlie. And the look of disgust he'd got from Emma as he sat.

The rest of the team seemed to be laughing at him. He couldn't tell whether they knew about the recovery plan, the flowers or whether it was something else. It could be anything, they were always laughing at him.

He'd agreed to another meeting with Charlie later that day to formalise their approach, but he was tempted to stand up and walk out now. It didn't matter what Charlie said, he knew it was over. He was close to tears and he needed someone to confide in, but that person would normally be Emma and she didn't appear to be impressed with him. Everything he did was wrong.

As first break came around, he was relieved to see that Emma had waited for him. Maybe he had misread the look she had given him.

"We need to talk, Darren."

"Did you like the flowers?"

"Did I like the flowers? The flowers happened to be my favourites."

"I thought you'd like them." Darren was relieved that his research had worked.

"And how did you know they were my favourites?"

"A good guess?"

"And how did you know what my favourite pizza was?"

"You must have mentioned it."

"And how did you know my address to send the bloody pizza to?" The volume was rising. "Are you stalking me, Darren?"

"Stalking? No, it was just basic research."

"Basic research? Darren, they are the exact same flowers I was sent by my friends when my Mam died."

Darren had found a picture of the flowers on Facebook and a comment from Emma saying she loved them. He'd never bothered checking why they'd been sent.

"It was meant to be a thank you for the help you've given me."

"You thank people by reminding them of their dead mother? Are you sick in the head?"

"I didn't think, sorry."

"Didn't think? You never do, Darren. But everybody else thinks though, don't they? What do you expect the rest of the team is thinking when you send me flowers? They've had a right old laugh at my expense this morning."

"You always tell me not to worry about what other people think."

"I was being polite. You can't spend your whole life going around not caring what other people think of you. I have to work here Darren. I've tried to be nice, I've tried to help you, and this is how you repay me? Stalking and humiliating me?"

"It wasn't stalking."

"Yeah, you've said, just basic research. Maybe you should do some basic research on how to behave around people. You can't go snooping around online, sticking your nose into their business. It's creepy."

"I'm sorry."

"Sorry isn't good enough this time. I'd appreciate it if you'd stop stalking me. I've deleted you from Facebook and you need to have a long hard think about your behaviour."

She stormed out of the double doors. Every pair of eyes in the call centre seemed to be on him. He rushed into the toilets, locked himself in a cubicle and sobbed.

That afternoon Charlie and Darren reconvened their meeting and Darren was relieved to get away from the frosty atmosphere between him and Emma. Charlie had missed the confrontation but knew something was wrong.

"Is everything okay between you and Emma?"

"Yes."

"I noticed the flowers, they are lovely."

"Glad you think so."

"Ah I see, a romantic gesture not reciprocated?"

"They weren't meant to be romantic." He wasn't one hundred percent sure if this was true.

"And she didn't like them?"

"You could say that. Everything I do is a mistake."

"That's not true."

"It is true. Everyone hates me, and I deserve it. I'm pathetic."

"That's not true either." She didn't sound convincing.

"I'm going to resign, Charlie. Thanks for giving me a chance but I've let you down. I've let everybody down. I don't know why I ever thought I could do this."

This made Charlie's life a lot easier. Her team's stats would improve overnight. She didn't need to deal with one member of the team who was an outcast and she would stop getting hassle from Michelle, albeit only briefly until she found something else to moan about. Most importantly, she didn't have to do this recovery plan which she knew would take up a disproportionate amount of her time.

But she wasn't ready to give up on Darren; not yet. Whilst she could do with an easy life, she refused to be dictated to by Michelle who didn't have the faintest idea how to manage people.

She wanted to give Darren a chance. She wanted to give herself a chance.

"It's been an emotional day, Darren. I know you feel like you want to walk out now but you'll feel different in the morning. Why don't we go through the plan first? Have a think about it tonight and if you feel the same tomorrow then you can go with my best wishes. I don't want you to make any rash decisions."

Darren's mind was made up, but he felt like he owed it to Charlie to go through the motions.

"Okay, if you say so."

He signed the recovery plan without fully understanding what was in it, grabbed his coat and left Phonetix for the last time.

****

Emma was stood at the bus stop when Darren left work, she wasn't carrying the flowers, so they were either still on her desk or in the bin. He didn't want the conversation, or the awkward silence so walked home. It was a lot further than he thought and a great deal hillier than he had realised when traveling by bus.

He now understood why people spent money on good shoes and didn't buy second-hand ones from the charity shop. It took him at least an hour and a half to reach the city centre and by the time he got onto the Wearmouth Bridge it began to rain. He stopped half way across where a withered bunch of flowers were tied to the railings. He looked down to the murky depths below and considered where his life had gone wrong.

He'd ruined everything. He didn't fit in and he never would.

The rain was getting heavier and it merged with the tears flowing down his cheeks. He was now standing on his tip toes on the base of the railings, his waist level with the top rail. He leaned forward. A Metro rushed past on the railway bridge. People going about their daily lives unaware of the mess he had made of his.

"You alright, mate?" A runner in his twenties stopped and removed his earphones.

"Yeah, just thinking," said Darren.

"You sure? I'm a bit scared of heights and you're making me nervous leaning over there."

"Sorry." He apologised for what seemed like the hundredth time that day and took a step back. "Been one of those days and trying to clear my head before I go home."

"As long as you're okay. We all have bad days but there's always someone to speak to." He drew Darren's eyes to the Samaritans advert pinned to the bridge.

Darren laughed. He thought about the Samaritans phones being manned by a call centre full of people exactly like him. "Thanks for your concern but I'm fine."

"If you're sure, mate. Don't spend too long stood out in the rain, you'll catch your death." He replaced his earphones, satisfied that Darren wasn't going to jump and ran off, casting the odd glance over his shoulder to ensure Darren hadn't plummeted to the water below.

Darren went to his inside pocket and removed the letter from his Nana. He didn't want to get it wet, but he needed to read it.

"I'm sorry, Nan. I've let you down like I let everyone down. I thought I could be the best like you said but I'm just the best at being an embarrassment."

He replaced the letter and took one last look over the railings.

He was soaked through when he got home and removed his sopping clothes, replacing them with his familiar jogging bottoms and sweatshirt. Luckily the letter from his Nana had survived due to its plastic cover. He'd thought it would bring him luck, but it wasn't working out that way.

There was another letter to consider. Brown envelopes on the doormat were never welcome and this one with no writing on the front was no exception. Darren had thrown it onto the table along with the pizza menus and offers to join the local Baptist church. He made himself a cuppa before bothering to check the contents. No good ever came out of a brown envelope so he was going to enjoy his tea first.

He ripped it open and removed the single sheet of A4 paper. It contained a simple message, printed in pink ink.

£2,000 cash by the end of the month or Ingham finds out that you hacked him and tipped off the police.

"Oh fuck."

Ingham was not a man to be messed with. Even now, when he was behind bars awaiting trial for murder, blackmail, shootings and the odd bombing, the man still had reach.

The story was all over the TV and the papers. One of the biggest trials in the North East for years but reliable witnesses were hard to come by. They all got a little twitchy when asked to testify against Ingham.

There was one crucial fact here, and Darren wasn't sure that it would make the slightest difference to Ingham, but he had never hacked him and never spoken to the police.

He had no idea who his blackmailer was, how they found his address and what they knew but the only thing that Darren was guilty of here was being an internet gobshite. And on this charge, they could throw away the key.

Yes, he claimed he knew Ingham. Yes, he claimed he had inside information on him. But he wasn't telling the truth, he never told the truth. That's what being King of the Internet was all about.

And now it was going to cost him. Whether it was financially or worse, he didn't know. He certainly didn't have two grand and had no idea how he would raise that sort of money.

The rain had cleared when Darren left the house. He limped to the bus stop. Blisters being the price he paid for charity shop shoes and his foolish walk home in the rain. He'd seriously considered not returning to Phonetix, but he couldn't return to his old life of farting and filth. He only had one other option and he hoped that he'd left that behind on Wearmouth Bridge. He couldn't remember what was on the recovery plan, he didn't even read it, but he needed to pull his thumb out of his arse.

He had to do it without Emma's help, she'd made it perfectly clear that she wanted nothing more to do with him. It was just him and Charlie, although he wasn't sure why she kept on giving him chance after chance. He realised that he needed to stop wondering why and start repaying her faith.

This was his last chance and he had to make it work.

CHAPTER THIRTEEN

Charlie was a little surprised to see Darren and it would have been a lot easier for her if he never returned but she was pleased that he'd turned up. If he was willing to listen to her advice and work on improving his stats, she was confident that he would get out of his recovery plan. She even believed that he could become one of those rare Phonetix employees who was willing to sit on the phones for the rest of their career.

What she really hoped for was that Darren's Phonetix career outlived hers. She was sick of the whole thing and wanted out as soon as possible; the photo of Sydney Harbour on her desk, taunting and tempting her once again.

Charlie grabbed Darren as he went for his break. "You've decided to stay and give it a go then?"

"I guess so."

"Glad to hear it, we're going to do this together. Focus on what we have discussed, come to me with any problems and you'll be out of the recovery plan before you know it."

Darren wasn't convinced that either of them believed it but he appreciated the effort that Charlie was putting in on his behalf.

Emma was a bigger challenge. She was still using the flowers as a physical barrier between them and hadn't acknowledged his presence all morning. He wanted to apologise but feared that he would make things worse. He remembered one bit of advice that Charlie had given him, 'People are very rarely angry at you. They are angry with other stuff and take it out on you because you are an easy target. Don't allow their anger to upset you.'

Good advice apart from that in Emma's case, it was very much him that had upset her. In call centre terminology, he had to 'park' this issue for now.

He sat alone at break, the only spare table being under the Star Employee notice board with Ryan's name highlighted right at the top. Darren's had slipped towards the bottom, but he needed to forget about it. It was no longer his concern. He looked around the canteen and watched the groups of people laughing and joking. For fifteen minutes forgetting the stresses of the job and having fun with their mates. He would never have that release, he was never going to have workplace friends. He was never going to have any friends. He had to make do with having a job that paid the bills and put a roof over his head.

The rest of his team went back to work, he thought that Emma may have glanced in his direction, but he had his head down and avoided eye contact.

He gave them a minute and returned to his desk.

Charlie grabbed a coffee with Lauren.

"So, Darren's staying after your little chat with him yesterday?"

"Yeah, I was a bit surprised to see him this morning. Glad to have him back though."

"Really? Recovery plans are a lot of hard work, can you be bothered with the hassle?"

"I want to give him a chance, Lauren. He's not a bad lad, he's just a bit—"

"Socially inadequate?"

"That's it. He wants to do well, his heart's in the right place, but he doesn't know how to interact with others."

"And you're going to turn around thirty odd years of anti-social behaviour in a month?"

"I've got to try."

"Why?"

"Because it's what I do best, and I refuse to be proven wrong by that daft bitch, Michelle. She doesn't have a clue what it's like out there on the shop floor. She introduces stupid initiatives like the Star Employee awards then gets surprised when people get distracted by it."

"Wow, she really gets under your skin."

"Everybody is just a cell on a spreadsheet to her, she doesn't understand people, doesn't understand what makes them tick," said Charlie.

"There is another option."

"And what's that?"

"You know what it is. Leave here and get on a plane. You're my best mate, Charlie, and I'll be gutted when you're not here, but you need to get away. You can't spend your life saving every lost soul in this place. You've got to save yourself first," said Lauren.

"You know it's not that simple."

"It is that simple. Hand your notice in and go."

"But what about my parents?"

"They'll cope, they'll have no choice. Don't open it up for debate, tell them you've made your decision and go."

"You make it sound like it's the easiest thing in the world."

"Because it is. Look outside; grey drizzle on a business park in Sunderland or sipping a glass of cool Chardonnay on Sydney Harbour? Which one would you choose?"

"If you put it like that."

"Promise me something. Promise me that Darren will be your last one. Get him through his recovery plan, prove everybody wrong, prove that you were right about him. Let upstairs see what you can do with the roughest of diamonds and then let them see what they have lost when you walk out of the door."

"You really want rid of me, don't you?"

"I want to come and visit my best friend when she is a successful businesswoman in Oz. Surely you're not going to deprive me of that?"

Charlie laughed. "I can't deprive my best friend a holiday, can I?"

"So, we're agreed?"

"I guess so."

"No guessing about it, you're doing this? You promise?"

"I promise, you've bullied me into it."

Lauren gave her a big hug. "I'm so proud of you, Charlie. I'll miss you."

"I'll miss you too, or at least I will if I ever work out how to turn Darren around."

****

"Are we allowed to do that?"

"Of course we are," said Ryan, "I mean it will be better to keep it amongst ourselves so people don't steal our tactics."

"It sounds a bit dodgy."

"Look mate, you'll never win the Star Award but I'm in with a good shout. Give your stars to me and there'll be a pint in it for you. I'll write up the nomination form for you, all you need to do is copy and paste." With the five-grand debt hanging over his head, Ryan wasn't leaving anything to chance.

"If you say so."

"Come on, who do you want to win? Me, your old mate, or one of the freaks from over there?" He pointed in the general direction of Darren and Emma.

"Okay mate, type it up and I'll send it."

"Cheers, pal."

Ryan was on a charm offensive. As cocky and as confident as he was, he knew he wasn't the best employee in the building, not even the best one on his team. He was however, the best at playing the system and he knew how to manipulate it, so he would win.

He surveyed the rest of the call centre and everyone else trying their best to impress customers in the hope that somebody recognised it and gave them a star.

"Idiots," he thought, *"I'm going to win this without even speaking to a customer."*

Emma could hear Ryan but tried to ignore him. She'd gained a few stars herself but hers had been earned by doing her job the way it was meant to be done. Trying to help customers on every call and assisting colleagues whenever she got the chance. She wasn't motivated by Employee Awards, but it sickened her to see others manipulate the system. The whole thing had the opposite effect, demotivating her and making her want to stop trying. The same thing happened every year, there was a big promotion by the top brass then somebody undeserving won it, angering the decent people amongst the workforce who try hard every day.

She could report Ryan, but she knew that it wouldn't do any good; management didn't want to know about stuff like that. She'd also noticed Darren behaving differently. Not just to her since she pulled him up about his creepy behaviour but to everyone. He'd barely said a word to the rest of the team, not that any of them noticed.

She'd seen him go into daily meetings with Charlie and she had a fair idea what that meant. The whole team got to see the stats and his weren't great. His confidence was shot, and it could only mean one thing. She would normally step up to help people who were struggling but she'd tried to help Darren already and he had misunderstood. He'd upset her with the flowers and the online intrusion and she wasn't prepared to let him off the hook.

He was on his own.

Darren delayed taking his break, so he didn't mix with his team, he'd managed to get his stats up to a respectable level and his call monitoring results had been good for the past few days. He was showing the signs of improvement that Charlie asked for, but he didn't want any distractions. The window of opportunity for apologising to Emma had passed and whilst the flowers had now gone, there was still a barrier between them.

He went for a quick walk around the car park. He'd bought a wristband that measured his steps in an effort to improve his fitness and he was becoming obsessed. He was easily hitting his ten thousand steps target each day by going for a long walk in his lunch break and getting off the bus a couple of stops early.

He was bringing sandwiches in each day and eating them whilst out on his walk. The fresh air and avoidance of canteen food was doing him good. Avoiding all human contact apart from his daily meetings with Charlie and talking to customers wasn't as good for his health but whilst he avoided speaking to people, they weren't mocking him.

Or so he thought.

He returned from his lunch to find a flower pot on his desk and a packet of flower seeds. His floral faux pas hadn't gone unnoticed and they'd been biding their time before calling him out on it. Most of the team were sniggering but avoiding eye contact. Emma couldn't have been part of it as she didn't appear to find it funny, it was another reminder of the embarrassment he had caused her.

He forced out a laugh in the hope that they would think he was going along with the joke, but he'd happily throw the plant pot out of the window or off somebody's head.

Actions, whilst satisfying, that may not be good for his employment prospects.

"Little update on the Star Awards," said Charlie.

Emma looked out of the window, she was sick of hearing about these stupid awards.

"Are we having an open top bus parade when we win?" said Adam.

"Nearly as good," said Charlie, "to go along with the £5,000 cash prize, there's going to be a celebrity presenting the award."

Emma sighed. She hated celebrity culture, hated the Z-listers who appeared on reality TV and became famous for nothing other than being famous. Yet another reason to hate the bloody Star Awards.

"Who is it?" said Adam.

"Anybody heard of Jon Radley?" Charlie sat back in her chair laughing.

"Who's that?" said Darren.

"H'away Darren," said Adam, "even I know who Jon Radley is and I don't watch the soaps. Our lass loves him."

"Only person to win the National Television Awards soap actor of the year three years in a row, Soap Magazines rated him as sexiest soap star again this year, born in Rochdale thirty-four years ago and recently single again after a split from his on off girlfriend Phoebe Truman who has been messing him around for years. That's who Jon Radley is." Emma even surprised herself.

"Wow, good knowledge, Emma," said Charlie, "you're a fan I take it?"

"Not particularly, I just like my soaps." Emma slid down in her chair as her face reddened.

"It's an added incentive, not that we needed one. Maybe you'll get to meet him if you win, Emma."

"I'm not interested in meeting him, I'm not bothered about celebrities."

The team knew she was lying, she knew she was lying, this put a whole new spin on the Employee Star Awards.

****

"What's this then, Dazza?" said Ryan picking up the plant pot.

"Nothing, just a joke," said Darren before taking another call.

As he was beginning his script with the customer, Ryan placed the pot on Darren's head. "Look everyone Darren's a pot head."

Darren tried to shrug him off but only succeeded in knocking the pot from his head and it smashing onto the desk and breaking into multiple pieces. The team laughed.

"Ryan, stop disturbing my team." Charlie was returning to her desk.

"Got to dash, I'm on a break," said Ryan, "see you, losers." He skipped off leaving half the team laughing and the rest, including Emma and Darren shaking their heads.

"You shouldn't encourage him," said Charlie, "he's nothing but a bad influence."

Everyone returned to their calls and pretended they hadn't heard her.

She noticed the debris on Darren's desk. "What's this? It's like working in a nursery school in this place sometimes." She placed a hand on Darren's shoulder before cleaning up the mess.

Darren and Charlie sat in the meeting room looking at his stats. They'd improved dramatically, and he was now in the top half of the team. His call monitoring scores were similar. He'd done everything Charlie had asked of him, but she still had concerns.

"What was that carry on with Ryan earlier?"

"It was nothing, he was just playing."

"Ryan is never just playing, what was it about?"

"Nothing, just attention seeking as usual, he was trying to get a laugh and used me to get it."

"I'm getting sick of this, did nobody on the team step up to defend you?"

"They were all on calls I think." He didn't want to admit how unpopular he was.

"Why did you have a flower pot on your desk anyway?"

"It was a present."

"Let me guess, another joke?"

"I guess so," said Darren.

"This is stopping now, I'm not having anyone on my team being bullied."

"I'm not being bullied."

"Darren, I can't have them laughing at you. They should be helping you. I don't know what's happened, I always used to have such a good team, but everything has begun to go off the rails. Maybe it's me, maybe I am losing my touch."

"It's not you, you're a great manager. It's me, I don't fit in, I never will."

"I don't believe that Darren and neither should you. It just takes a little bit longer to get to know you."

"I think they like me less now that they do know me."

"That's not true either. I'm going to have a word with Ryan's manager to keep him away from you."

"I'd rather you didn't, I don't want to draw more attention to myself."

"Don't worry, I'll keep your name out of it but someone needs to put him back in his box."

"Thanks."

"I know it's tough, nobody likes being laughed at but trust me, it will get better. We're coming to the end of your recovery plan and you are well on target. Keep your spirits up and ignore anyone who is distracting you. You are doing a good job, keep it up and we'll win the team around."

Charlie went for a chat with Ethan, Ryan's manager.

"He's disturbing my team and I need it to stop."

"He's not doing anything wrong, he's only having a laugh."

"He's not having a laugh, it's bullying and I'm not standing for it."

"Come off it Charlie. You can't tell me that you haven't had a laugh at someone else in the office."

She couldn't argue with this one, everybody had a laugh behind someone's back every now and then. "Not like this though. He's targeted the weakest member of my team and is deliberately picking on him." As soon as she said it, she realised that she had broken her promise to Darren to keep him out of the conversation.

"Who, Darren? He brings it on himself, look at the state of him. God knows why you employed him in the first place."

"I'd much rather have Darren on my team than Ryan."

"Yeah, well I'd much rather have a man who is top of the Star Employee Awards, is loved by senior management and is popular with his colleagues. Darren's got as many mates as I've got unicorn tears."

"Regardless, I want him to keep away from my team."

"That's just how he rolls."

"Just how he rolls? He's not in a street gang in LA, he's in a call centre in Doxford Park."

"Whatever, Charlie. Are you finished?"

"Are you going to speak to him?"

"You look after your team and I'll look after mine." With that, he walked off.

Charlie stifled a scream.

She knew she could humiliate Ethan, see how he liked it. She could tell everyone about his tattoo saying, 'Pull here for pleasure'. Or his tiny dick that resembled a ring pull more than something that could create pleasure. Or the strange grunt and whistle combo that he emitted on orgasm thirty-seconds into the act. All those things that could humiliate him if it wasn't for the fact that it would remind the whole of Phonetix that she had once been intimate with him. The humiliation would be all hers.

She knocked on Michelle's door.

"What is it Charlie? I'm busy."

"I need to talk to you about Ryan."

"He's doing well, isn't he? Good to see someone buying into the Employee Award programme."

"He's not buying into it, he's manipulating it for his own benefit."

"The rules are the same for everyone, we encourage creativity amongst our staff."

"He's bullying my team."

"And why are you telling me instead of his line manager?" said Michelle.

"I have told his line manager and he doesn't think he is doing anything wrong."

"If he is doing nothing wrong, I don't see why you want me to get involved."

"I want you to have a word with Ethan."

"I thought you said Ryan wasn't doing anything wrong?"

"I said Ethan doesn't think he is doing anything wrong."

"You seem a little confused Charlie, sounds like you need to get a better understanding of what your team is doing."

"The problem isn't my team."

"Sorry, Charlie, I don't have time to listen to this. It's the senior management ball tonight and I need to pick my dress up from the dry cleaners. If you need any advice on how to manage your team properly, maybe you should ask Ethan. His team seems to be doing really well."

****

Charlie watched Michelle flounce out of the building and felt like smashing the windows in her office. Her concerns had been ignored and she knew why. It was because Ryan's stats were good, the one and only thing that mattered. The fact that he manipulated the system and used every possible scam didn't matter. This was the sort of devious behaviour they encouraged, he was on the fast track to management. She wouldn't hang around to work alongside him if that happened.

She called a team meeting. There was nothing like time off the phones to galvanise the troops.

Richard, the resource manager tried to intervene. "This isn't scheduled in, Charlie."

"Sorry, it's an urgent meeting, I got it authorised by Michelle. Ask her if you like."

He looked towards her office and it was empty. "Okay, but I'm not happy about it."

"You don't come to work to be happy, I think that has been made abundantly clear."

She led the team into the meeting room and began laying out her strategy. A strategy that she hadn't thought through, a strategy that didn't amount to much more than one line. One line that she knew would hurt Ryan the most.

"I don't care what it takes but somebody on this team is going to win the Star Employee Award."

"What do you mean, you don't care what it takes?"

"Exactly what I said."

"Including cheating?" said Adam.

"Including being creative, I'm not having someone from another team abusing us and getting rewarded for it. I will back you in whatever you do to win. The only thing I ask is that we keep this to ourselves and work as a team. Do whatever you can to help your teammates."

"What happens if we get caught?"

"Let me worry about that. As long as we are being creative, I'll handle any flak we get," said Charlie.

There were excited murmurs around the room.

"Would be funny to put Ryan in his place," said Adam.

Everyone laughed. Whilst they played along with him to his face, it was clear that he was unpopular amongst the majority.

"We're all agreed then? Any questions?"

Darren raised his hand. "Does this mean everybody on the team has to go for it?"

"Yes, I don't care who it is but someone in this room is winning that award. You've already got some stars on the board, let's see if we can build on that."

Darren couldn't hide his smile. He was back in the game. He didn't want to get distracted, but he still had a few gold stars, he was still in with a chance.

When the team went for their break, they all went together, including Darren. None of them really spoke to him but they didn't object either. They were trying to work out how to beat Ryan, but they weren't getting anywhere.

Until Emma spoke.

She wasn't comfortable with the new directive, but she understood where Charlie was coming from. Ryan was nothing, but a bully and she didn't want to see him rewarded for his behaviour.

"I've got an idea. I heard Ryan talking about his tactics the other day. All his team's awards are going to be given to him making his lead almost unassailable. We could do the same."

"He'll know what we are up to and bully a few others, so he still wins."

"Not if we keep them spread out amongst the team. We don't need to transfer them until the last minute. We can collect as many stars as we can between us and make sure that as a team we have more than Ryan. He won't suspect anything because none of us will individually be near the top of the leader board. When the time comes, we'll see who has the most on our team and transfer the lot to them."

"That's a great idea, he won't be expecting it."

"We'll need to ensure that we have the justification written up when we do transfer them, but Charlie will sign off anything."

"You're really quite devious under that sensible exterior, Emma."

"Not devious, just pragmatic. I'd rather not be involved but we're a team and it's time we acted like one."

Darren didn't know if that let him off the hook but didn't push his luck. He would stay silent and go along with whatever they said.

"So, we're all agreed," said Emma.

"Agreed."

Darren's enthusiasm was deflated as soon as he stepped through the door of the flat and found Colin the landlord sat there. His mood dipped further when Colin outlined why he was there.

"You can't do that," said Darren.

"I can do what I like, it's in the contract." Colin sat with both hands down his shorts.

"What contract? I can't remember anything about you being allowed to increase the deposit."

"The evil is in the detail, Darren. That's what separates successful entrepreneurs like me from the dregs of society like you."

"The devil is in the detail."

"Indeed it is." Colin stood and walked around the room whilst moving his hands to the back of his shorts.

"Not evil, you said evil," said Darren.

"And that's where the detail is." He removed his right hand, sniffed it and raised his eyebrows as if in surprise.

"I give up. What happens if I don't pay?"

"You get evicted. Simple as pie, there's plenty of people lining up to pay the going rate. People who know how to keep a house clean and tidy. People who know how to conduct themselves in public." With that, Colin stuck his left index finger out of the bottom of his shorts and laughed to himself.

"How long have I got?"

"End of the month."

"To raise one thousand pounds? How am I meant to do that?" He already had the two grand blackmail hanging over him, this would kill him.

"You told me that you were the top employee at Phonetix Mobile, ask them for a raise."

"I can't do that, they'll..." Darren couldn't finish his sentence, his mind was racing ahead to the thought of being homeless.

"Anyway, got to rush, time waits for nomad."

Colin offered his hand, but Darren declined, knowing where it had been.

"It's time waits for no man, you fucking imbecile," said Darren as he heard the front door slam behind Colin.

Darren had some thinking to do. He wanted the Star Award before, now he needed it.

****

"Hi, Darren, I've got a Mr Proctor on the line, says he needs to speak to you about a credit on his account. Says he won't speak to anybody else."

"It's okay, I know who he is. Put him through." This was the last thing Darren needed. His stats were back on track and his call monitoring scores had all been above ninety percent. This could throw a real spanner into the works. "Good morning, Mr Proctor, how can I help?"

"Hello again, Darren, it's about that monthly discount you said that you were putting on my account."

"Monthly discount?"

"Yes, last time we spoke you said that you were applying a monthly £50 discount for the inconvenience you have caused me. I've checked online and there only seems to be a one-off payment. It's an easy mistake to make, would you be able to correct it please?" Spencer leaned back in his chair and gave a gesture to the receptionist for her to make him a cuppa.

"I'm sorry, Mr Proctor but as you will remember, that was a one-off goodwill gesture. We didn't agree a monthly discount."

"Come on now, Darren, surely you aren't suggesting that I am lying." Spencer was enjoying himself. The Police hadn't been back, George wasn't in a position to question his paperwork and he was on his way to getting himself a monthly £50 credit.

"Not at all, Mr Proctor, maybe just a misunderstanding."

"It's okay, it's easy for you to get confused in such a high-pressured job. If you could apply the discount and I'll let you get on with your day."

"No, I'm sorry. I meant that you must have misunderstood. There was never an agreement for a monthly discount." Darren tried not to raise his voice. He could feel himself getting angry, but he was still on his recovery plan. He couldn't afford to lose his temper.

"I remember it quite clearly, Darren. You apologised for the inconvenience you caused me, and I have to say, I'm feeling a little inconvenienced right now."

"I'm sorry you feel like that. The notes on the account clearly state that it was a one-off goodwill gesture."

"I'm beginning to feel a little upset, Darren. It feels like you are trying to bring my good name into disrepute. Trying to suggest that I am pulling some sort of scam."

"I'm not suggesting that, Mr Proctor, merely reminding you of the previous discussion we had."

"I'm quite angry that you would insult me like this, Darren. I'm not one of those people who sits in their grubby little flat phoning call centres to get their kicks. Add the discount now and I won't take this any further."

The inference was clear. Add a discount to his account or Spencer would expose Darren's previous dealings with Phonetix. Even if Darren wanted to add the discount, he didn't have the authority to do so. He looked to Emma, but he wasn't in any position to ask her for a favour. The only other person was Charlie but there was no way he could ask his line manager to apply a fraudulent credit.

He was out of options.

"I'm sorry, Mr Proctor but I will not be adding any further credits or discounts to your account. The £50 discount was a one-off and I now consider the matter closed. If you do want to take this matter further, we have a complaints procedure. I can give you the details."

"Don't bother. I already know them and Phonetix are about to find out exactly who you are." Spencer hung up and swore as the receptionist was delivering his coffee.

Darren was shaking as he came off the call. He looked up to see Charlie looking straight at him.

"Everything okay, Darren?"

This could be the end of his Phonetix career. "Yes thanks, just a difficult call." He went straight onto his next one so he didn't have to discuss it. He knew he was buying time until he could think up a believable cover story.

Darren and Charlie sat in his daily one to one and both knew what the discussion would be about. He'd spent most of the day thinking up a plausible reason why this customer was picking on him but none of them were convincing. For someone who had spent so much of his spare time lying to Phonetix Mobile, he couldn't bring himself to lie again to Charlie. He owed her the truth, even if it cost him everything.

"I've got a confession to make."

"Go on," said Charlie. She thought that she had turned a corner with Darren, but this could be fatal depending on what he told her.

"It's not about what I've done since I've been here, apart from one call. It's about my past."

Charlie didn't like the sound of this. HR did criminal record checks on all new starters, so it couldn't be that. What had he done? "Okay. I'm not going to like this, am I?"

"Worse than that, I think you'll hate me." Darren tried to keep himself from sobbing. He was upset that he was going to lose his job, but he found himself being more upset that he was letting Charlie down. She had trusted him and believed in him when nobody else did. "Before I joined Phonetix I was a customer. I used to phone customer services a lot."

"Okay," Charlie wasn't sure why this was a problem, "so you have some empathy with our customers when they get upset?"

"Thing was, I never had any genuine complaints, I was taking the piss. I used to enjoy phoning up to annoy the staff, to get credits that I wasn't entitled to." He sunk back in his seat, embarrassed. "Think of the worst call you've ever heard, that was probably me."

"You Darren, you were a troll?" Charlie couldn't contain her rage. "You, snivelling little shitgoblin."

****

Spencer came in from work in a foul mood but wasn't prepared to tell Rebecca what it was about. She wasn't prepared to listen anyway, she had other things on her mind. The whole Thomas thing was getting on top of her and her colleagues had begun to notice that something was up.

Spencer on the other hand wouldn't notice if she placed a signed confession in front of him.

Everything was in place now for her to leave. The deposit had been paid on the rental property, thanks to a loan from an understanding friend once the route through work was closed. The moving in date had been agreed and she'd even arranged for a man with a van to help her move.

The only thing left was to tell Spencer and the kids.

Spencer took a beer from the fridge and slumped on the settee with the laptop. He was on that bloody message board again. Rebecca couldn't understand why a grown man spent so much time chatting to strangers on the internet yet didn't have any time to speak to his wife or children. She decided to leave the discussion for another day. Leave him to his online family.

She grabbed her own laptop, opened a spreadsheet and tried to work out what the hell was going on with their finances. If she was to become a one parent family, sacrifices needed to be made. Rebecca looked over to the settee and watched Spencer. She wondered what she had ever seen in him. At one time, he'd seemed exciting but that soon wore off after they got married. Then he became a convenience, a father to their kids albeit one who only put the effort in when it suited. Then he became an irritation, the little things he did grew to be an annoyance. And now, now he was a risk, a risk to her future and a risk to her sanity.

She couldn't work out what he was doing with his money, but it wasn't going into the joint account. Sooner or later mortgage payments would get missed and the house would be at risk. She couldn't allow the children to grow up with this hanging over them. It was better to get out now and make a fresh start with what she had than wait for it all to come crumbling down around her.

The fact that Spencer hadn't even been up to see the kids was telling. Yes, they were in bed and yes, they should be asleep but they both knew that they tried to stay awake to see their Dad when he came in. She knew he would make some feeble excuse about not wanting to wake them if he went up, but she knew that he couldn't be bothered. Far more interested in what was happening on that bloody message board than he was in his own children.

Spencer posted a new thread on the forum.

Should you tell your employer that you have defrauded them in the past?

He knew the heading would get attention. People hoping that he was making a confession. Hoping that he would trip himself up.

STONE POSES: What have you been up to DB10? Been charging a penny extra for a Twix in the tuck shop?

LAST KING OF SUDDICK: They'll not be happy if you've been nicking Fairy Liquid from the kitchen in McDonalds again.

DAFT AS A THRUSH: Have you claimed for a new broom handle when the old one wasn't even broken?

He allowed the thread to gather momentum, with at least thirty replies before he bothered saying anything.

DB10: Not me. A well-known poster on here has previous for defrauding a company, getting credits on his account and has openly admitted his crimes on this very board. He now works for that company. Wonder if he got the job through the workers there that he pretended to know during the recent siege?

I'm sure his new employers would be very interested to find out.

Without naming him he'd left enough clues for it to be obvious who he was talking about. Somebody else would name Darren soon. He hoped the thread lasted long enough for Darren to see it before the moderators pulled it. He might cop a ban for posting the thread but as he hadn't named anyone, he would hopefully get away with it.

Darren saw the thread pop up. He hadn't been on the message board much recently but knew that something would happen after his run in with Spencer. It was as predictable as it was unwanted. He could report the thread to the moderators but let it run its course. He'd created the mess, he needed to deal with it.

As expected, there was a flurry of activity, he got named about sixty posts in but by then the thread was heading in about four different directions. Most people seemed to have read the first post and replied to it rather than read the whole thread. **DB10** was coming in for a lot more abuse than he had anticipated. Very few people referenced Darren and then the thread was gone. The moderators had clearly had enough of the abuse that was being dished out. Darren had got off lightly.

He had bigger things to worry about. After his confession to Charlie, he had to wait until the morning to find out what she intended to do.

CHAPTER FOURTEEN

There's not a single call centre worker who hasn't at one time wanted to do unspeakable things to a customer. There were a fair proportion of the workers at Phonetix who would like to do that to Darren once they discovered who he was. He couldn't blame anybody but himself, so he was willing to accept his fate.

It was a sad end to a short career.

By the time he got into the meeting room with Charlie, he'd stopped being nervous. He knew what was coming.

"I've had a long think about what you told me yesterday Darren, and I have to say that I am disappointed."

"I'm sorry, Charlie."

"We've had our problems, but I've always consoled myself with the fact that you are a good guy, trying to do your best." Charlie was trying not to raise her voice. "To find out that you used to phone in to abuse the staff has really upset me. I trusted you. I'm beginning to wonder if your whole employment here is another way of mocking us and wasting our time."

She had a point, why should she trust him? "Now I know how it feels to be on the other end of it, I wouldn't wish it on anyone," he said.

"You have no idea how it feels."

"I know you've got to sack me, so tell me what I need to do to make it easier for you," said Darren.

"Who said anything about sacking you?"

"I thought, with you knowing my history, that you'd have no choice."

"We always have a choice, Darren. Luckily for you, HR don't have a policy on whether employees have phoned customer services before they joined the company. Please tell me you haven't rung since you've joined?"

"No, never."

"Good, then I don't think it is a disciplinary matter. We can't sack you for something you did before you joined us."

"Thank you." Darren didn't think thank you was enough, but he didn't know what else to say.

"It doesn't mean we are out of the woods yet. This customer, Proctor? What's his next move?"

"I don't know."

"Of course you know, Darren, you used to be him. Think like you used to. What would you do in his situation?"

"Well, he tried to expose me on the message board last night but nothing much came of it."

"And if you were him would you contact the employer to report the past as he threatened?"

"No, that would be too much effort. It was always idle threats designed to put people on edge. As long as the threat is there you can manipulate them."

"So, we don't need to worry about Mr Proctor if he contacts you again. You know what his next move is, so you are always one step ahead."

"I hadn't thought of it like that."

"You've already told your manager, so his threat is null and void. I'll help you deal with him if he ever calls back."

"Thanks," Darren mumbled without looking Charlie in the eye.

"We have another problem."

"What?"

"If he exposed you on the message board last night, what's the odds of someone who works here having seen it?"

"The thread is gone now but there is a good chance that somebody saw it. There will be other references to it over time, so it will always be hanging over me."

"So why don't we tackle it head on?" said Charlie.

"What do you mean?"

"Before it becomes common knowledge, we go public with it ourselves."

"But people will hate me," said Darren.

"Let's be honest, you about as popular as a Jack Russell at a cat convention. You have nothing to lose."

"But what good would it do?"

"We get to control the news. We sell you as poacher turned gamekeeper. Like companies employing hackers to tighten their security."

"Do you think people will buy into it?"

"Who cares, it will be fun finding out." For the first time in the conversation, Charlie allowed herself a smile.

The team sat open mouthed during the team meeting as Darren told them everything. What tricks he used to get credits, how he would put people under pressure, how he would identify and exploit their vulnerabilities. He was worried that it was going to get violent as some didn't take the news well. It was to be expected but Charlie controlled the meeting.

"I realise that a lot of you won't be happy, but Darren has been very brave standing up and telling you the truth. He could have kept it hidden and none of you would be any the wiser."

"How is he brave? Dickheads like him are the reason most of us hate this job." Adam wasn't impressed.

"I understand that. You might not trust Darren yet, but I hope you all trust me. I believe Darren when he tells me that he has changed and that he is willing to help."

"How can an arsehole like him help us?"

"Next time you get one of those calls where you think the caller is pulling a fast one, you speak to Darren. He will be able to spot whether they are genuine or not."

"So now we're relying on the sixth sense of a proven liar? A troll who's been taking the piss out of us for years?" said Adam.

"Not a sixth sense," said Charlie, "experience. He can say whether the caller is behaving in the way he used to."

"Like a lying wanker? Have you any idea how close I come to walking out every day due to dealing with people like him?"

"I understand your frustration but this way you won't have to deal with these customers ever again," said Charlie.

"How do you mean?"

"Whenever you get a caller you hate, or a caller who hates you, give it to Darren. Ask for his advice first but if you can't get rid of them, pass them over to Darren."

The mood lightened a little when they realised what this could mean for them.

"Really," said Adam, "will that not bugger his stats up?"

"I'll not repeat this outside of this room but bollocks to Darren's stats, the team's are more important. This is his final chance and Darren knows it." She looked straight at him. "He needs to help the rest of you if he has any chance of surviving at Phonetix Mobile."

****

The team was shocked by both Darren's confession and Charlie's suggestion on how they were going to use him. It was all they talked about on their next break when Darren thought it wise to give them space to talk it through. Charlie knew that she had given herself a logistical headache. Darren's stats would get worse as he helped other people but at the same time, the team's overall stats should improve and his might sneak under the radar. Now that she had given him a different way of thinking about customers and the autonomy to give chancers short shrift, his stats should improve anyway. She knew that she would be in trouble once senior management found out, but she was using her initiative. If it worked as she intended, the proof would be in the stats and she would be untouchable.

It wasn't long before Darren's assistance was called for. An irate customer demanding to speak to a manager about incorrect charges. Darren listened in for a couple of minutes whilst he checked the account. The call history showed that they'd been with the Phonetix a long time and rarely called.

"They're genuine."

"Really?" Adam was hoping that they weren't, so he could get rid of the call, but this at least changed his approach. Once he believed the customer, the call became easy, the incorrect charges were removed without question and the customer went away very happy.

The next one that Darren was asked to help with was definitely trying it on. Multiple calls about minor issues always ending in credits to the account or long drawn out arguments according to the notes. When Darren listened in, the customer was constantly interrupting, not giving the call handler time to think or compose themselves. Once Darren gave his view, they were free to get rid of the customer as quickly as possible as long as they didn't use the release button.

"Aah, Frumpty Dumpty, my favourite call centre spinster." Ryan placed his hands on the back of Emma's chair.

"Go away, Ryan," said Emma.

"Just passing the time of day, no need to be rude."

"I've got to go." Emma packed her remaining sandwich back in its Tupperware box and placed a bookmark in her paperback before shoving it in her bag.

"I've been chatting to a friend of yours."

Emma pretended to be disinterested, she couldn't imagine that any of her friends would speak to Ryan, but she was mildly concerned. "That's nice for you."

"Yeah, we had a good old chat whilst my girlfriend was cutting her hair."

Emma knew immediately who he meant. Not so much a friend as her next-door neighbour who had an unhealthy fetish for new hair colourings and an even unhealthier interest in unsolicited gossip. "Like I said, I have to get back."

"She told me loads about you, like how you've never had a boyfriend."

"That's not true." It was but Ryan didn't know that.

"And how you've plans to do the deed before you reach forty."

"I don't have to listen to this."

"She even went as far as to say you had your eyes on someone at work to help you out."

"Leave me alone." Emma tried to push past Ryan.

"I'm flattered but I've already got a girlfriend."

"As if I'd choose you to take my virginity." As soon as she said it she knew what she'd done. Confirmed exactly what Ryan was hoping she would despite the fact that she'd never discussed it with her neighbour. Any conversation they'd had would be speculation and nothing more but now it was a cold hard fact, and one that Ryan had hold of.

"That hurts, Emma, that really hurts. But if it's not me, who is it?"

"Get out of my way." Emma shoved Ryan in the chest.

"Oooh, so you're into the rough stuff? You're after someone a little bit kinky? I guess there's a fair few of them about in here."

"Piss off, Ryan." Emma grabbed the handle of the door. "Unless it's that fat mess, Darren."

Emma paused just for a second before opening the door.

"It is," said Ryan, "I'm right aren't I? You want to do the business with Chubby Checker. Guess it doesn't get much kinkier than that."

"I'm reporting you to HR," said Emma. She was crying now and raced towards the lifts.

"Don't be like that, I can help you." Ryan ran after her.

"I don't need your help."

"You really want to go to HR and make it official that you want kinky sex with Dazza?"

"I never said that."

"Look, I can tell that you're embarrassed, but this doesn't have to go any further. We can just keep it between the two of us."

"Tell who you like, nobody will believe you."

"You sure of that? Everyone loves a bit of gossip, especially when it involves kinky sex. They'll lap it up and it'll be all round the call centre before you've even whipped Darren's arse."

"What do you want, Ryan?"

"Nothing, like I said, just passing the time of day." As they reached the lifts he looked up at the display screen in reception showing the Employee Star leader board. "Look at that, I'm very close to winning, it's only going to take a couple more votes."

The implication was clear. The lift pinged, and the doors opened. Ryan stood aside to let Emma in. She knew what she had to do.

"I see your stats have been improving," said Michelle, "I'm glad you finally listened to my advice."

Charlie couldn't think of a single thing that Michelle had said that was worthwhile. "Advice?"

"Yes, I told you to improve your stats. Good to see that you took some notice for once."

Charlie wasn't sure how that constituted advice but wasn't prepared to argue. She didn't want to reveal how her team's stats had improved and wanted to keep Darren under wraps for as long as possible.

She'd taken a risk on trusting the team with Darren's past and it seemed to be paying off.

Maybe she needed to take more risks.

****

It wasn't long before news of Darren's skills spread to other teams. Charlie had hoped to keep it quiet but the improvement in stats was dramatic and the other Team Leaders asked for her secret. She tried to be coy, but people talked. Her own team had learned quickly from Darren. So much so that they rarely asked for his help now, just followed a few tips that he had given them for identifying trolls.

He'd used his initiative to type a crib sheet of things to look out for. Behaviours which were present with all trolls. It wasn't just the anger and shouting; genuine customers could get angry and frustration manifested itself in many ways. It was the constant belittling of the person they were speaking to. The undermining, the attempt to unsettle them, to make them doubt themselves. Skills rarely seen outside of a doctor's reception.

Darren realised how much of an art it was. He'd been doing it for fun, but he'd been honing his skills and he'd known how to spot a weakness and exploit it. He felt both proud of how he'd taught himself those skills and ashamed at how he had used them. At least now he was putting them to good use, spotting the patterns, recognising the behaviours and turning them against the caller.

The one thing he realised that they all had in common was how pathetic they were. When you stripped away the bluster and the false air of superiority, it was insecurity that drove them on. Trying to find a weakness in others to make them feel better about themselves. The message board was the same. It took him putting some distance between himself and the forum to realise how sad he appeared.

That was in his past, he was a new person now and he hoped, a lot more positive.

Someone from the next team called him over. "What do you think of this one, Darren? He's arguing blind that the charges are wrong on his account, but they all look right to me."

Darren listened in and had a quick look at the account. The customer sounded frustrated and upset but the charges also seemed correct. Crucially, the customer had been with the company for six years and this was the first time they had phoned. This was the most difficult type of call. "They are genuine," said Darren, "but they are wrong."

It occasionally happened that someone could get confused by something on their bill that they weren't expecting. They would be so convinced that they were in the right that their opinion couldn't be shifted. They weren't deliberately trying to defraud Phonetix, they'd just used a service that was chargeable, and they hadn't realised.

"Cheers, Darren, time for a little discretion I think." He gave Darren the thumbs up and returned to the customer.

"Hello, Mr Shepherd, first things first, I'll remove that charge straight away," it was only £15 and worth it as a goodwill gesture to get him off the call, "however the charge was applied correctly. Would you mind if I took a couple moments of your time to explain how it happened, so you don't get charged again?"

With that slight change in approach, the customer was back onside. For the sake of £15, there wouldn't be repeated calls into the call centre, he would remain a customer of Phonetix for years and crucially, he knew never to trust his grandchildren again when they asked him to download an app to his phone.

Darren's simple approach to identifying trolls was spreading.

It wasn't long before Ryan noticed as well.

"Not sure why he's getting praise from everyone. He should be sacked for being a troll, we don't want his type here."

The rest of his team murmured agreement but a lot of them would be quite happy to use his services if the chance arose.

"He's only been here two minutes," said Ryan, "and we're supposed to believe that he is some sort of expert capable of understanding customers? He's blagging it just like he did when he used to phone in to get credits on his account. They should take those credits out of his wages."

Nobody was listening to him now, they all had their headsets on and were taking calls or at least pretending to so they didn't have to listen to Ryan's rant. Darren could hear Ryan but chose to ignore him. If he could teach himself to ignore the trolls, he could ignore someone like Ryan.

The unexpected bonus of Charlie's new initiative with Darren was that the Employee Stars were rolling in. Mainly for Darren but for others in the team as well. They were all creeping up the league table. Not enough to draw attention to themselves just yet but enough to make the stealthy approach she had called for to unseat Ryan from the top. She did a quick tot up of the scores and the team wasn't that far behind Ryan's total. There was a chance that her plan might come to fruition.

"Good work today, everyone," she said as the day drew to a close. It was days like this when she thought that the job wasn't too bad. She knew that feeling wouldn't last.

Before she'd shut the front door, her mother was in the passageway holding a tea towel. "Good day, love?"

"The usual."

It was the same routine each night, there was no point in expanding on what sort of day she'd had. Her mother wasn't interested, she only cared that the status quo was maintained. That she left at the same time every morning and returned at the same time every night. Any disruption to that routine was unwelcome.

But disruption is what she was going to get, because despite Charlie's good day, she was now determined that it was time to leave.

****

It was a sad day for George. A successful career in car sales tarnished by one foolish mistake. It was a foolish mistake he'd made plenty of times before but this time he got caught out. Borrowing a car from the showroom for an illicit afternoon with a barmaid was one thing. Losing the car was another thing entirely.

The police had investigated and whilst the case wasn't closed, they didn't think George was guilty of anything other than stupidity. Unfortunately, his bosses thought otherwise. He was the top man in the showroom; he had to lead by example and extra marital affairs and stolen cars weren't the example the company wanted him to set.

As soon as the police were involved he knew his time was up. When the F-Type never materialised it merely confirmed what he already knew, and he tried to go with as little fuss as possible. The area sales manager sat in his office as George cleared his things away. There was no animosity, just an acceptance that this was the way it had to be.

Spencer looked on from his own desk on the showroom floor, trying to suppress a smirk. He'd never liked George. Whilst he'd allowed everyone to get away with the odd thing, he was strict. Especially with sales targets and he never let up when Spencer was struggling. He should have felt guilty about what he'd done but car sales was survival of the fittest and he needed to keep this job. It might turn out better than he'd hoped as the frostiness between him and the departing George was evident to everyone and might stand him in good stead when they looked to replace him. Everyone else was fussing around George, saying how sorry they were to see him go. Even buying him a leaving present but Spencer wanted no part of it. George had brought the company's name into disrepute and Spencer wanted to maintain the highest standards or at least that was the impression that he wanted to give.

The police seemed to have given up, they hadn't been back, there was no trace of the car and he was confident there never would be unless somebody took a holiday to Dubai and stumbled into it. He was in the clear and he would be collecting his payment very soon.

While everyone was distracted he did some paperwork. He was chancing his arm a little bit, but he forged George's signature on a couple of documents, no reason why Spencer shouldn't profit from his departure.

It had been a tough few months financially, but things were turning a corner. Maybe Rebecca would trust him again.

"Got any ideas on what you will do next?" said the area sales manager.

"Good salesmen are always needed and there's a few old friends that will help me out. Won't be quite the same as this place but I've got nobody to blame but myself."

"Despite everything, I am sorry to see you go, George. You are one of the good guys and I've enjoyed working with you."

"I appreciate it. Sorry it couldn't have been in better circumstances," said George.

"Me too." They shook hands.

"Look, I know you don't think I run a tight ship here, but I was looking into something before all this kicked off and it might be worth keeping an eye on." George took a pile of documents from his drawer.

"What's this?"

"Spencer's sales have been falling for months but they had a little bump recently. A bump that coincided with us employing a promising junior salesman."

"Go on."

"We got rid of Callum because he wasn't making any sales, but something didn't feel right."

"How do you mean, didn't feel right?"

"I had a look at Spencer's recent sales and they were nearly all from the used car pool, not his usual area."

"Could he have been sealing deals that the junior couldn't close?"

"That was his story, but it doesn't add up. Once Callum left, Spencer's figures dipped again."

"Interesting. Thanks for this George, I'll keep an eye on it."

"Sorry for dumping another problem on you but there's something not right about him."

"Yeah, he's a bit too arrogant, even for a car salesman. Did you tell the police any of this?"

"The police, why would I involve them? It's an internal matter."

"The paperwork might be but this sort of behaviour suggests that he is having money problems, and if he is, does that not give him a motive?"

"A motive for what?" said George.

"The F-Type."

"I'd never thought of that."

Of course, this wasn't strictly true. He'd thought of very little else recently.

He gathered his things and took them to the waiting taxi, he no longer had a company car. He said his goodbyes and accepted the good wishes of his former employees. He fought back the tears as the taxi pulled out. He took one look back and stared Spencer in the eye. He knew he was right.

With George out of the way and the police uninterested in the F-Type anymore, Spencer decided that it was time to cash in. He made a call and arranged to meet in Durham Services again.

He pulled in and waited, like before, until he saw the black Range Rover pull up. He was dealing with some bad people here; he was nervous, but he'd kept his end of the deal, so he was confident that he would be okay. A large figure got out of the driver's door, walked past his car and threw a brown envelope through the passenger window as agreed. He continued walking into the service station. Spencer didn't bother to open the envelope, but it was a lot thicker than he was expecting. He put it in the glove box and pulled out of the services.

When he got home, knowing that Rebecca was still at work and the kids at school he looked for somewhere suitable to hide the cash. He couldn't bank it, so he had to risk hiding it in the house somewhere. He thought about the loft, the children's bedrooms, the garage but none seemed right. He needed to get back to work so shoved it in the suitcase on top of the wardrobe; it wasn't like they were likely to be going on holiday anytime soon.

****

Charlie surveyed her team, happy that they all seemed to be getting along now. They had all bought into the new initiative with Darren and it was paying off with improved stats and plenty of nominations for the Employee Awards. It was also keeping Michelle off her back for a while. Charlie wasn't sure what she had done to Michelle to be made a target but everything she did, she seemed to do wrong. Even if it was exactly what Michelle had told her to do.

Lauren reckoned that it was because Michelle saw her as a threat but that was ridiculous. If Michelle's team was doing well, surely that strengthened her hand rather than weakened it but she didn't seem to see it that way. Charlie was trying to stick to the advice she had given Darren to stay under the radar, but the success of the initiative and the Employee Awards might bring her into the spotlight again.

Charlie drained the last of her coffee and checked the clock on her monitor screen, it was that time of the week again, the Team Leader's meeting. Whilst the team couldn't wait for a team meeting to get off the phones, the managers dreaded the idea of being preached to, patronised and reminded of how worthless their opinions were in the hour they spent with Michelle each week.

Her rants were random and unpredictable. She could state something as fact one week and unequivocally and categorically deny any knowledge of it the next, throwing everybody into a state of confusion. Charlie had learned to ignore whatever instructions were given as they were bound to change. She had also learned to keep her mouth shut and not argue.

Most of the time.

"The Employee Star Awards are not getting enough traction," said Michelle.

"In what respect?" said one of the new Team Leaders foolish enough to open his mouth.

"Nobody knows anything about it. I saw someone in the toilets yesterday and asked if she had any stars and she said she didn't know what I was talking about."

"Maybe she was a little intimidated."

"Intimidated?" Michelle raised her voice. "I'm not intimidating. Who says I'm intimidating? Raise your hand now if you are intimidated by me." She glared at everyone individually, daring them to raise their hand. Nobody did. "See?"

"One person isn't indicative of the whole call centre. There's posters, balloons, big screens, everybody is talking about it."

"You aren't socialising the information to your teams."

"Socialising?"

"You aren't telling your teams about the awards."

"Right, you're saying there is a communication problem."

"No, I'm saying that you aren't socialising the information," said Michelle, slowly and deliberately.

"But socialising doesn't mean–"

"Maybe we could reiterate the importance in our next team meetings?" Charlie butted in to save the new Team Leader from the horror that would follow on from correcting Michelle.

"You are solutionising, Charlie. I need you to stop solutionising."

"Okay, what do you suggest?" Charlie struggled to hide the sarcasm in her voice.

"Stars."

"Stars?"

"Everyone who is on the leader board should wear a big gold star to identify them."

A couple of people stifled sniggers, others gasped. Charlie knew that she needed to challenge it but it was going to get ugly.

"Isn't that slightly inappropriate?"

"Inappropriate, what on God's earth are you on about?"

"The Jews?"

"Are you being racist, Charlie? I will not tolerate racism in this call centre."

"Not at all, the Nazis, World War Two, ring any bells?"

"You need to unring that bell right now and start listening," said Michelle as she thumped the table, "everyone on that list will be wearing a gold star. Are we agreed?"

A few mumbles of nervous agreement went around the table.

"See," said Michelle with her face turning to a smile as if the previous exchange has never happened, "I knew you would come up with a solution."

Charlie returned to her team, trying to keep her temper in check. Once again Michelle had humiliated her, and she had done nothing but try and protect her from making a ridiculous mistake. There was no way she was making anybody wear a gold star and she knew that none of the other Team Leaders would either. To do so would lead to a dressing down and possible disciplinary action when Michelle denied all knowledge of it a week later.

As she sat she looked once again at the glorious blue of Sydney Harbour and opened a Word document. Her half-finished resignation letter. She began typing then closed it again. "*Don't do it in the heat of the moment,*" she thought.

Instead she concentrated on the one small problem in the team that she still needed to resolve; Darren and Emma. She'd paired them up when Darren first arrived, and Emma had been a great mentor. Especially good considering the baggage that Darren brought with him.

Despite Darren's recent success, Emma had long been the top performer on the team and Charlie hoped she would be for a long time to come. She didn't seem happy at the minute and Charlie needed to do something about it.

It had started when Darren had sent her flowers. Whether it was a romantic gesture gone wrong or something else, Charlie wasn't sure. She maybe should have spoken to Emma at the time but didn't want to pry. She wasn't sure of the solution either. She could move one of them to a different seat but that drew attention to the issue. She'd hoped that it would have resolved itself by now, but they still didn't seem to be speaking. She could get them to work together on something, but Emma would see right through that and would resent the implication that she could be conned so easily.

It was a tricky situation, but Charlie knew that she would resolve it, she always did. She had a one to one meeting coming up with Emma soon and she was going to take a leaf out of the training manual for dealing with customers. Instead of assuming to know what they want, take some time to find out. She may have totally misread the situation and making Emma uncomfortable would only make things worse.

Charlie liked a challenge and she was determined to conquer this one.

****

After what seemed like a never-ending stream of one to one meetings, including a one-way discussion with Emma, Charlie was joined by Darren in the comfy seats. They had a view out over the car park towards the few trees that gave the impression that they were somewhere rural and blocked out the sight of the dual carriageway behind it. She'd tried to talk to Emma about Darren, but the shutters had come down and she hadn't been prepared to discuss it.

Time for Plan B.

"Hi Darren, how's it going?"

"Good, I think." There was a little hesitation in his voice as he'd been caught out before when he thought he was doing well.

"It's been a good couple of weeks, you're storming up the charts with the Star Awards. I noticed that you made it onto the leader board."

"Yeah, I was hoping not to draw attention to myself," said Darren.

"I think it's unavoidable now, but you have to keep on doing what you are doing."

"If Ryan notices he'll try and cause trouble for me again."

"I'll deal with Ryan when the time comes, don't worry about him," said Charlie.

"Thanks."

"There was one thing I wanted to bring up with you." Charlie shuffled her chair in closer.

"Yeah?" Darren knew there was something, there always was.

"Emma?"

"Emma?" He blushed and fidgeted with his sleeve.

"Is everything okay between you two? You don't seem to get on as well as you used to."

"Just a bit of a misunderstanding; it was my fault, not a lot I can do about it now."

"Have you tried apologising?"

"Sort of."

"What do you mean, sort of?" said Charlie.

"She doesn't appear to be talking to me so I don't think she would listen."

"You won't know if you don't try."

"That's the problem, whenever I do try to speak to people I get it wrong. I always put my foot in it."

"You need to try harder."

"It was trying harder that got me into this mess in the first place," said Darren.

"It's none of my business what went on and neither of you seem willing to share but you are both on my team and I care about you. I want you to sort it out."

"How can I sort it out?"

"By saying sorry?" said Charlie.

"It isn't that simple."

"It is if you mean it. Maybe instead of trying hard, try being yourself."

"Is that a good idea? Being myself is usually what gets me into bother."

"Yes, it's a good idea. If you come across as natural and genuine, she is more likely to listen."

"I'm not sure."

"Darren, you've been speaking to hundreds of customers and you've worked out that it becomes a lot simpler when both sides are honest about what they want. It's the same in real life. You might not always get what you want but it's a lot easier to communicate that way."

"What if she doesn't want to speak to me again."

"At least we'll know for sure but I very much doubt that is the case."

"She seemed pretty upset."

"Then it's up to you to put it right."

****

Darren recognised the knees that had taken up position in his kitchen. Colin the landlord was back.

"You can't keep letting yourself in like this," said Darren.

"We've discussed this before, it's my flat, I can do what I like." Colin raked about in his shorts readjusting himself with his right hand whilst he held a cigarette in the other.

"I thought we weren't allowed to smoke in here."

"Do as I say, not do as I do, Darren. You'd do well to remember that."

"But the rent's paid, the flat's tidy, you've got no reason to be here."

"Just checking on you. I had noticed you'd had a bit of a spring clean, have you finally got yourself a woman?"

"No, not that it's any of your business."

"My flat, my business. Can't have you subletting without me knowing about it."

"I'm not subletting."

"I believe you, I've had a look about and there doesn't seem to be any women's stuff."

"Women's stuff?"

"Pants and that."

"You've been searching my flat for women's underwear?"

"My flat, not yours. Just keeping an eye on my investment." Finally satisfied that everything was rearranged, Colin let the waistband of his shorts snap back with a twang. "Where've you been anyway? All dressed up and that."

"Work."

"You've still got a job? My God, thought they would have sacked you long ago."

"I'm on my way to being Star Employee."

"Of course you are, Darren. You keep on believing that, son."

"They love me there, I'm doing really well." Darren knew this wasn't true, he was far from loved, but he didn't want to lose face to Colin.

"Well, if you ever fall off that high horse of yours, don't come running to me with a broken leg. I'm not losing rent and that extra deposit because you've lost your job."

"I'm not losing my job and you haven't brought me the new contract yet, so I can check whether the demand for the extra deposit is legal"

"Look at yourself, Darren. You might have squeezed yourself into a suit, but you can put a top hat on a turd, doesn't make it a leprechaun."

"Leprechaun?"

"You lose that job and there'll be no more second chances. You'll be gone like a priest in the night."

"Priest in the night?"

"Anyway, thanks for the tea." Colin dropped the cigarette butt into a mug where it sizzled briefly. "And open a window, it stinks of smoke in here." Colin zipped his anorak and put up his hood despite it not raining outside.

"Are you going to bring that contract?"

"I'll bring the contract, you make sure you have my money," said Colin whilst shoving his hands in his anorak pockets. "See you soon, Darren. And remember, I'm always watching."

CHAPTER FIFTEEN

Darren rehearsed what he was going to say into the mirror in the gents, but he couldn't get it right. It sounded false and he didn't want to make things worse. He knew that Charlie was right, and he had to apologise to Emma, but he worried that he would put his foot in it and make the situation irretrievable. He owed Emma the apology, he owed Charlie for believing in him and he owed it to himself to put things right with Emma. There were a lot of debts riding on one conversation. Someone came in and Darren pretended to be straightening his hair. Given that his hair looked like a bucket of worms fighting over a bird's nest, he didn't know if that looked worse than talking to himself.

Emma was at her desk and it was still five minutes before their shift begun.

"Morning, Emma," said Darren, "do you mind if I have a word please?"

"What is it, Darren?" She didn't look up from her book.

"In private?" He nodded towards the soft seating area.

"I'm about to log-in."

"It will only take two minutes, I promise. It's important."

She sighed and put her book down. "It better be quick, I don't want a black mark for logging in late."

They walked down the call centre in silence. Darren tried to break the ice. "Did you do anything nice last night?"

"That's none of your business."

She had a point. That was the very reason they were having the conversation in the first place.

"Thanks for agreeing to speak to me, Emma." He sat.

"Hurry up, Darren, we've got to log-in in a couple of minutes." She seemed reluctant to sit but relented.

"I wanted to say sorry," he rubbed his hands against the chair fabric, "for what happened before. The flowers and everything"

"Is that it? I think you've already said that."

"No, I mean really sorry."

"Were you not really sorry before?"

"That's not what I meant. I'm trying to explain why I did what I did," said Darren with an air of desperation.

"I'm not sure that I want to know."

"I know how it seems. All I wanted to do was make you happy, but I got it wrong."

"You can say that again."

"I always get things wrong, it's not always deliberate."

"So, you didn't deliberately pry into my private life?" said Emma.

"I did, but at the time I thought I was doing the right thing and I realise now how wrong I was."

"How could you not know that spying on someone was wrong? And weird. And creepy."

"I didn't think. I guess I've never thought much about the consequences of my actions," said Darren.

"You don't seem to have thought about it at all."

"I know and if I knew a way to put it right I would. But I don't know how to put it right so all I can do is apologise."

"It's a little late for apologies, you really upset me."

"I'm not expecting you to forgive me or forget what I did but I want you to know that I did it with the best intentions, no matter how misguided they were."

"Are you finished? I need to log-in."

"Yes, I guess that's it."

They returned to their desks in silence. Darren's apology didn't have the effect that he'd hoped but at least he'd tried. He'd said what he'd intended. Maybe not as smoothly as he had wanted but he'd got his point across. If Emma wanted to ignore his apology, then that was her decision and he would accept it. He would maybe ask Charlie to move him to another team to make it easier for her.

Emma was angry. Angry at Darren and angry at herself for letting this go on so long. Darren had upset her, but she was punishing him for being shy, hopeless and socially inadequate. What he'd done wasn't out of malice, but it was still hurtful and their walk down the call centre hadn't gone unnoticed by Ryan.

Maybe it was time to ask for a move to another team, to start again. She liked Charlie and she was by far the best Team Leader in the building, but she couldn't work in this atmosphere. She wanted to get her head down, take calls, do a good job and go home. She didn't need any drama, she would have a word with Charlie when she got a chance.

Charlie watched Darren and Emma return from their chat. Their body language didn't look promising and they logged in without speaking. She wanted to get them in a room and bang their heads together. She wasn't convinced that splitting them up would help. Darren had done well recently but she wasn't confident that another Team Leader would be as understanding of his unique personality. Emma would fit into any team, but Charlie didn't want to lose her best performer.

Michelle and the rest of senior management always thought that management was about stats, call queues and bonus schemes but to Charlie it was about people. Understanding people, understanding what they want, what they are thinking and trying as best she could to remove any obstacles to them doing a good job. If she couldn't resolve this dispute, then she wasn't the manager she thought she was. She kept thinking about the age-old mantra she had always had. Look after your staff and your staff will look after you.

To get any job satisfaction before she left, she needed to step up and sort this.

****

Rebecca had taken a half day from work and arranged for one of the other mothers to pick the kids up from school. Everything was sorted, and she had the keys to the new house. Today was the day she moved out.

It would be essentials first. A few trips in the car with most of the children's things then enough stuff for her to survive. She would come back in a couple of days with a van. She didn't intend to clear Spencer out, but she needed to make the new house habitable until Spencer accepted what was happening and hopefully moved out of their home.

She had to tell him to his face. It would have been easier to go and leave a note but that wouldn't be a great start to her long-term plans. She needed to keep things amicable. A dignified exit would also give her the moral high ground. Thomas' disciplinary was in two weeks and she no longer cared what happened, she just didn't want to give Spencer a get out of jail free card. Better to leave now and avoid the whole scenario.

She wasn't looking forward to the conversation with Spencer, she had no idea how he would react. He could fly off the handle and that's why she was keeping the kids out of the way. On the other hand, he may be resigned to it and not care. Rebecca possibly feared that more.

It was surprising how much stuff she could fit in the car with the seats down. It was a pain taking the kids' seats out in the first place, but it was a necessary evil. She got the children's mattresses, bedding, clothes, a selection of toys and crucially one of the smaller TVs in the back and another bag of stuff on the passenger seat.

She made the first run and returned for another load. She probably should have got some help but didn't want to burden anybody else with her problems, didn't want to get them involved in taking sides. She'd got the basics for the kids and needed to think of some essentials for herself. Her mind had already drifted to what they were having for tea. It would need to be takeaway as she didn't even have any pans or much in the way of cutlery. Pizza would distract the kids long enough for them to stop asking questions about why they were moving without Daddy.

She took the case from the top of the wardrobe.

The brown envelope didn't register at first, just some old travel documents from a holiday long ago perhaps. But it was too thick for that.

She opened it and stared. It was thick with notes.

She didn't bother counting it, all she needed to know was that there was money that Spencer was keeping from her. It was bad enough that he wasn't paying into the joint account but now he was secreting wads of cash around the house.

She ripped the room apart to see if there was any more.

After his last encounter, Ryan didn't want to go to the gym, but he had little choice knowing that he was being monitored by his Caitlin. He couldn't win.

He decided that getting his limbs removed by two thugs was the lesser of two evils when compared to the humiliation he would get from his girlfriend if he didn't work on his physique.

Putting his bag in the boot gave him a stark reminder as to why he didn't want to go. He'd left the box he'd been given in the car as he couldn't risk leaving it in the house. He'd already swerved awkward questions from Caitlin by persuading her that they should take her car to Sainsbury's on the feeblest of excuses. His excuses wouldn't last for long.

Knowing the people, he was dealing with, he suspected the box contained something criminal, but he also knew them well enough not to take a peek inside. The less he knew the better.

But now he had a bigger issue, it had begun to smell.

He'd noticed it the day before, the sort of whiff you get driving past a farmer's field, but he was in a built-up area. It was more pungent now; the signs weren't good. Whatever it was he wanted rid of it but he wasn't in a position to say anything until he'd paid his debts and there's only one way he could do that.

"What are you doing?"

Rebecca jumped. She'd got so distracted that she'd lost track of time. So much for a dignified exit.

"What am I doing? What are you doing?" She threw the envelope at him and the notes spilled out across the carpet.

"I can explain." But he couldn't, and he wasn't sure if he even wanted to.

"What's going on, Spencer? Is it drugs? Gambling? What are you up to?"

"You wouldn't understand."

"I'm not sure I want to. Wherever it has come from, me and the kids want nothing to do with it."

"It was you who put me up to it, you who was complaining about money not going into the joint account."

"Don't try and pin this on me," said Rebecca, trying her best to keep her voice down.

"George had it coming to him anyway."

"George? What's it got to do with George?"

"I was going to lose my job because of him, where would we be then? He's out of the picture now and we have a bit of spare cash. Where's the problem?"

"Out of the picture? Don't tell me you were involved in that car going missing."

"It can't be traced back to me, the police aren't interested, and the garage have got rid of George, case closed."

"If you think the police or the garage are going to forget about a sixty-grand car you are off your head."

"They can't link it to me, I didn't physically take it," said Spencer.

"But you arranged for someone else to."

"Sort of."

"And how did you do that?"

"Just a quick phone call, it was nothing."

"You're an idiot, Spencer. An absolute fucking idiot!"

****

No expense had been spared for the Star Employee Awards leader board. It had been moved from the whiteboard to a large TV screen with the leaders being updated in real time. Ryan was still in the lead, but he hadn't gained any new stars for a couple of days. He'd persuaded all his team to hand theirs over to him, but they weren't earning any new ones.

Darren had moved into second place, still some way back but all his stars had been earned and it didn't take into account the ones that the team could potentially transfer to him at the last minute as per Charlie's plan.

When Ryan's name flashed up in first place, his team gave him high-fives, looking forward to the pint that he had promised them all if he won, but he knew the battle was far from over.

He cast a nervous glance over to Darren. How could this shambles of a man be anywhere near to catching him? He looked a mess, had no friends and he was so socially awkward that Ryan was surprised that he wasn't living in a cave.

Charlie sat daydreaming in the Team Leader's meeting, wishing she could be anywhere else. Someone was giving an update on some initiative or other and was trying to fit in as many buzzwords into their presentation as possible. It was as if they had stumbled upon a bag stuffed with management speak and they were trying to use it all up before the owner came and asked for it back. They'd been talking for at least twenty minutes without saying anything. People were making notes as well. Charlie had no idea what they could be writing, he hadn't made a single coherent point. She made a note of her own. **I need to get out of here.**

The agenda moved on to the Star Awards and Charlie grimaced as Michelle praised Ryan.

"He's doing a great job there, Ethan, well done."

"I've trained him well."

They both let out a nauseating laugh. Why couldn't they see what a divisive little creature Ryan was? Maybe it was because he was made in the same mould as them.

"Charlie, this Darren character in second place, he's the weird one on your team, isn't he?" said Michelle.

"I wouldn't say weird but, yes he is one of mine. He's quite new but he's doing very well."

"For a troll," said Ethan.

"What was that, Ethan?" said Michelle.

"Nothing, just thinking aloud."

"Do we want a new person winning," said Michelle, "what sort of message does that send out to the people that have been here a long time?"

"That they should work a bit harder, try and be a bit more helpful?" said Charlie.

"Have you seen the state of Darren," said Ethan, "he looks like a beer belly dressed in a bin bag."

"And that's relevant why?" said Charlie.

"At least Ryan is presentable."

"Yes," said Michelle, "Ryan is well turned out and quite handsome."

"We are giving awards based on looks now?"

"No, but there will be a lot of publicity around the winner and photos. We need to present the company in the right light."

Charlie shook her head, there was no point in arguing anymore.

"Makes no difference, Ryan is way out ahead. Nobody can catch him," said Ethan.

"We'll see."

Charlie was more determined than ever that Darren would win. If they tried to deny him the prize, they had one hell of a fight on their hands.

She returned to her desk attempting to keep her temper in check but was cheered when she saw that Darren had gained another two stars. Emma was also on the leader board now. Whatever her differences with Darren, she hadn't let it affect her work.

"Well done you two," she said pointing to the screen, "I've just come from a meeting where they were praising you for your efforts. You're gaining on the leader, I think one of you will catch him."

She was well aware that she said it loud enough for Ryan to hear. Maybe it wasn't wise to upset him but she was sick of him being built up as some call centre superstar when he was anything but.

"Well done," said Darren to Emma, "you'll overtake me soon."

"I doubt it."

She put her headset on and took a call before he could continue the conversation. He wasn't going to push his luck. She hadn't accepted his apology and dishing out praise or engaging in small talk wouldn't change things, he would only annoy her more. He had to accept that she wasn't going to forgive him no matter what he tried. He'd been an idiot and deserved everything he got.

Emma looked at the leader board. She wasn't one for awards or recognition, but it was nice to see her name up there. She was a doing a good job and her colleagues and customers were recognising it. She'd got on the leader board without trying. She'd got there by doing her job well and that's the way it should be. She hadn't chased the awards like Ryan or stumbled across them like Darren.

She didn't begrudge Darren his place on the leader board, but it was mainly due to his previous life as a troll. He seemed to be getting rewarded for terrorising the call centre in the past. It wasn't the reason why she had fallen out with him, but it was another annoyance to add to the list. She'd been happy at Phonetix until Darren arrived on the scene. She'd been foolish to allow him to get under her skin, but the damage was done now.

She took one last look at the leader board and noticed Ryan watching her with a smug grin on his face; she took another call.

****

Spencer sat with his back against the bedroom wall, his elbows resting on his knees and his hands hiding the world from him. Rebecca had gone, walked out and taken the kids with her. Not even a hint that anything was wrong. Yes, she might have complained that he hadn't been paying into the joint account, but she was always moaning about something. Was it really a reason to leave?

She still left even after he explained that he was doing something about it. Even after she discovered that he already had done something about it and got a very healthy ten thousand pounds into the bargain. She said she didn't want anything to do with it, didn't want to touch the money or know any more about where it had come from. How was he meant to pay the bills on this house if she wasn't there? She never explained whether she intended to continue to pay her share.

Worse than her leaving with his children, worse than the financial uncertainty she had left him in, worse than everything she had done to him was the fact grenade that she had dropped into his lap. His perfect crime; the masterplan where he avoided CCTV, couldn't be seen talking to the criminals and was in the showroom when the car was taken had one fatal flaw.

He had used his own phone.

He had no idea why he had been so careless. Maybe it was because he wasn't a proper criminal, maybe he was concentrating too hard on the prize at the end, maybe he was just lazy. Whatever it was, it was a big problem.

He could try and forget about it. He'd assumed that the police had given up but what if they were biding their time? What if they had made the connection to some serious criminals being in the service station car park at the same time as him? What if they were building a case against him?

It wasn't just the thought of prison time that bothered Spencer although that terrified him. It was the thought of what the gangsters would do if they knew he was the weak link, the one who had led the police to them. Everybody in Sunderland knew who they were. They may have hidden behind legitimate businesses, but most people were aware that the majority of their income was less than honest. The police will have been waiting for an opportunity to connect them to a crime and Spencer had done just that. He might not even make prison and if he did, he was unlikely to survive inside. He needed to do something about it.

He took out his mobile, the mobile that threatened to betray him. He scrolled through the recent calls until he found the number he needed and pressed dial. He navigated the options, choosing lost and stolen to bypass the queues and finally got to speak to a human.

"I need to speak to Darren Updike."

"I'm sorry, sir, we don't usually transfer calls, is there something I could help you with?"

"No, Darren is dealing with my case exclusively, he knows all about it."

The adviser had a quick look on Spencer's account and Darren did seem to have dealt with the last couple of enquiries although there wasn't any note saying he was the only person who could deal with Spencer. She wasn't in the mood for an argument so looked up Darren's number and transferred him.

"Hello, you're through to Darren, how can I help?"

"It's me, Spencer Proctor, I need you to delete a few calls from the system."

"I'm afraid that's not possible."

"Do we need to go through this whole charade again, Darren? Just do as you are told."

"That's not going to happen, Mr Proctor."

"Look, I haven't got time for arguments right now. Why don't we agree on a truce? I'll make it worth your while if you help me out."

"I don't think you understand, Mr Proctor, it's not physically possible to delete the calls from the system."

"Of course it's possible, it's just a computer."

"It's not possible, we aren't able to delete anything."

"Well, speak to someone who can."

"Like I said, it's not as simple as that. If you think there is a discrepancy on your bill I could look into it."

"There's no discrepancy, I want any trace of the call deleted from the system, I'm happy to pay."

"Even if I could delete the calls, Mr Proctor, which I can't, there would still be a record elsewhere. The mast you logged onto when you made the call, the phone you dialled, even your own phone will have a record somewhere if you delete it from your history. It isn't physically possible."

"My life is in danger here, Darren. Come on help out a mate, we're all on the same side, aren't we?"

"If your life is in danger I think you should be calling the police, not me."

"Darren, you better delete those calls now or I'll tell everyone at Phonetix who you are and what you used to get up to."

"They know."

"What do you mean they know?"

"I confessed. I couldn't have it hanging over me and decided that honesty was the best policy. It's worked out quite well, you did me a favour."

"You're not deleting the calls?"

"I've already explained that it isn't possible."

"I'll find out where you live," said Spencer. "You're going to regret this,"

"It appears that one of us is. Was there anything else I could help you with?"

Spencer hung up and dropped his phone to the floor. This could be the end for him. He'd always been a success but now he was without a wife, without a family, very likely to be without his freedom and if his criminal acquaintances got hold of him, he could be without breath. He looked at the scattered notes spread across the bedroom, he'd risked everything for ten thousand pounds.

He put his head back in his hands and sobbed.

****

Ryan didn't like the way the leader board was looking. Yes, he was still at the top by some margin, but Darren was edging closer each day. There were only a couple of days left but there was still a chance that he could be toppled from top spot and he wasn't having it. He couldn't have it. He thought about the debt and the threats and the metal box in the boot of his car that he might end up in.

"Morning, Darren, done any trolling lately?"

"Go away, Ryan."

"Just asking because, you know, with the competition and everything, people are getting a little suspicious."

"Suspicious of what?" Darren knew that he should ignore Ryan but couldn't help but get dragged into the conversation.

"Most of your stars seem to have come from helping people who are receiving calls from trolls, bit of a coincidence, isn't it?"

"Coincidence?"

"Yeah, people are thinking that maybe you have got your troll friends to phone in just to give you an opportunity."

People weren't thinking that, Ryan was making it up on the spot, but he knew that if he planted the seed, the rumour would grow.

"That's nonsense, I don't have any troll friends."

"I guess the idea of you having friends is a little far-fetched, but all you weirdos stick together. I imagine you all have a little place where you meet on the internet to discuss your pathetic lives."

"Was there something you wanted, Ryan? I've got calls to take."

"Just having a bit banter, Darren, where's your sense of humour?"

"Bye, Ryan." Darren put on his headset.

Ryan noticed something sticking out of the inside pocket of the suit jacket that was on the back of Darren's chair. He snatched it. "What's this, Darren? Ahh, isn't that sweet? Carrying a letter around from your little old Nana?"

"Give it back, Ryan." Darren made a grab for it but was caught up in the lead from his headset.

"You can be the best. Isn't that lovely, your poor old Nana lying to her pathetic little grandson to try and boost his confidence."

"Don't talk about my Nana like that."

"Does she still tuck you in at night and tell you what a brave little soldier you are?"

"She's dead."

"Probably died from embarrassment having you as a grandson."

"Give it back." Darren had thrown his headset to the ground and was now face to face with Ryan.

"Ooh, look who's being all big and hard. Think you can take me on?"

"Just give me the letter and leave me alone."

"You'll never be the best, Darren. You're not even close. I've got this competition sewn up."

The whole of Darren's team was watching but none of them intervened.

"We'll see," said Darren.

"We'll see? You think you are competition for me? There's winners and losers in this life Darren. I'm a winner and you are very much a loser. Everything about you screams loser. When the Employee Awards are over you'll crawl back under whatever bridge you came from and you'll never be heard of again."

"I don't care about the competition, just give me my letter back."

"If you don't care then you won't mind when I wipe the floor with you."

"Whatever, I've got calls to take." Darren retrieved his headset.

Ryan noticed Charlie approaching via the double doors. "Anyway, like I said, Just a bit of banter." He slapped Darren over the head with the envelope, ripped up the letter and threw it in the bin before walking off.

Darren gripped the desk until his knuckles went white to stop himself from punching Ryan. He'd never hit anyone in his life, but the rage was building inside of him, he needed to control himself.

"What did he want?" said Charlie as she sat.

"Nothing." Darren was fighting back the tears.

"Are you okay, Darren?"

"I'm fine."

He was far from fine. That letter was the one link he had to his Nana and Ryan had destroyed it.

Charlie surveyed the team. Everyone had their heads down, there was no chatter, no playing around. They had all witnessed whatever happened between Darren and Ryan and nobody had done a thing to stop it. She was disappointed in them. She thought she had a good team who worked for each other, maybe she was wrong. She looked at Emma, the one person who she could always rely on for integrity, but she also remained silent.

Charlie had thought the team had turned a corner, but it was falling apart.

Emma couldn't concentrate on her call. She was ashamed of herself. She'd sat back and watched as Ryan bullied Darren. Watched as Ryan destroyed the most precious thing Darren owned and she did nothing. All because of some petty dispute that had got out of hand.

He hadn't deliberately set out to upset her, quite the opposite, it's just that his actions were down to his social ineptitude. And now she had sat back and watched as somebody had exploited his weakness for no other reason than because he could. Ryan was everything she hated in a man, but she'd stood by and let him carry out his bullying right in front of her because she wanted to save face, was scared of the repercussions. That wasn't who she was.

It was time she stepped up. Time she showed who she was rather than letting the bullies take over.

CHAPTER SIXTEEN

Darren could feel himself getting annoyed. His blood pressure was bubbling just under Vesuvius levels and he felt dizzy. His voice was getting louder.

"I've tried to explain this to you three times already. The charges are correct because the Britain's Got Talent voting line is a premium rate number. It doesn't matter that the person you voted for didn't win, you still need to pay for the calls."

"It's a fix."

"That's something you'll need to take up with Simon Cowell."

"Put him on the phone then."

"He doesn't work here I'm afraid."

"Why are you telling me to speak to him then? Sounds to me like you don't know what you are doing."

Darren massaged the bridge of his nose. He had a searing pain in his temples and his vision was going blurry.

"All I can suggest is that you write in to ITV and explain your concerns to them."

"I will do. And next year I'm going to watch The Voice, then you'll be sorry." With that the line went dead.

Darren felt a hand on his shoulder. "Are you alright?" It was Emma.

"Yeah, I'm fine, just an awkward customer." Darren went to take another call, but Emma stopped him.

"Come on, it's only a couple of minutes until break time. Let's bend the rules for once and nick off early, I'm sure Charlie won't mind."

Charlie pretended that she hadn't heard but had a little smile to herself.

Darren didn't need another invitation and logged out. "You're right." He immediately felt his blood pressure dropping to a less critical level.

"Tough call?"

"Shouldn't have been. It was straightforward, but I allowed myself to get wound up."

"It happens to the best of us."

They grabbed a drink and chose a spot in the corner of the canteen away from where the rest of the team would sit when they came down. This was the first time they'd spoken since the flowers fiasco apart from Darren's attempt at an apology. Darren was grateful.

"Thanks for looking out for me up there. If I'd taken another call I would have lost my rag and possibly my job. You saved me."

"I should have stepped in earlier when Ryan was picking on you."

"It wasn't your problem, you don't want to get on the wrong side of him."

"His behaviour was disgraceful and I'm ashamed at myself for not sticking up for you."

"You shouldn't be, I deserved it."

"You deserved it? Don't be stupid Darren. He's a bully and he needs to be dealt with."

"I'd rather keep out of his way."

"That'll never happen; people like him don't give up when they smell blood. You need to take the fight to him, you need to win that Employee Award," said Emma.

"I'm miles behind Ryan."

"Yes, but you've still got all the team's stars to add to yours, that'll take you way past him."

"The team don't want to give up their stars to me though, they'd rather see Ryan win."

"Believe me, nobody wants Ryan to win. My stars alone will get you close, I'm in the top five now."

"I don't want to take your stars, Emma. You've earned them the right way, you should be recognised for what you do."

"I don't care about stuff like that, I want to see the best person win and that person is definitely not Ryan."

"It's not me either."

"It is, you'll see. From now until the end of the competition I'll do everything I can to help you win."

"Why?"

"For all your flaws and bad judgement, your heart is in the right place," she placed a hand on his arm, "I shouldn't be punishing you for that."

"Thanks. And sorry again for that business with the flowers and stuff."

"I'm willing to forgive you," said Emma, "but only if you beat that prick Ryan."

Charlie was getting a coffee from the machine in the canteen and nodded over to Emma who smiled back. It looked like her team was back on track.

Darren returned to his desk and glanced in the bin, but the cleaners had already been and emptied it. The last link to his Nana was now gone. It was time for him to move on.

"Take some deep breaths, stay calm and let's go and win you that award." Emma gave Darren a wink.

He logged in, relaxed and confident. Ryan no longer bothered him, the customers weren't going to upset him. The letter from his Nana might be gone but he could still do her proud. Whatever happened from now on, he knew he could rely on Emma and that meant more than anything. He'd been an idiot, but she'd forgiven him, he wouldn't mess it up again.

****

As always when a team brief was called first thing in the morning, nobody much cared about the subject matter, it was time off the phones and they would milk it for what it was worth.

Darren was no different to the rest so was pleased for the break and walked along to the meeting room with Emma. "Any idea what this is about?"

"No, it'll probably just be some product update."

Once everyone had settled, Charlie started. "Thanks for coming everybody. For once, you don't have to listen to me. It's a team brief and I'll let the team do the talking. Adam, do you want to kick off?"

"Yes, thanks. As you know a handful of us have been on this team a long time, quite a few of you are relatively new but since Charlie has been our Team Leader, we've always been tight as a team and looked out for each other. I think it's fair to say that we've let ourselves down a bit lately."

There were some murmurs and, not for the first time, Darren felt like there had been a discussion that he had been excluded from.

Adam continued, "Darren, I don't want to put you in the spotlight here but yesterday we all sat by and watched Ryan take the piss."

"It's okay." Darren blushed and looked at the floor, he didn't like the attention.

"No, it's not okay, mate. Fair enough some of the new guys not standing up to him but I should have, and a couple others feel the same."

"It's not a problem, honest."

"It is to me; I hate bullies, especially Ryan the fucking prick."

"Adam," said Charlie, "watch your language."

"Sorry, as I was saying, we didn't step up yesterday but I'm apologising on behalf of the whole team. It won't happen again."

Everybody nodded their agreement.

"I appreciate it," said Darren.

"I know this is a bit shit, but we did try our best." Adam shoved a piece of paper across the meeting room table towards Darren.

It was his Nana's letter. Crudely taped back together but legible nonetheless.

"Thank–," Darren felt himself welling up, "I don't know what to say."

"I'm afraid none of us are particularly artistic and we got into a bit of a mess when we stopped back last night to fix it. Still it's a lot better than it was."

"It's brilliant."

"Think yourself lucky the miserable get in charge of the stationery cupboard didn't allow us any glue or it would have been a lot worse."

"It's great, thank you."

"Anyway, Ben here is a bit handy with Photoshop, I think we're a bit more suited to digital stuff than the practical side. We scanned it and he had a bit of a mess about, it's not the original but this looks almost as good as new." He passed him another piece of paper.

"You stopped back to do this for me?"

"Turned into a bit of a laugh once we got going, bit of a team building exercise if you like. Shame you weren't there. Sorry again for yesterday."

"You don't need to apologise, it was Ryan who was being a prick. Sorry, Charlie."

"I'll let that one go," said Charlie, "because he is one."

Everyone burst out laughing and they got some funny looks from the team sat opposite the meeting room.

"Don't worry about Ryan, we've got plans for him," said Adam.

"Plans?"

"We're going to make sure you win the Employee Award."

"There's no need, I'm not bothered about it."

"You might not be, but we are. You've helped us all and we should repay you, I think we'll all enjoy taking him down."

"Should I be listening to this?" said Charlie.

"Trust me, it'll all be squeaky clean."

"Are you going to share these plans?"

"It's your idea really, Charlie. Darren has helped us all, so we can legitimately transfer our stars to him as long as you're happy to sign it off."

"Of course, but were we not waiting until the last minute, so he couldn't do anything about it?"

"But where's the fun in that?" said Adam, "A couple of us are doing it today. Just enough to get Darren within touching distance and to light a fire under Ryan."

"Then what?"

"That's up to Ryan but if he behaves the way we expect, the prize is Darren's"

"You okay with this Darren?" said Charlie.

"I guess so, but I really don't mind if I don't win, I just want to do a good job."

"But it would be nice to finally put Ryan in his place though," said Adam.

"I can't argue with that."

They returned to work rejuvenated. Their plan in place and a new-found team spirit.

"Was this anything to do with you?" Darren said to Emma.

"Surprisingly not, they told me about it and I stopped back to help but they made their minds up at break time after your run in with Ryan. They're not a bad bunch."

"How do you think Ryan will take it?"

"Really, really, badly I hope."

Charlie caught up with Lauren on the way back to her desk.

"They look happy," said Lauren.

"Just a spot of team bonding."

"So, it wasn't you telling them you were leaving then?"

"No, not yet."

"But you will be doing it soon?"

"I need to find the right time. I need to tell my parents and they won't take it well. Then there's the conversation with Michelle."

"Surely that's the fun part?"

"I don't even want to be in the same room as her. She will probably tell me how wrong I am and what a mistake I am making, as she always does," said Charlie.

"And therefore, proving it is the right thing to do."

****

Darren carefully folded the original letter from his Nana and put it back in his pocket. It was going back into the drawer at home and it wasn't leaving again. He pinned the copy by his PC, so he could see it every day. He didn't care if Ryan saw it or even if he tried to destroy it, he wouldn't get upset by him again.

He was moved by what the team had done for him and had got quite emotional. They didn't need to do it and he had no idea why they would do such a thing for him, but it meant a lot. He was back on speaking terms with Emma, finally accepted as part of the team and whilst he claimed it didn't bother him, he was in with a chance of winning the Employee Star Award. It meant more than he would ever let on. It would prove that he was good at something, prove his Nana right and if he could beat Ryan, all the better.

He wasn't sure what the full plan was, but his team was convinced that he would topple Ryan. They'd already started transferring their stars and Charlie was signing them off straight away. Each time he got a new one, the screen flashed. He was gaining on Ryan, he was within touching distance. Ryan hadn't failed to notice either. He removed his headset and stared at the screen as Darren's numbers started climbing.

"What the fuck's happening here?" said Ryan, "He must be cheating."

"Scared of a little competition, are you?" said Charlie.

"This is bullshit."

Ryan sat back down again, rattled as predicted by the rest of the team. They had smug grins on their faces, they knew how this would pan out.

Darren logged in and his first few calls were a breeze. Even potentially difficult ones were easy due to his good mood and positive outlook. His stats were good, his calls excellent, this was going to be his best day ever.

Another call came through.

"Hello, can you hear me, son? I haven't got my hearing aid in, so you'll need to speak up."

"Hello, you're through to Darren, how can I help?"

"I'd like to make an appointment please."

"An appointment?"

"Yes, please."

"What sort of appointment?"

"Ooh, I'm not sure I want to discuss that with you."

"I need to get some details before I can help."

"If you must know, it's my lady bits. They've sprung a leak."

"I'm sorry. I'm not sure I understand."

"Men never do. It comes to us all when you get to my age."

"I'm sorry but I really am lost here," said Darren. He looked around the team to see if he was the victim of some sort of prank.

"Told you I shouldn't be discussing it with you. I should be discussing it with the doctor, she'll understand."

"Yes, maybe you should."

"Have you made my appointment then?"

"Appointment for what?"

"The doctor, have you not been listening?"

"The doctor?" said Darren.

"Yes."

"I'm sorry, did you think that you had got through to the doctor's surgery?"

"Yes."

"I'm not sure how you've done this, but you haven't rung the doctors. You've rang the Phonetix call centre." Darren was baffled. Most people struggled with the automated menu system when calling. To navigate it and get to speak to an operator when you were trying to get the doctors was quite an achievement.

"So, you're not the doctors?"

"No, sorry."

"So why were you asking about my lady bits? Are you some sort of pervert?"

"No, I think it was a little bit of a misunderstanding. Do you want to hang up and try ringing the doctors again?"

"I've been trying all morning and I couldn't get an answer."

"And you thought you'd ring us instead?"

"Those doctor's receptionists can be quite rude and you sound very polite, despite your unhealthy interest in an elderly women's private parts. Can you not make the appointment?"

"I wish I could, but I don't work for the doctor's surgery."

"But I've been trying all morning."

There was real disappointment in her voice. Darren glanced at the letter from his Nana. This woman could be the same age and she was just a little bit confused. It would ruin his call stats, but he'd had a good day so far and, strictly speaking, it was as far from the procedure manual as he could get but he was going to try.

"I'm not meant to do this, but you remind me of someone special so let's see if we can sort you out. First things first, who is your doctor?"

"Dr Symmons."

"Okay and when would you like an appointment?"

"Whenever you can get one, love. Are you sure you don't mind?"

"Not at all, I need to put you on hold and I could be a little while, you know how difficult those receptionists can be. Enjoy the hold music and I'll be back as soon as I can."

"Thank you, you're a star."

Darren wasn't one hundred percent sure what he was doing or if he should be doing it, but he'd promised her now. He had the elderly lady's name and address details that came up when she dialled from her handset. Now he needed the help of Google.

He typed in **Dr Symmons, Burton** and hoped that the doctor was in the same town as she lived. Luckily there was only one hit, he clicked on it and got the number for reception.

After holding for five minutes, arguing with the receptionist for another five, he finally had an appointment.

"Mrs Wilcox? Are you still there?"

"I'm still here, I was quite enjoying that music."

"Would 11am on Thursday be okay for you?"

"That would be wonderful. Have you really managed to sort that out for me?"

"I have, and it's been a pleasure doing it."

"I should ring you every time."

****

Ryan was furious when he saw how close Darren was getting to overtaking him on the leader board. He'd been creeping up for a few days then there was a surge when half the team transferred their stars. He should have seen it coming.

"I'm not getting beaten by that fat simpleton," he thought.

He'd conceded defeat with Emma despite his intimidation. *"There's no way the Dowdy Doris is going to offer hers up."*

He'd also exhausted most avenues and had charmed as many people as he could to get stars from them under false pretences. Short of going out and earning them properly, which was unlikely in the timeframe, there wasn't much he could do.

There was one slight glimmer of hope. Half of Darren's team had donated their stars at the same time, so it must have been a team decision. But that meant that half had chosen not to donate them, maybe Darren wasn't quite as popular as he thought. The leader board on the main screen only showed the top ten. Ryan had approached everybody on it except Darren and he obviously wouldn't give anything up.

He logged onto the Employee Stars site on the intranet and had a look a bit further down the list. Darren's team still had a lot of stars between them. If Ryan could get his hands on them he'd have an unassailable lead. It was mainly lads who he had spoken to in the past, the type of lads who were bound to favour him over Darren. He had to be careful how he approached them, especially as the whole team appeared to have breaks and lunch together.

He caught up with one of the lads who was late going on his break so was sat in the canteen on his own.

"Alright, mate. How's it going?"

"Canny, Ryan. You?"

"Sound as a pound mate. Can I ask you a quick question?"

"Fire away."

"What are you doing with your Employee Stars?"

"What do you mean?"

"You're not getting into one of the prize-winning positions now, so your stars are worthless. How would you feel about transferring them to your old mate Ryan? There'll be a pint in it for you."

"Why do you need them, thought you were well ahead?"

"I was, but that weirdo on your team is catching up fast."

"Darren?"

"That's him. What sort of message does it send out if he wins?"

"Aye, there's a few on our team want to see him win."

"I thought that when they transferred their stars over. Bit of a shifty move that. We'll just be balancing the books a bit."

"I don't see why not. I don't get why he's become Mr Popular all of a sudden, he's always been a bit dodgy. Got to get back on the phones now but remind me when I'm at my desk and I'll send them your way."

"Cheers, mate, I appreciate it."

One down, another five to go and the competition was his. Ryan went back from his break five minutes early to work on the rest of them. He fired a quick instant message to the lad he had been speaking to in the canteen.

Ryan: Don't forget to transfer the stars mate. I'll email the wording for you to put in the document. You don't have to do anything but copy and paste. Ethan will sign it off.

He pressed send and the lad immediately put his thumb up. Now to work on everyone else.

Ryan: Hi mate, any chance you could transfer your Employee Stars to me to stop Darren winning? There'll be a drink in it.

Kieran: Isn't that against the rules?

Ryan: Not if we do it properly. I've got a system where we won't get found out, got half the call centre sending theirs my way. It'll get signed off. Don't worry.

Kieran: As long as I'm not doing anything wrong.

Ryan: You're not mate. I'll send you the wording to use.

Kieran: Okay mate, send it over.

He messaged the others and got similar responses. They weren't keen to break the rules but once Ryan convinced them that they wouldn't be caught, they all agreed. Despite the whole team agreeing to help Darren, a lot of them were still clearly unhappy at his past life as a troll. Darren's brief spell of popularity was going to be cut short. If half of his team didn't even like him, he had no chance with the rest of the place. Ryan knew it would be easy, all he had to do was wait and watch himself pull away at the top of the leader board.

After an hour, the scores hadn't changed. Everybody was busy on the phones, but he didn't want any to be missed. He sent a message to Ethan.

Ryan: Hi mate. Has anybody transferred any stars over yet? Convinced a few and given them the wording. Can you sign them off as soon as they come in like the others? We need to beat that mong Darren.

Ethan: Nothing's come through yet. I'll sign them off as soon as they do. Agree that we need to destroy that freak.

Ryan waited another hour and sent another round of messages to hurry them up. Michelle and the Head of HR were at Ethan's desk, so he didn't want instant messages to pop up on his screen, Ryan tried the others first. Ryan wasn't getting any responses and Ethan was away from his desk now, he'd gone into a meeting with Michelle and the HR woman.

He'd need to wait.

He was surprised to see Michelle approaching. He kept in with the senior management, so they quite often spoke to him, but they rarely approached him on the floor.

"Can I have a word please, Ryan?"

"No problem, Michelle, what's it about?"

"In the meeting room, I'd rather discuss it in private." She glanced at the leader board.

"Probably wants to suck my plums, even that little dumpling wants a piece of her star employee," thought Ryan. "I understand." He walked away with a swagger.

When they went into the meeting room Ethan was already there with the Head of HR.

"Hi, everyone, what's up?"

Ethan nodded towards the table.

The table that was covered with screenshots of instant messages that Ryan had sent to Darren's team.

Screenshots incriminating him and Ethan.

****

Rumours spread like wildfire. Had Ryan and Ethan been sacked? Suspended? What had they done? The rumours ranged from illicit phone upgrades to adding credits onto friend's accounts. They'd only left the building two hours ago, both ashen faced and silent and led out by the Head of HR. People had even searched the Echo website for any unsolved crimes they could be implicated in.

What was clear was that Ryan's name was no longer at the top of the leader board, it was nowhere to be seen. Darren was the clear leader and with Ryan gone, the rest of his team had no need to transfer their stars even though they all had legitimate reasons to do so if they wanted.

"Well done, Darren."

"Well done, mate."

"I'm really not bothered about winning, but thanks everyone, your plan worked perfectly."

They hadn't let Darren in on what they were up to and the half a dozen who hadn't transferred their stars had put on Oscar worthy performances when Ryan had approached them. They had no intention of offering their stars to him but were more than happy to give him enough rope to hang himself. By putting the pressure on him they knew he would make mistakes. It was a lot easier than they had hoped and the fact that he was more than happy to send instant messages and emails explaining exactly what illegal behaviour he was getting up to made collecting evidence a piece of cake.

The fact that Ethan was stitched up into the bargain was the cherry on top of that cake.

Michelle's reputation was also tarnished after so publicly backing Ryan and Ethan. That's why she acted swiftly when the evidence was put to her, she couldn't risk any of it sticking to her. She cut them adrift at the first opportunity.

Now all Darren had to do was keep his nose clean for another day, keep his stats above average and not accidentally release any calls. He touched his Nana's letter before leaving for the night. It was an odd set of circumstances, but her prediction was coming true.

Amongst all the celebrations, Charlie hadn't said much. She knew that it was nearly the end of the road for her. She took more pleasure than anyone in seeing Ryan and Ethan's downfall, but she knew that Michelle wouldn't forgive Charlie for publicly shaming her. She'd pushed her into a corner with the evidence against them and she didn't appreciate it. It would be a rough time. Sure enough Michelle called her into the office.

"I want to see all the paperwork on Darren's stars. I can't believe that someone like him is in the lead."

"No problem."

It was a problem because it was a lot of work, but Charlie knew that it was watertight. She had double checked every form, checked the wording. Added account numbers for the accounts that colleagues said Darren had assisted with. Provided links to any calls that were recorded relating to Darren's stars. Whilst she may have nudged people in the right direction, Darren had earned his place at the top of the leader board and she wasn't going to let Michelle's bitterness spoil it.

She stopped back and spent a couple of hours gathering the evidence then presented it back to Michelle. She couldn't argue with any of it, but she wasn't happy.

"You put me in a very awkward position today. I'm going to have to explain all of this to Henry when he comes up next week."

"Surely it was Ethan and Ryan who put you in that position?"

"If you hadn't got your team involved, none of this would have come to light."

"I'll pass on your thanks."

"Don't try and be funny, Charlie, I'm not thanking anyone. This discredits the whole Employee Star Awards, made us look very foolish. I'd have preferred it if you had left it well alone."

"And let cheats win?"

"They weren't cheats. They were being creative but unfortunately they crossed a line."

"I guess we'll have to agree to disagree on that one."

"You don't get a choice on when you agree with me and you'd do well to remember that."

"Was there anything else, I should be getting home?"

"I won't forget this, Charlie."

"I wouldn't expect you to."

Charlie tried to hide her temper as she stormed out to the car park. "Night, Frank."

Frank looked at his watch. "Thought you were never going to leave."

"I thought that once as well."

She got home to the usual barrage of questions.

"Where've you been?"

"Work."

"You're two hours late."

"I had things to do," said Charlie with a sigh.

"You could have phoned. I was worried sick, anything could have happened," said her mother, still clinging to the tea towel, "Maureen from the club had her Yorkshire Terrier snatched by gypsies, they used it for dog fighting. I thought something like that had happened to you."

"Like I said, I was busy."

"Are they paying you for that extra time?"

"It doesn't work like that, Mam."

"I feel like writing your boss a letter, you shouldn't be expected to work late for free."

"It wasn't detention, Mam. I'm not at school anymore."

"There's no need to talk to me like that. Your tea is ruined."

"Give it to the dog then."

"We don't have a dog."

"Maybe you should think about getting one for when I leave. Keep it on a lead so you know exactly where it is every minute of the day."

"What do you mean leave? You're not going anywhere."

"I'm going to my room."

She ran up the stairs two at a time, so she didn't have to deal with any more of the interrogation. She'd had enough. Enough of Phonetix, enough of Michelle and enough of her interfering mother. She needed to get away and she needed to get as far away as possible. She'd done what she set out to do at Phonetix. Her biggest challenge, Darren, was now an accepted part of the team and a valued employee.

It was time to look after herself for once.

****

Spencer was tempted to phone in sick, but he knew it would look bad. Whatever happened he had to keep up appearances that everything was fine. He wouldn't let on that Rebecca had left but it was going to be hard to keep on top of things. He didn't even know how the washing machine worked so he would be out of clean shirts by the end of the week if he didn't learn. He could always ask on the message board, but he would only make himself a target, something he could do without.

He caught a glimpse of himself in the rear-view mirror. He'd forgotten to shave. A big crime in the sales industry but he'd bluff it out. They hadn't appointed a replacement for George yet, so he might get away with it. It was more important than ever that he got George's role as he didn't know if he could rely on Rebecca's wage still paying the bills.

He pulled into the car park and noticed a customer car already there, a Mondeo. The showroom wasn't officially open yet, but they must be inside and if he was quick he might nab them before anybody else. Mondeo drivers were usually prime targets for an upgrade to a Jaguar.

He practiced smiling in the mirror, smoothed his hair and sauntered in as if he didn't have a care in the world. The illusion of confidence was all important. He scanned the showroom for the customers, but they were already in the office; George's office.

They were looking through files. They weren't customers, it was the police.

"Morning, Spencer." The receptionist was more cheerful than usual.

"Sorry, left something in the car."

He ran outside.

"Shit, shit, shit!"

He jumped back into the car and head butted the steering wheel.

"What do they want?"

He tried to compose himself. What could they find in George's office? There were documents showing he'd forged signatures, but he could argue that was normal practice in the showroom to push deals through. It might give them a slight motive, but it still didn't link him to the stolen F-Type. The only link to him and the car ringers were the phone calls. He rang the call centre and demanded to be put through to Darren again. He came up against some resistance at first, but his usual belligerence won through and it wasn't long before he was speaking to Darren.

"How can I help, Mr Proctor?"

"It's about those calls I told you about. I desperately need them deleting."

"As I explained the other day, there is no way I can delete them."

"What is it you want, Darren? Money, I can give you money. Enough to get you out of your poxy bedsit."

"I don't need money."

"Cars, I work for a Jaguar dealership. I can get you a cracking car, it'll attract all the birds and you can't tell me that a fat sex pest like you doesn't need the help."

"I can't drive."

"What is it you want, name it?"

"I don't want anything. As I've explained, those calls can't be deleted."

"Don't mess me about, Darren, this is a matter of life and death."

"Yours?"

"It could be yours if you don't delete those calls."

"Are you threatening me, Mr Proctor?"

Charlie's ears pricked up immediately and she put on her headset and listened in.

"I'm not threatening anybody Darren, but I am not ending this call until you delete those records."

"I'm afraid we're at an impasse as I can't delete them."

"Can't or won't?"

"Both," said Darren.

"I guess we're stuck here all day then."

Darren checked his stats. His average was quite good but one bad call could ruin it and put his chance of winning the Employee Star Awards in danger.

"If there's nothing else I can help you with Mr Proctor I'm ending this call."

"You're not ending this call Darren and we both know it. You can't press the release button without setting alarm bells off all over the call centre, I know how these things work. You're stuck here."

Darren was silent, he didn't know what his next move was. If he released the call it would be flagged, and he wasn't stupid. He knew that Michelle was out to get Charlie and would be looking for any excuse to discredit him to get to her.

"Not got anything to say, Darren," said Spencer, "still the pathetic loser you've always been?"

Darren's finger hovered over the release button. It would be worth losing the award just to hang up on him.

Then another voice came through his headset.

Charlie.

"Good morning, Mr Proctor. You are speaking to Charlie, Darren's manager, and I would like to make you aware of a couple of things."

"Who was speaking to you? I was talking to Darren."

"Now you're talking to me or rather I am talking to you and you are going to listen. Darren is worth a hundred of you and Phonetix could do well to get shot of customers like you."

"I spend a fortune with Phonetix."

"I don't care. You are pathetic, Mr Proctor, a pathetic bully who needs to phone a call centre to try and validate his life. I bet you don't have any friends, or a family that loves you. You're a pathetic nobody acting like you are something."

"You can't talk to me like that."

"I think you'll find that I can and I am. I've made a note that you've tried to delete some calls and we've refused just in case the police or whoever come snooping. They should know that you were trying to hide something."

"Don't, it will ruin me."

"I hope it does. This will be the last time you phone Phonetix Mobile and if I ever hear of you calling again I will personally cut your phone off and pass the information onto the police."

"You can't do this."

"Goodbye, Mr Proctor."

With that, Charlie released the call.

****

"Don't worry," said Charlie, "the released call will go against me not you."

"How will you explain it?"

"He deserved it, the bloke's a prick."

"Will Michelle buy that?" said Darren.

"I hope not." She winked back at him. "Go on, get some more calls taken, you need to keep your stats up."

Charlie took a deep breath, she knew that it was game over for her. Released calls were automatically flagged for review and the way she spoke to Mr Proctor was unacceptable. No matter how much he deserved it, she should have remained professional. She knew it and she had done as soon as she intervened in the call. She'd dealt with hundreds of clowns like Spencer Proctor over the years and never lost her temper once.

And she hadn't this time, she knew exactly what she was doing, and it felt good.

She unpinned the picture of Sydney Harbour and put it in her bag along with the rest of her personal effects. This was the last time she would be setting foot inside of Phonetix Mobile. She wouldn't wait to be called in by the call monitoring team or sit in an office whilst Michelle talked down to her. She was done with all that. She was going to have one final break with her team, say her goodbyes then see out the rest of her shift before disappearing to the other side of the world.

The team were shocked when she explained but they wished her well. She had been good for them, but she made them realise that they didn't need her anymore. They had shown that they had grown as a team and as individuals, they could now go on to bigger and better things.

Darren couldn't help but feel guilty.

"I'm sorry, Charlie. If I'd dealt with him better, you wouldn't have had to intervene."

"Don't apologise, Darren, you gave me the excuse to do something I should have done a long time ago. I'm proud of you and everything you've achieved since you've been here. I'm leaving happy with you at the top of the leader board."

"Thanks for everything you've done for me Charlie. I wouldn't have achieved anything if you hadn't believed in me."

"It was my pleasure."

"This might be a little cheeky, but could I ask one small favour before you leave?"

"Why not? Your wish is my command."

There was a knock on the car window. Spencer didn't need to look up to know it was the police. He wound the window down.

"Could we have a word please, Mr Proctor?"

"What about?"

"I think we both know what about."

Spencer got out of the car and they handcuffed him whilst reading him his rights.

"You have the right to remain silent..."

He remained silent because there was nothing left to say. They put him in the back of the Mondeo and drove off. He glanced back at the showroom for the last time.

It was getting towards the end of the shift and everyone was watching the leader board. They'd almost stopped taking calls, so they could see Darren crowned champion.

"Well done, Darren, you deserve it," said Emma.

With one minute to go the screen flashed.

The score against Darren's name had changed to zero.

The intake of breath across the call centre could have created a vacuum.

Michelle was out of her office looking at the screen along with everybody else.

"What's happened? Darren, why have they taken your stars from you?" said Ben, casting a glance towards Michelle.

Everybody's attention turned to Darren, the whole floor was watching for his reaction. Nervous chatter spread and got louder.

Darren stared at the screen.

The screen flashed again.

Darren's name had been replaced with Emma's.

Darren slapped his hand on his desk and rocked back in his chair. "It should always have been you."

Emma's face was white with shock. "Darren, what have you done?"

"Don't worry, it's all above board. You've helped me from day one, you even helped me when I was in training. I had hundreds of examples of you being a star. It was easy to get Charlie to sign it off."

"I don't deserve this."

"You do. You were always going to win, I wanted to leave it until the last minute, so you didn't have a chance to turn it down. I never wanted to meet Jon Radley anyway."

"Congratulations, Emma," said Charlie, "I thought Darren deserved it but when he spoke to me earlier I realised that he was right. Nobody deserves this prize more than you. You've made me very proud today; all of you. I'm going to miss you."

Charlie wasn't sure if it was her who cried first, or Emma, or Darren. It didn't matter, they were a team.

"If you lot have finished getting all emotional," said Ben, "can we tempt you to a quick farewell drink?"

Everyone agreed, and they left as one. Michelle was storming down the office after receiving Charlie's resignation email, but Charlie wasn't hanging about to discuss it with her. She'd dreamed of this day and had worked out a speech of some home truths she would give Michelle, but she realised that it wasn't worth it. She was happy, and she was leaving on a high.

She gave a bemused Frank a peck on the cheek as she walked out for the final time and accepted the offer of a lift to the pub. The team was buzzing. They were genuinely sad to see her go but understood her reasons. Darren was joining in with the banter with the rest of the team. An equal member now, not just the weird new starter.

Charlie's phone buzzed. She checked the message from an unknown number. On any other day she would have thought it a prank, even alarming, but the way things had gone today, she was willing to take it at face value.

Hi Charlie, we've been watching Darren's progress from afar and would like to say thank you for everything you have done. If there's anything we can do for you, please let us know.

She was going to delete it but had a thought.

I'm not sure if this is possible but...

She finished the message and put the phone back in her back wondering what she'd done.

"You alright?" Charlie said to Emma who was sat quietly with a glass of lemonade.

"Yeah, great thanks. It's been quite the day, hasn't it?"

"That was a nice gesture from Darren."

"It was lovely, he's not a bad lad, is he?"

Ryan parked in a lay-by, a popular fly tipping spot. He checked that nobody was around and heaved the metal box from the boot of his car.

It clattered to the ground and he slammed the boot shut before running to jump back in the car. But he stopped.

The lid of the box had sprung open and something was spilling out. The smell was horrific.

His need to get away was superseded by his morbid curiosity. He went back to look at the box, both terrified and fascinated with what he might see.

What he didn't expect to see was dead fish, hundreds of them. The gangsters had been laughing at him all along, he was a nobody to them. They'd still want their money back, but they'd never trust him with anything serious. He was a joke.

His phone buzzed in his pocket, he didn't want to take it out. He knew it would be Caitlin and he was in trouble.

He couldn't ignore it.

Caitlin: Where are you? I know you aren't at the gym, I've checked your app. Why am I seeing rumours on social media about you being sacked? Why are you so pathetic, Ryan? I don't care where you are, just don't bother ever coming home. You are an embarrassment, you always have been.

He was a joke to everybody, his ex-colleagues, Caitlin, the local criminal fraternity, every single one of them was laughing at him.

He caught another whiff of the fish and heaved his guts over the lay-by.

After two glasses of wine, Charlie was in no mood for an interrogation. She ran up the stairs before even taking her coat off.

"Sorry, got something to do," she said to her mother before she could even ask where she'd been.

She slammed the bedroom door shut and fired up her laptop. The page was saved in her favourites, she'd looked at it every night for the past two years. She took out a marker pen and put a big cross on the calendar, two weeks from today. She then removed her debit card from her purse, typed in the details and pressed confirm.

She was going to Australia.

She printed her confirmation and headed downstairs. It wouldn't be an easy conversation, but she wasn't giving her parents the opportunity to try and change her mind. She'd left work and now she was going to leave home and she felt great. This was freedom, this is what she'd wanted for a long time and now that she had it, she wished she had done it sooner. She wasn't wasting any more time.

"Mam, Dad, sit down, I've got something to tell you."

CHAPTER SEVENTEEN

"Are you looking forward to finally meeting him?" said Michelle as she fussed around straightening banners for the Employee Star Awards.

"I guess so." Emma was a bit taken aback. Michelle had never as much as acknowledged her existence never mind entered into friendly chit chat about her favourite soap star.

"He's really handsome, isn't he?" Michelle dragged a stand with the Phonetix logo on under the big display screen whilst simultaneously firing a wheeled chair across the call centre floor with her buttocks.

"Yes, he is a little." Emma was playing down what she really thought. She hadn't slept with the excitement of finally meeting Jon Radley.

"It will be so inspirational for the staff to get to speak to him in person."

"Really?" As much as Emma loved Jon, inspirational wasn't a word she would use to describe him. Gorgeous, definitely, talented, he was a much better actor than people gave him credit for, but inspirational? She wasn't sure how he was going to inspire people to deal with an angry pensioner who doesn't understand their mobile phone bill.

"Of course, Henry is the perfect example of what can be achieved if you work hard."

"Henry? Who is Henry?"

"Henry Towns, our Chief Operating Officer. Who on earth did you think I was talking about?"

"Jon Radley, the soap star who is presenting the award today."

"Soap star? I don't watch that nonsense. Soaps are for imbeciles and morons. I wouldn't watch Jon Radley if he smothered himself in butter and jumped in a bacon sandwich."

"Michelle," said Frank the security guard as he approached from behind her, "this is Jon Radley."

Michelle couldn't help but let out a snort of derision, begrudgingly holding out her hand whilst looking over his shoulder. "Henry!" She barged Jon out of the way, bundled her way across the floor and embraced Henry Towns with an enormous bear hug.

"Wow," said Jon, smiling at Emma, "she's a bit, err, different."

"You could say that. I'm Emma." She offered her hand.

"Our award winner? I've heard so much about you." Jon took her hand and leant in to give her a peck on the cheek. "Is there anywhere I can grab a coffee?"

"We do have a vending machine," said Emma blushing. Not sure if she was embarrassed to meet her crush or by the state of the coffee. "But it's not the best."

"I noticed a coffee shop on the way in, do you fancy nipping out for a quick cuppa before the madness starts here?"

In a rare show of compassion, Emma had been given the morning off the phones for the award ceremony and photo shoot. She was fairly sure it didn't extend to leaving the building, but she wasn't going to miss this opportunity. "Of course."

And that's how she found herself in a coffee shop on a business park in Sunderland, chatting with the UK's most famous soap star about her cats and weird neighbours as if it was the most natural thing in the world.

They returned forty-five minutes later, their laughing brought to an immediate halt by Michelle who was waiting for them. "Where have you been? Henry hasn't got time to waste hanging around for the likes of you."

"We needed a coffee," said Jon.

"That might be acceptable in soap land but here we have call queues and we can't have people swanning off for coffees whenever they feel like it. Let's get this rubbish over with, Henry is taking me out for lunch."

They gathered under the big screen that displayed the Employee Awards logo. The top ten in the Employee Awards had charitably been allowed fifteen minutes off the phones and the audience had been swollen by the compulsory attendance of every team due on a break.

The local newspapers, radio and TV news crews were also in attendance. Drawn by the appearance of a soap star and also the carrot of possible advertising revenue if they showed Phonetix in a positive light.

Henry stepped up to begin his speech.

"I recognise him," whispered one of the girls in the audience.

"He does look familiar," said her friend.

"Good morning, everybody. My name is Henry Towns, Chief Operating Office of Phonetix here in the UK. This is my first visit to the Sunderland office and I hope to spend a lot more time here in the future."

"We hope so too," shouted Michelle with a grin so wide her ears were in danger of falling off.

"I don't want to keep you from our lovely customers any longer than I need to, so I'll hand straight over to our guest, Jon Radley to present the award."

Cheers, whoops and a round of applause went up, much to the annoyance of those still on the phones, and Jon stepped up.

"It's a true pleasure to be here today. I've been lucky enough to grab a coffee with our winner and I don't think I could meet anyone more deserving. Ladies and gentlemen, can we have a round of applause please for Emma Bennet?"

More cheers went up, everyone genuinely pleased with Emma's victory. Camera flashes went off and call centre rules were flouted as some of the staff got their phones out to video the occasion. Jon gave her another peck on the cheek and handed over the award.

At that moment, Emma didn't know if she had ever been happier.

Darren stood at the back of the crowd, possibly happier still.

Henry took the microphone back from Jon and addressed the audience. "Well done, Emma. I'm sure we can all agree that we can do even better. I'll soon be socialising the information on how Phonetix will not only be delivering world class customer service but aiming for universe class customer service."

He'd hoped for an enthusiastic cheer but was greeted by confused murmurs. The screen flickering above his head had also put him off his stride. The Employee Awards logo disappeared, and the screen went black momentarily before being replaced with a partially pixelated image.

There was little doubt as to what was under the pixelated part and no doubt at all as to who it belonged to as the face and naked torso of Henry Towns appeared.

"That's where I recognise him from."

His suggestive message was there for all to see despite Michelle's best attempts to prevent it. "Stop looking, stop looking everybody. I forbid it." She clambered onto a chair to try and stand in front of the screen but instead rolled across the floor, desperately trying to reach out for the screen and her career that was gradually slipping away.

Camera flashes went off from all angles and the whole call centre put their calls on hold to watch this unfold. Girls started opening dating apps and showing the many almost identical messages they'd received from Henry Towns in the past few weeks. He'd definitely been playing the numbers game.

He tried to slope off in the chaos, but the news crews had him cornered.

"I haven't had this much fun in years," said Jon Radley, "we'll have to do it again sometime." He handed his card to Emma. "If you ever find yourself in Manchester, that's my private number. Give me a shout and we can have a catch up over lunch if you have time."

Darren caught the exchange and allowed himself a small grin. *"So, this is what it feels like to be happy for other people."*

****

Darren heard a key in the front door.

He recognised the knees as soon as they entered the living room.

"Colin."

"Morning, Darren. Hope you didn't celebrate your win too hard last night."

"My win?"

"The Star Employee thing. That was yesterday wasn't it?"

"I didn't win."

"What do you mean you didn't win? I was banking on that money, you owe me three thousand pounds."

"Three thousand, I thought it was only one."

"Err, yeah, sorry that's what I meant. Slip of the gums."

"I'm sorry but I don't have the money."

"But I need it and I need it now."

"I can get it, but I'll need a copy of the new contract first."

Colin unzipped his anorak and produced the contract from his inside pocket. "I've come prepared."

"Pink ink? That's unusual."

"I ran out of black and I haven't got money to waste on new printer cartridges, I just thought I'd use the other colours up first."

"Luckily I had some black ink in my printer and I've printed my own contract out," said Darren.

"Your own contract?"

"Yes, I've made a couple of amendments."

"Amendments? I'm no legal beagle but I know you can't make amendments."

"I ran it past my legal people and they were very interested in the pink ink situation."

"Situation?"

"You see, this isn't the first time I've seen pink ink. The last one was just as demanding but not as polite. I suspected someone else, but I realised that he had no idea where I lived."

"I've no idea what you are talking about."

"I'm sure Mr Ingham won't mind having his name used as leverage to get money out of someone."

"I never used his name," Colin played with the zip on his anorak, "that blackmail demand wasn't from me. I don't know who hacked his computers."

"But you do know what was in the letter."

"Bullocks."

"It's only a couple of simple amendments, nothing for you to worry about."

Colin now had both hands down his shorts and a worried look on his face.

Darren pushed the contract over to Colin and handed him a pen.

Colin removed his hands from his shorts and signed with the air of a man who had bigger things on his mind.

Darren logged out of the message board and shut down his PC. It had been quite a couple of days. First there was the plot to oust Ryan. It was clever but in hindsight it was obvious how he would react to Darren catching up on him. He had little sympathy for him.

Then the call with **DB10** that could have ruined his career. There were rumours flying around the forum that he had been arrested. The moderators were having a hard time keeping up and as soon as one thread was closed, another popped up. Darren had some inside information, and, in the past, he would have been all over it, but he didn't feel the need. Whatever had happened with Spencer wasn't any of his business and as much as he had enjoyed the forum, now was the time to bow out.

His timing was ironic due to the email he had just received. The hackers, who started the whole thing were giving him his old message board account back along with old email accounts and everything else. Even his spreadsheet. They assured him that his PC was virus free, they were no longer spying on him. No explanation, no apology, other than a screenshot of a post on a message board from what seemed like a lifetime ago.

DAZZLED: Maybe I could help. In situations like this, I think it is always best to go back to the beginning and find out what I have done wrong. Only once I realise where I've made the mistakes can I begin to recover the situation. Hope this helps.

Along with the screenshot was a list of log-ins, the spreadsheet and most importantly, his Nana's photos.

He spent five minutes browsing them before backing them up to the cloud, in two separate places, to his external hard drive and then ordering some prints online. He was going to frame them and put them up around the flat. He deleted the spreadsheet before closing the PC. He no longer needed it, that was the old Darren. He was a lot happier with the new one.

He didn't know how many hours he had wasted arguing online, trying to prove he was something that he wasn't. His online experience was a lot easier when he'd decided to be honest with everyone. The people he thought it was important to impress online weren't important at all.

He opened the drawer, looked at the letter from his Nana.

"You were wrong, Nan. I'll not be the best at anything, but I'll be the best I can be."

He finally understood what she meant.

He closed the drawer and ran his finger along the desk, checking for dust. A new habit he had picked up. There wasn't an abandoned sock or empty Coke can to be seen in his bedroom now. At most there was a glass of water by his bed. His clothes were ironed and hanging in the wardrobe. His bedding was freshly laundered. He liked the new Darren.

He wandered into the sitting room. A sitting room no longer covered with dirty mugs and takeaway cartons. A clean carpet that he could now see, he was surprised to find that it had a pattern. The windows were clean and the surfaces polished. He'd even installed a plug-in air freshener.

Instead of a pig sty it was now somewhere he was comfortable, somewhere he could be proud of. There was music playing in the background, something he'd had no interest in before and if he was honest, he couldn't tell who was on the radio, but he liked it. He was open to new experiences. He made himself comfy on the settee and took in how his life had changed.

Not just his life; maybe inadvertently but he'd helped Charlie make the move she'd always wanted to and he would never forget the smile on Emma's face as she chatted to Jon Radley. He'd somehow had a positive impact on other people's lives and he liked the feeling it gave him.

Darren didn't know if his happiness would last but he wasn't letting anything spoil his mood tonight. His life was on the up.

The Troll life was over.

The End

Acknowledgements

Susie, Monkman and Bill, once again, your feedback has been invaluable.

Iain and the rest of Holmeside Writers, especially Lisa, Ray and Tom, thanks for all the encouragement, problem solving and feedback.

Liver and Bunions, you are a constant inspiration.

To my Twitter and Facebook friends, thanks for sharing, encouraging and keeping me in check whenever I came close to being an online book bore.

Finally, to the SMB, without you Darren would never exist. I'm sure he lives on in all of you, thanks for the inspiration.

Thank you for reading Troll Life. If you enjoyed it, please leave a review, I would really appreciate it.

You may wish to read my other novels.

You can follow my website and blog at www.alan-parkinson.com and follow me on Twitter @Leg_It.

Leg It

Fifteen years since Peter Wood left school and disappeared, he returns.

Is he back to make peace or is he back for revenge?

Childhood in the eighties was fun for but nothing lasts forever.

Running away seemed like his only option; as did his return fifteen years later.

Will his old friends forgive him for going?

Will his enemies forgive him for coming back?

Will Pete win back the life he thought he had lost or will he Leg It?

A classic laugh out loud tale of love and friendship, revenge, gangsters and rubber pants.

Alan Parkinson's debut novel Leg It is set in Sunderland and mixes crime and humour in the style of Christopher Brookmyre and Colin Bateman.

Alternating between the lead character's schooldays and the modern day, it gradually reveals his reason for moving away and motivation coming back.

A fast-paced comic thriller that will bring back memories for anybody who went to school in the eighties and will strike a note for anyone who ever wanted to put right what happened in their teenage years.

Available on Kindle, iBook and in paperback.

Idle Threats

Liam hates his job working for Phonetix Mobile. Fighting for every second and battling with every customer, he is close to the edge. Bumper's business is going under. His debts are rising, his drinking is getting worse and his wife has had enough. Jodie is unemployed and is desperate for work to give her son the life he deserves. Her mobile phone on the other hand, appears to have no intention of working.

They are all brought together by an armed siege that could change their lives forever.

The long awaited follow up to Leg It, Alan Parkinson's debut novel. Idle Threats, set in Sunderland, is a fast-paced tale of guns, bombs, gangsters and sombreros.

Comic crime fiction in the style of Chris Brookmyre and Colin Bateman, Idle Threats will have you on the edge of your seat.

A must for anyone who has ever suffered either working in a call centre or spent hours on the phone to one.

Would you take it one step further and take a gun into a call centre to settle your grievances?

Available on Kindle, iBook and in paperback.

Life In The Balance

How far would you go to make amends?

Manuel Frost is obsessed with right and wrong. Each day he logs good and bad deeds that he witnesses into a ledger that nobody is allowed to see. Each night, if the books don't balance, he sets out to perform deeds of his own to even them up.

He interferes in events until they inevitably spiral out of control and he has to make the ultimate sacrifice to balance the books.

A comic contemporary novel in which socially awkward Manuel takes his obsession too far, often with hilarious results.

His relationships with his overbearing mother, his boss Chloe and his colleagues often leave him confused. The one thing he has that he can rely upon is his ledger. Except his attempts at keeping the books balanced don't go as planned and he is forced into a series of increasingly ridiculous situations.

Oliver and Tony are hapless ex-cellmates who barely tolerate each other. In debt to the local gangster they need a plan to escape the life they have created for themselves and try and repair the damage with their families.

But they hadn't factored Manuel into their plan.

Will Manuel listen to his mother or follow Chloe's advice? Or will the cat be the one to save him?

Offset all the misery in your life and read Life In The Balance.

Available on Kindle, iBook and in paperback.